I0822521

Bad Apple

iBooks
Habent Sua Fata Libelli

iBooks
Manhanset House
Dering Harbor, New York 11965

bricktower@aol.com • www.ibooksinc.com

Library of Congress Cataloging-in-Publication Data

Ozeroff, Barry.
Bad Apple

p. cm.
1. Fiction. 2. Thriller—Fiction—
Fiction, I. Title.

978-1-59687-438-1, Hardcover

May 2017

---

iBooks are published by iBooks, an imprint of J. Boylston & Company, Publishers
Manhanset House, Dering Harbor, New York 11965 •www.ibooksinc.com•

Bad Apple

Barry Ozeroff

Table of Contents

Prologue

I eat meals I can't afford. It started when I won a raffle at work for an all-you-can-eat dinner at Morton's Steakhouse in Portland. I ordered their most expensive cut, along with several appetizers and a couple of side dishes, and it was the best meal of my life. With drinks and dessert, it came to just over two and a half bills, but it didn't cost me a thing. Even the tip was covered. When you love food like I do, you don't forget a meal like that.

Sometimes, I can just taste that dinner, completely out of the blue. It's called a gustatory memory. The appetizers themselves were better than most main courses I've ever had. I drool like one of Pavlov's dogs every time I think about it.

Even though I can't afford to eat like that on my own nickel, I've done it several times since then—twice at Morton's and once each at El Gaucho and Ruth's Chris. Next on my list is Portland City Grill. I'll probably go before my next paycheck, which will really screw up my budget. Damn the financial consequences; my craving is just too strong to resist.

Sometimes, my other urges are like that, too.

Chapter 1

March 15, 2014

The end of life as I knew it came on a Saturday. The urge had been coming on strong for over a week, just like the gustatory memory. But I was slow to respond because satisfying this particular craving does not come easy to me. My anxiety had been increasing for days, ever since the urge started coming on. I usually feel like that right up until the moment I do something about it; at which point, everything suddenly makes perfect sense, and I'm back in my comfort zone. It happens every time.

Somehow or other, I made it through the workday. It was pouring and unseasonably cold when I left the office. March in Oregon can be like that. They say it only rains once a year in the Pacific Northwest—from October 'til May. Weather-wise, the one thing you can count on is that it's predictably unpredictable. Tomorrow will probably be sunny and seventy.

I'm a carnivore, and I was hungry after work, starving actually. There wasn't a lot in my apartment that could still be considered edible. In my place, red meat isn't bad for you. Fuzzy, green meat is bad for you. I sat in my car and tried to decide where to go.

Some of the guys at work had been raving about a place called Killer Burger in Northeast Portland. I liked the name, so I looked the place up. I found it at the corner of NE Tillamook and Sandy, which was a few miles out of my way, but I figured it might be worth the trip.

I pulled up and noticed the streets surrounding the place were mostly empty, probably because of the weather. A couple of pickups, a soccer mom van, and a lowered 90's Nissan were the only vehicles parked nearby.

There were only three people in the dining room, a young couple in their twenties and a well-dressed guy about my age. As for employees, I only saw three: a multi-pierced teen whose name tag said NICK, a pimply girl about twenty years old scrubbing down the grill, and a young man in his mid-twenties. There might or might not have been another kitchen scullion somewhere in the back.

As I tried to decide what to order, the urge slapped me hard in the face, and at that moment, I just knew. It was going to happen, right here and right now, and it would be a doozy. In a flash, I was as taut as a guitar string.

I wasn't prepared for this, but that only heightened my excitement. For a moment, I thought it might not happen, but then I knew there was no stopping it.

"Welcome to Killer Burger," said NICK. "What can I get you?"

And then it happened.

Chapter 2

My gun, a beautiful fourth-generation .40 caliber Glock 27, came out in a smooth, well-practiced draw. "Your complete and utter cooperation," I said quietly to Nick and the girl. "You can start by not moving a muscle, either of you." I had my back to the dining room, so the couple at the table was still oblivious to what was going on.

I pushed open the aluminum door and leaned into the storage area. There were no other employees. "This is a robbery," I declared, unnecessarily. By now, the manager knew what was going on. His hands were held the highest of them all. "All of you, get down on the floor—right here on this side of the counter. Do it now!"

They did it now.

Keeping them in view, I stepped back into the dining room. The young couple had both stopped chewing, their mouths agape midbite. He was a hipster, pure Portland: scraggly beard, black-framed glasses, funky hat, shorts, and Birkenstocks with dark socks. She was a ginger with bland orange hair, empty blue eyes, and freckly skin so pale she looked sick. The other man was still blissfully unaware.

"You two! Dinner's over. Get back here, and get down on the floor. You too, buddy," I said, addressing the other guy. "Let's go. On the floor behind the counter. Right now."

I now had the undivided attention of everyone in the restaurant. It took a moment to sink in, but then they all nervously stood and obeyed. They'd all watched enough TV to know that the proper way to lie on the floor when ordered by a robber is facedown.

"You!" I said, pointing at the ginger, "You're going to lock the front door. If you try to run, I will shoot your boyfriend. Do you understand?"

"Y-yes," she said, crying. From her right nostril glistened a small snotcicle, slowly making its way toward her upper lip.

"Manager, what's your name?"

"Eric Saunders, sir."

"Eric, give her your keys. The cameras . . . real or fake?"

As he handed them to the girl, he said, "They're real, sir."

I put the barrel against her boyfriend's head, and she got up and began fumbling with the door, trying to find the right key.

"Ok, good. Now this is exactly what's going to happen here. When—"

The bathroom door unexpectedly burst open, and a fat guy in a cowboy hat came charging out, shouting. He looked scared, but determined. He held a smallish pistol, a Walther PPK maybe. It was pointed right at me.

I'd been a Ranger in the army and spent my entire life around weapons, but this is where training worked against me. Action, I know, is faster than reaction, and any fight, even a gunfight, is won more in the head than with guns or anything else. This man wasn't mentally prepared for what he was trying to do. I was. He probably expected me to drop my gun, maybe put my hands in the air.

I did none of those things. I just acted—faster than he could react. Had I not been so well trained, I would have taken a moment to think about it, and I am sure I wouldn't have shot him. I didn't *want* to shoot him. But I didn't think; I just did what I'd been trained to do. I don't even remember doing it. As I pulled the trigger, my mind registered his last words: "Deputy sheriff! Drop the gun!"

I scored two center mass hits just under an inch apart, dead smack between the nipples. A perfect double tap. He went straight to the floor in the little alcove between the front door and the bathroom.

As the shots echoed into silence, I was as confused as everyone else in the restaurant. What the hell just happened? I looked at the body on the floor, and when I realized that I may have actually just killed a cop, I almost vomited.

I hadn't been in the restaurant for two minutes.

I have an irrational and completely uncontrollable urge to take risks. I don't seek thrills. I take real, actual risks. I do something crazy or ballsy that could have dire consequences. The more that's on the line, the better.

This . . . condition, for lack of a better word, has plagued my entire adult life. I've always considered it an ailment, a mental illness, maybe a psychological disorder of some kind. Whether it's real or not, it no doubt stems from my screwed-up childhood. Regardless of the cause, the urge gets so overpowering I do extremely stupid things to satisfy it. Every time I do something to satisfy the urge, the risk factor has to increase, or the satisfaction is muted and unfulfilling. Like an opiate addiction, sooner or later, you're gonna need a bigger dose.

About a year-and-a-half ago, I graduated to armed robbery. It had been building up to this for years. Like Nixon, I feel the need to say that I am not a crook. At least, not in the classic sense. Criminal activity is just my newest way of satisfying the urge. I don't do it because I'm bad or need the money. I do it to satisfy an unquenchable thirst.

I had committed six armed robberies in the past eighteen months. Every one went down the same way. Pull the gun, get compliance from everyone present, clean out the register, take care not to leave evidence, and skedaddle. One time, I passed the police on their way to the crime scene. I pulled over and laid across the seat while lights and sirens whizzed by me. I never felt more alive.

It's all about the risk.

Nothing has ever gone wrong. The consequences have always been out there, and that's where they've remained. But by its own definition, a risk is an action that when taken, might go wrong. Otherwise it's not a risk; it's a thrill, and thrills don't do it for me.

That's why my world ended when I realized what I had just done. Now things had gone wrong. Now I had to act or face the consequences. I had to fix this, or . . . well, it would be bad. Real bad.

Tonight's performance was more spur-of-the-moment than the other times. Normally, I scope out a place and do a little planning first, but this time, the urge had been building for so long, a spur-of-the-moment job just kind of felt right. The higher the risk, the greater the reward. So much for feelings.

I've often considered the ramifications of getting caught. Fantasizing about that was part of the satisfaction of taking the risk. Pardon the adolescent simile, but otherwise, it would be like jerking off without fantasizing about having sex. But just like sex, you can imagine what it will be like all you want, but until it actually happens, you'll never truly know.

Now, as they say, the shit just got real. Now something had gone wrong.

Now it was time to pay the piper.

I had just killed a man. If he really was a deputy, then I had just killed a law-enforcement officer who was engaged in the performance of his duties. It didn't matter if he was in uniform, or actually on duty or not. And, it was all done right in front of the security cameras, not to mention the six witnesses. The way a run-of-the-mill stickup is investigated by the police is a lot different than the murder of a police officer. The same holds true for the way these cases are prosecuted. In other words, I had very little chance of getting away with this.

The people on the floor remained oddly silent. They all had their heads buried like a child who farted out loud and is old enough to be embarrassed about it. If they couldn't see me, then maybe I couldn't see them. Floating along in that scary place between having a nightmare and realizing it was just a dream, I looked back at the man in the cowboy hat on the floor. A small red flower had bloomed in the middle of his yellow button-down shirt. The stain wasn't getting bigger, and that said all I needed to know. The dead don't bleed unless the hole is at the bottom. When the pump stops working, gravity takes over.

He was on his back, arms outstretched. One of his boots was pointed up, the other to the right. The gun lay next to him. I watched him for a long moment, my weapon still leveled. His chest did not rise. I lowered and re-holstered the Glock under my jacket.

I walked the fifteen or so feet to the body and confirmed that he was indeed gone. There was no pulse or respiration. He already had the waxy, mannequin-like appearance and the lifeless, open-eyed stare of the recently deceased. It wasn't the first corpse I'd seen, but it was the first that I had made dead.

I picked up his pistol. It was a Sig Saur P223, not a Walther—a nice little gun. I patted him down, and that's when I found the silver sheriff's deputy badge and ID card in his wallet: "Benton County Oregon Sheriff Department, Reserve Sheriff's Deputy."

I had actually killed a cop.

Shaking, I took the gun and put his wallet in my pocket.

I looked up, and that's when I realized the ginger was gone. She'd left the door ajar, the keys hanging in the lock.

I consider myself a smart guy with a lot going for me. I knew that if I bolted at that moment, I would get away before the police arrived, but I also knew they would quickly find me. The spent shell casings on the floor held my fingerprints. The bullets in the deputy would match my firearm. There was the video and the witnesses, one of whom was already gone.

It seemed that I was screwed either way.

I shook my head to ground myself, considering my options. I could run, or I could try to clean this up some. If I ran, they'd catch me sooner than later. If I cleaned this up, I might still stand a small chance of getting away with it. I had maybe three minutes before this place would be flooded with cops.

I locked the door.

I figured the witnesses would be a lot less reliable than the surveillance system, so I needed to take care of the cameras before I left. I'd need the computer that was storing the footage. While I was at it, I thought, I should still get the money. After all, this was a robbery.

Before doing anything else, I picked up my brass, dumping the two casings in my jacket pocket. That done, I addressed the manager: "Where's the computer?"

"By the office, sir. On the wall."

I started to go back there, but then realized that if I did, it would give the hostages a chance to escape. I was caught in a moment of indecision. Go for the laptop and hope the hostages stay put, or secure them somehow, then go for it. I tend to get stressed when too much piles up on me too fast, and when that happens, I make simple, but devastating mistakes. At such times I can't see the proverbial forest for the trees. I have to constantly be on guard for this.

It took me another few seconds to see the solution. I needed to slow down, start thinking straight. I couldn't afford any more mistakes.

"Get up. All of you. We're going to the office."

There was a group hesitation.

"Move it!"

They all did little pushups and stood up as a group then went to the office. Next to the door mounted to the wall, the camera cables all came together at a junction box, which was connected to a Sony laptop.

I unplugged the laptop and herded everyone into the office. There was barely enough room for all five.

I didn't know how much time had passed, but realistically, I knew it was at least a minute since the girl had run out—far too much for me to still be there. I'd be lucky to get to my car before the police showed up. Forget the money.

I was halfway to the door with the laptop when an idea occurred to me. Perhaps I could intimidate the witnesses into silence. If I took their driver's licenses and threatened their families, maybe they'd feel compelled to forget some of the details.

Another conundrum. This would add at least thirty seconds, but it could prove to be well worth the time. I might be able to grab the cash on the way out. Cursing, I sprinted back to the office and opened the door.

The Portlandia-looking guy was talking on his phone, a deer in the headlights expression painted on his face. How could I have put them in a room without searching them and taking their phones? There was even a cordless phone sitting on the desk! What if one of them had had a gun? I was stressed, and now I was making mistakes.

The guy's voice trailed off into silence as I unholstered the Glock and pointed it at him, holding my left hand out in front of me. He handed me his iPhone, which I put to my ear.

"Sir? Are you still there?" came the tinny little voice on the other end. "Can you tell me if he left? Hello? Ok, if you can't talk, then just stay on the line. Please don't hang up. The police are arriving now, and I want you to stay on the line until they contact you. Ok? Can you still hear me? Is he—"

I disconnected.

"God damn it," I shouted to the group with real fear in my voice for the first time. "Give me your phones! All of you! And give me your wallets, too. *Shit*!" I punctuated this last epithet by pointing my gun at the Portlandia guy's head.

I put my own phone in my back pocket and crammed the rest of my pockets full of smart phones and wallets. Lastly, I grabbed the landline handset and closed them back in the office.

The police were here. That was a game changer.

I was safe in either the kitchen or the storeroom, where my witnesses—hostages, now—were securely tucked away in the tiny office. Because of the way the place was set up, only the dining room and the area immediately adjacent to the counter could be seen from outside. I looked at the monitors; nothing seemed to be any different. The glass entry door was still closed and locked, the deputy still lay dead on the floor, and I could see no flashing lights outside.

I plugged the laptop back in. The dining room cameras gave a very limited view of the street as seen through the front door. It was dark now, so beyond the doors, I couldn't see anything.

The dispatcher said the cops were already here, and she wouldn't lie. They wouldn't roll right up to the front door with lights flashing, nor were they about to just bust in here blindly, so it was no surprise that I couldn't see anything. They would likely park down the street or around the corner and approach on foot. By now, they were either lined up outside the door, or more likely, they were hiding behind their cars while more cops poured into the area. In fact, it probably wouldn't be long before they called for a SWAT team.

This was bad. Real, real bad. It wasn't about to get any better.

I wanted to enter the dining room and have a peek for myself, but I didn't dare. Adrenaline had been flowing freely for the past ten minutes, and now it all caught up to me. My hands and feet began trembling, and my breathing became rapid and shallow. I forced myself to calm down and take several deep, slow breaths.

The hardest part of all this was that I pretty much knew how it was going to go. There was no decent way out of this one. I've always known that one day I might not get away with it. And now that day had come.

There were only two ways for me to leave this restaurant—dead or in custody. At forty-two years old, I was too young to die, and I had way too many years left to spend them all in prison.

Essentially, I could choose to die now, or I could choose to die later in prison. I couldn't decide which I wanted. If I chose to die now, I could shoot myself, or I could make the police shoot me. One was quick and easy, and the other didn't require me to do anything harmful to myself other than pose a threat to the police. I couldn't decide which would be the easiest. To die in prison, all I would have to do is to give myself up. Would I die there naturally, or by homicidal violence, or capital punishment?

Then I realized that I didn't have to make any snap decisions. I may be screwed, but right now, I was still in charge.

The telephone handset I had forgotten about began ringing in my hand. I looked at it, but I didn't answer. It rang twenty times then stopped.

I paced the kitchen thinking. My mind was racing as was my pulse. I made myself slow down and take a few deep breaths. I thought about the cops outside. Did they feel like I did? Were they scared? Exhilarated? Did they wish it was just over?

My back pocket vibrated.

It was a text from my own personal cell. I closed my eyes and deflated.

Of course it was. This was the call I'd been waiting years to get, only the circumstances were just a little different than I had anticipated. Shaking my head at the irony of it all, I fished the phone out of my back pocket and pressed the flashing text icon.

SERT CALLOUT: FULL TEAM ACTIVATION. BARRICADED HOSTAGE SITUATION WITH SHOTS FIRED. KILLER BURGER RESTAURANT, 4644 NE SANDY. COMMAND POST: TILLAMOOK EAST OF SANDY. TACTICAL UNIT AND HOSTAGE NEGOTIATORS RESPOND DIRECTLY TO THE SCENE. SAFE APPROACH FROM THE EAST.

Chapter 3

My name is Dean J. Appleby, affectionately known to all as DJ. I am a police officer with the Portland, Oregon Bureau of Police. I've been a cop for eighteen years. I'm currently assigned to the patrol division out of East Precinct. I'm a field training officer with a tactical background, which means I've been on the SERT team. SERT stands for Special Emergency Response Team, which is Portlandspeak for SWAT. I spent three years as an operator on the team before switching over to CNT, which is the crisis negotiation team. For the past eight years, I've been the lead negotiator.

I'm the guy who talks to the bad guy. Well, I was. Now I *am* the bad guy. Shoe sure feels different on the other foot.

My phone buzzed again. This time it was Darren Roberts, the CNT team leader, initiating a private talk group for the negotiators. "Ok everyone, you've all seen the page," he started. "What they didn't say is there's a man down in the restaurant. I'm twenty minutes out from the command post. I need everyone to check in."

"Williams, fifteen out," said Darth Vader. His real name is Darren, but we call him that because his voice is so deep. We don't put him on the phone with really timid people or females because his voice is so intimidating, but we do like to use him with really aggressive people. He's black, and from his voice, you'd expect him to be six foot six and three hundred pounds, but really, he's about five ten and skinny. We're pretty good friends.

"I'll be there in five minutes," came the voice of Beth Quinlan next. She just lives a mile or so south of here, so I knew she'd get here first. That means she'd probably be the one to call me, which ought to prove interesting because she's my partner on the team. Whenever a negotiator is on the phone, he has a coach listening in, making suggestions on sticky notes, even whispering in his ear. Beth's been my coach for more than four years.

One by one the rest of the team checked in. I stayed off the air.

"DJ, you get the page?" Darren asked.

My heart was racing. I couldn't think of how to answer him. I could ignore the call, but I have not missed a callout in all my years with SERT, and everyone knew it. I wanted to say I was on the coast, or drunk, or otherwise unavailable, but I had just gotten off work, and I don't drink, which they know. So, I just ignored it. They'd know why soon enough.

"Anyone know where DJ is?"

"He was at work today," said Roger Cantwell, a negotiator who works East Precinct with me on dayshift.

"If he's not there in thirty minutes, I'll have a unit go by his house," Wilson said. "Ok, here's the scoop. This info comes from Lieutenant Jacobs, who briefed me before the page came out."

Lieutenant Noah Jacobs is the swing shift watch commander. He'd be in charge of the scene until SERT arrived or someone with brass shinier than his took command.

Darren continued, "It looks like a botched robbery. Patrol's got the place surrounded, and they are reporting absolutely no movement inside. A female customer managed to get out, and she said four or five shots were fired, with one person down. She says there's one hostage taker and an unknown number of hostages, probably between five and ten. Our H-T is a white male, five ten, one eighty, and has a black semi-auto. There were maybe four or five people eating there and a couple of employees present at the time of the robbery.

"One of the first officers on scene was Jose Menendez. He had a pole cam in his SERT rig, and he says that the guy who's down appears to be dead by multiple gunshot wounds. Based on that, Jacobs has ruled out a rescue attempt. Given the circumstances, they're just not going to risk it. Jacobs already tried calling the place once, but there was no answer. Break."

He gave others a chance to ask questions. When there were none, he continued, "First one on scene, I want you to call the restaurant. Beth, that's probably going to be you. Get with Jacobs; he'll give you the number. Next on scene, meet with the escaped hostage and start me an intel workup. Third on scene, join Beth as her coach. When DJ gets there, he'll take over as primary, and Beth will become his coach. Everyone else, circle wagons at the command post, and I'll dole out assignments when the van gets there. Until then, you guys all know what to do.

"Remember, people, there's a guy holding hostages in there, and one of 'em's already dead. SERT's not gonna want to go in. They're going to leave this one up to us. This is the big one, folks. We're gonna do it by the numbers."

The phone fell silent.

Darren was right on one account. This *was* the big one. It was a lot bigger for me than it was for them. But he was wrong about the other thing.

I was pretty sure this one wasn't going to go by the numbers.

There was a back door off the kitchen storeroom, which I was able to secure by means of a heavy iron bar that fit into brackets welded to the frame. A little red sign on the wall said, "Fire Door to Remain Unlocked During Business Hours," but I wasn't exactly following all the rules. I didn't want SERT doing a covert entry while I was occupied on the phone.

Next, I checked on my hostages. They were all fine. The older man had usurped the manager's authority and had become the de facto spokesman of the group.

"Look," he said when I checked on them. "You don't need all these people here. Why don't you just let us go, ok? Everyone here has families they'd like to get back to. What do you say?"

"Sorry, pal, not going to happen. But I'll tell you this. It's not my intention to hurt anyone. If that guy hadn't come out like John Wayne, I'd be gone by now, and so would all of you. But things have changed. Just try to relax, and don't do anything stupid."

To his credit, he tried again: "Listen, if you think you need a hostage, I get that. But you don't need five. Let the others go, and just keep me. I won't give you any trouble. I promise. You can tie me up if you want. But give the others a break. They're just kids."

"What's your name?"

"Robert Stillwell. *Doctor* Robert Stillwell."

"You keep these guys calm now, Doc. I need some time to figure out exactly how to handle this, and until I do, I'm not gonna do anything.

You guys just stay put, don't do anything stupid, and you'll all be out of here soon enough."

I closed the door without giving him a chance to respond.

I leaned against the door and closed my eyes, taking a few deep breaths and counting slowly to ten. I have to admit that despite being terrified, the feeling of being alive was more intense than I'd ever experienced. Apparently, this was the high I'd been chasing all along. Nice as it was, I wished I had never found it.

It is my nature to not consider the long-term consequences of my actions—to only take care of my immediate needs. I tend to not care so much about others and concentrate only on what's best for DJ. That may sound cruel or selfish, but it's just who I am. I let that nature wash over me now. What will I need to do to survive the next five minutes? The next half hour?

I was hungry. Starving, actually. That's what had brought me in here in the first place. Dropping to my hands and knees, I crawled out of the kitchen to the counter area. There was a bag sitting on the counter under the pickup sign. I figured it belonged to the deputy. He'd probably been waiting for his food when he went to the bathroom.

I pulled my hoodie up over my head and wrapped a dish towel around my face. Exposing myself for no more than two or three seconds, I popped up, grabbed the bag, and returned to the kitchen.

It was easy to see how the deputy had gotten so fat. Two bacon double cheeseburgers, a large order of fries, and a large Coke. I attacked the food. It wasn't exactly a Porterhouse at Morton's, but it was probably the best burger I've ever had. *I ought to eat here more often*, I thought wryly.

Halfway through the first burger, the phone started ringing again. Once again, I chose not to answer it. This time, it rang for a solid minute. That would be Beth, hoping to establish what we call verbal containment. Basically, it meant if I was talking to her, I wasn't shooting hostages, or preparing a defensive position, or thinking about how I might resist or escape. I was occupied talking to her, while SERT was free to do all the things *they* needed to do.

I wasn't ready to be verbally contained yet, but I knew I couldn't hold off forever. I decided to answer next time they called.

I finished the food and wished there was something sweet to eat. By then, a creeping anxiety had eroded the excitement and left me depressed and overwhelmed. I had killed a man. A cop. A *fellow* cop. And now I could kill myself, or I could give up. Of those two very bad options, I wanted neither.

On the face of it, the idea of dying didn't bother me. I held no beliefs in the afterlife, or judgment, or any such thing. I'll admit I didn't want to die badly, but once it was over, it wouldn't matter to me anymore. As far as I was concerned, I'd no longer know or care.

The strongest feeling I could muster about the possibility of death was regret. Simply put, I wanted to live longer. There were some things I wanted to do before I checked out. I wanted to go to Europe, for example. Mostly though, I wanted to see my daughter graduate from high school, which was only two months away.

Her name is Grace, after her mother's mother. I met her mom when I was twenty-three, and Laura was twenty. She got pregnant right away, and I agreed to marry her, which was a huge mistake. We barely knew each other and certainly didn't love one another. As it turned out, Laura and I weren't even compatible. We gave it a good try, but the marriage didn't last two years.

A year after Laura and I split up, she married a guy named Todd. I wasn't exactly what you would call daddy material in those days, and I hardly ever saw Grace. This marriage lasted eight or nine years, and during that time, I only saw my daughter once every couple months. Usually, I'd just stop by for a few hours and play with her in their apartment, or maybe take her to the park.

Laura and Todd's breakup was bad—hard on all of them.

About a year later, when Grace was ten, Laura married her current husband Jake. Jake, in my estimation, is a weenie who lets her dominate him. I've met him exactly twice. The first time, he copped an attitude because I decided I wanted to see Grace on her twelfth birthday and went to their house without calling in advance. I kind of crashed her birthday party, and it turned ugly when Jake asked me to leave. I got in his face and challenged him to fight, and I would have beat the hell out of him, but Grace intervened.

As it turned out, Grace hated Jake about as much as I did and watching me challenge him to a fight actually served to draw us together. What was it Jesus said? The enemy of my enemy is my friend. Or maybe it was that fat Chinese war god; I can't remember. History's never been my thing.

The next time I saw Jake, he treated me a lot nicer. It didn't matter. The guy meant nothing to me. But Grace and I have gotten closer and closer ever since. Now I see her maybe every two weeks, and she's taken over the spare room in my apartment. I bought a bed and lots of frilly girl things for her. She spends a few days or a week there a couple times during the summer and sometimes on school breaks, too. She's the only person I love.

As far as going to prison, well, the major problem is that cops don't do well in prison. In fact, they are often isolated in solitary confinement for their own protection. Most people would hate that, but it held a certain appeal for me. I live a pretty isolated life anyway. My biggest regret would be the effect on Grace. I actually like having a daughter, and she really looks up to me. I hate the idea of losing that.

I know myself pretty well, and I think I would do ok behind bars. I wouldn't like it, but I can pretty much adapt to anything. Part of who I am is not having any kind of real identity. Mostly, people identify me as a cop—a smart guy who loves his job, they say. The truth is, I see that only as my current station in life, certainly not who I actually am. Other than Grace, I have no one in my life, and that means I am free to be whatever, and whomever, I want.

I have one basic precept I try to live by. I am brutally honest with myself. I may lie to your face and not bat an eye, but I don't lie to myself. I make no bones about who I am. Monster or saint, it's like Popeye says, "I yam what I yam."

The circle of things I care about is very tight. I care about me, and I care about Grace. Being a cop, doing good, doing bad, being free, or being incarcerated—none of that really matters.

With that in mind, I decided right then and there that eating my gun or going out in a blaze of glory wasn't going to happen. I still didn't know how exactly I was going to handle it, but knowing that I'd rather live than die was enough to get started.

There was no way around it. My days of freedom, and life as I had known it, were over. The window for me to escape had long since closed. The only place I'd be going from this building was to the backseat of a squad car, and from there, to jail. I'd probably make occasional side trips to the Multnomah County Courthouse downtown, but my next and final destination would be the Oregon State Penitentiary.

The man I shot was a police officer, and by his statement, he was clearly acting in that capacity when I killed him. Under Oregon law, that made my crime aggravated murder. Aggravated murder is the only crime in Oregon for which you can get the death penalty. It's either that or life in prison without the possibility of parole. And because *I* was a police officer, there's no way the DA's office would go for life without the possibility of parole. No way.

Probably the only way I could turn a date with the needle into a life sentence would be by bargaining the lives of my hostages for a signed declaration by a judge and the DA for a guaranteed sentence of life without parole. Either way, I would die in the pen. It was just a matter of when.

The thought of feigning insanity and fooling my way into the Oregon State Hospital briefly crossed my mind. The stress of the job, my sad childhood, a mental breakdown—all combining to make me lose touch with reality. Guilty by reason of insanity. Just a temporary break, but the only thing that would matter is my state of mind at the time I committed my crimes, not how I was later in court. If I could pull it off, they couldn't sentence me to death. I might go from the hospital to prison, but at least I'd be spared the cocktail.

The problem with that lies in doing it. I don't have the foggiest notion of how to convince a battery of psychiatrists that I'd lost my sense of reality. I'd have to be more than merely convincing. I'd damn near have to be insane, and even then, it would be tricky. Once they have a cop on trial for something like this, they'll want to drink my blood. No amount of pretending could possibly do it.

I next thought about shooting myself and saying I was among the hostages, and one of the other guys was the bad guy. I didn't give this option a second thought though because it was as impossible as it was ridiculous. I'd have to kill everyone in here, but then, there was still the one that got away.

I couldn't think of any other ways out. No, bargaining the lives of the hostages for a life sentence was my only hope. If I was honest with the police and showed regret and was willing to let the hostages all go in exchange for a guarantee of a life sentence, then maybe, just *maybe*, I could pull it off.

With that resolved, I settled in to wait. They'd probably call soon.

The minutes ticked by, but they didn't call. I thought about why, and the only thing that I could come up with was, since there had been no more shots fired, they were ostensibly giving me a chance to stew in my own juices while they got their collective act together, preparing to have a sniper take me out once CNT could talk me into looking out a window.

Someone knocked on the office door from the inside. "Excuse me," came the voice of Dr. Stillwell. "The young lady here needs to use the restroom. Hello?"

The way this place was laid out, you couldn't see the bathroom from the safety of the kitchen. The bathroom was very close to the front door, just past the body of the fallen deputy. I didn't want the police to see the hostage going in there, and I didn't want the hostage trying to run out. Therefore, there would be no bathroom trips. So how the hell was I supposed to handle this?

I opened the office door and stepped back, gun in hand.

"What's the problem?" I demanded, clearly irritated.

"Please try to relax," said the doctor. "She just needs to go to the bathroom, that's all. She can't help it. Surely you can understand that, right? It's going to happen to all of us sooner or later if you keep us here."

"Yeah, well, that may be, but I've got news for you. Nobody's going into the restroom. What's your name, young lady?"

"Crystal," she said dully, studying the floor.

"Can't you hold it, Crystal? I hope it won't be that long."

"No, I can't. I had to go before you came in, but it was too busy. Then Eric asked me to clean the grill, so I was going to go after that. Then you came in. I can't hold it any longer, and I really don't want to pee myself."

"Well, no bathroom trips. This door doesn't lock, and I'm not having everyone pile out of here while I babysit you in the toilet, and I'm not having you run out the door while I'm in here babysitting them. If you really need to go, you can go in a pot or something right here in the kitchen."

She looked up at me in terrified disbelief. "I'm not going in a *pot*," she said defiantly.

"You're kidding, right?" said the doctor. "You're not seriously going to make her do that, are you? My God, I'm going to have to take a crap if this goes more than an hour or two. I suppose you're going to make me take a dump here in the kitchen? What kind of a . . ."

His voice trailed off due, I'm sure, to the expression that clouded my face. I advanced toward him menacingly. "You better listen to me, and listen good. Don't you ever talk to me like that again, or you will be the first one to go. In case you haven't noticed, there's a fuckin' *dead* guy in the dining room. If you ever talk to me like that again, I will shoot you between the eyes, and it will only diminish my bargaining power by one-fifth. You all are going to do *exactly* as I tell you, or by God, you will die in this building tonight. Do you understand me?"

"Yes. Yes, I do."

"Do *all* of you understand me?"

There was a dull chorus of yeses.

I addressed Crystal once again. "Now if you have to go tinkle, then I suggest you get out here, and close the door behind you. If you can hold it, then stay there and close the door behind you. Which is it going to be?"

Crying, she stepped out and closed the door. I looked around, but this was a fast-food restaurant, not a soup kitchen. There were no pots. There was, however, a drain on the floor near the fryer.

"There," I said, pointing to it. "And make it quick."

She looked at me like she was waiting for me to turn around. There were enough knives in here that I wasn't about to do that, and I'd already lost a gal who decided to bolt. That wasn't going to happen again. I pointed again and said, "Well?"

"Please don't watch," she begged.

I softened, but just a little. "I'm sorry, Crystal. Look, just so you know, I'm not going to touch you, and this isn't about me getting off watching you pee. I hope you can see that, but if you can't, then think what you will. Either way, pee, or don't pee. Just make it quick because one minute from now, you are going back in that room, and unless you'd rather pee in your pants in front of the others, you'd better do it right now."

Wiping her eyes, she turned her back to me, lowered her pants, and squatted over the drain. She choked back a sob as she let go. Man, she really needed to pee. As she was doing so, she said, "You know, I wish *you* were a hostage and had to pee, so you'd know how humiliating this is."

"Spare me the sentiments, and just hurry up."

In one motion, she stood and pulled up her pants. "Can I at least wash my hands?" she asked defiantly.

I had to admit the kid had moxie. "Just shut up and get back in the office." My words were hard, but my tone was almost friendly, though I'd be surprised if she noticed.

After they were all safely tucked away, I thought about what she'd said.

And that's when another option occurred to me. I pulled out their wallets and cell phones and rooted around until I found the ones I wanted.

Thank you, Crystal.

Chapter 4

Forty minutes after I walked into Killer Burger, the Bearcat rolled up to the front of the restaurant and parked twenty-five or thirty feet off the main windows. It parked perpendicular to the traffic lanes, blocking both of them. The Bearcat is an advanced, fully armored urban assault vehicle, purchased through a grant from the Department of Homeland Security. It has extremely sophisticated cameras, a highly directional PA system that concentrates the sound to a narrow cone that can penetrate walls, extremely bright flood lights in all directions, glass than can take multiple rounds up to .50 caliber, and a battering ram capable of punching through reinforced doors or cinder block walls without much effort. It's a neat little $350,000 dollar urban armored personnel carrier.

I can't count the number of times I have either driven the Bearcat or sat in it parked off some location just like this, making various announcements via the loud-hailing system. I've focused the cameras into windows over a half-mile distant and still had a picture clear enough to recognize the face of the bad guy from a wanted bulletin.

I'd been expecting the Bearcat any time, but I was still surprised at how intimidating it is from this point of view. I've seen it before from this angle, but only when I was playing a bad guy in training scenarios. The real thing is infinitely different.

Now I was the bad guy, and this was no training scenario. To my friends at the command post and inside the Bearcat, this was the big one—a robbery gone bad, with a cop killing hostage taker holding five innocents and refusing to make contact. If they knew who their H-T was, trust me, it would be *the* big one.

Speaking of SERT, even now they were fervently discussing and finalizing all manner of tactical plans on how to deal with every possible contingency. These plans would include anything from making a covert entry and gaining a foothold, to making coordinated, multiple point dynamic entries through each doorway. They would discuss having the bomb squad blow a hole through the wall from the business next door and making a dynamic entry though that. They would also discuss forcing a sniper initiated tactical resolution. The most likely scenario, however, would be to inundate me with gas in an effort to drive me out or incapacitate me before taking me out and rescuing the hostages.

Their first, and hopefully only, tactic would be to negotiate. In a case like this, they would take all the time they needed to talk, talk, talk me into surrendering—any option other than risking the lives of the hostages. Nobody wanted to see that. They would do nothing more than plan those other scenarios until I dictated they use them, either by overtly threatening statements or actions, or by stalling the process of negotiations long enough. Until then, the word of the day would be to negotiate.

Since I hadn't answered the phone yet, now would come the loud-hail pleas to do so. I've made those loud-hail announcements literally hundreds of times and knew exactly what they were going to say.

As if on cue, they began. I even accurately guessed whose voice would be making them.

"Attention inside Killer Burger," announced the voice of Darth Vader. For the intimidation factor, you see. "This is the Portland Police Bureau SERT team. You are surrounded. You are ordered to put down your weapons, and exit the front doors with your hands up and empty. You will be told what to do when you are outside the restaurant. Do it right now."

Darth Vader made the announcement three more times, then switched gears. "Look, if you're unable or unwilling to come out, you need to pick up the phone. There's a police officer on the other end. This doesn't have to end badly, you know. It can end easy. But the only way that can happen is for you to either come out peacefully, or answer the phone. We're calling now. Please, answer the phone."

The moment he stopped talking the phone began to ring. Having already made up my mind what I was going to do, I closed my eyes and answered it.

"Yeah, I'm here," I twanged in a voice other than my own, silently thanking Crystal and her urinary ruminations for the idea.

I've always been great at doing voices. Sometimes, I think I missed my calling. I could have had a career doing voiceovers for cartoons and such. I do foreign accents pretty well, and I'm also very good at imitating people. I had to be careful here; I've disguised my voice dozens of time playing the role of a bad guy in training, and my teammates were used to it.

After wracking my brain for something new, I decided on a David Allen Coe kind of thing crossed with my father's brother, who sounded like a goofy Oregon country boy, even though he himself was a hardened criminal. I needed to fool these guys one last time, and I was betting my life on my ability to do so.

"Thanks for picking up," said Beth Quinlan. Who better than my own partner to be able to recognize my voice? "My name's Beth, and I'm with the Portland Police Bureau. Are you ok in there?"

"Yeah, sure. Just dandy. Hell, I got all the hamburgers a man could ask for. What the fuck could be wrong in here?"

"Look," she said, "I know this has got to be terribly stressful for you. I'm pretty sure you didn't intend for things to go wrong or for anyone to get hurt. What we've got to do now is just slow down, try to relax, and work our way through it, ok? I know it won't be easy, but together, we can do that. One step at a time. No pressure, no hurry, ok? I don't know what to call you. Would you mind giving me your first name?"

Beth was good. She'd already shown empathy for me, allied herself with me by telling me she realizes I never intended for things to go this way, and given me subliminal hope that it could get better, all while taking the pressure off and laying the foundation for a rapport.

"Bob."

"Ok, good. Thank you, Bob. So, Bob, I want to get this out there right off. Other than being scared and stressed out, are you ok? Do you need any medical attention or anything?"

"Medical attention? No, I don't need medical attention, Betty. What I need is to get out of here."

"It's Beth, Bob, not Betty. Anyway, I hope you'll let me discuss that with you. Because that's what we both want, for this thing to come to an end without anybody else getting hurt. But how about the others? Are they ok? Do any of them need medical attention?"

"Nobody needs anything, Beth. And yeah, since I'm sure you already know all about it, the dude out front ain't as lucky. But that guy tried to *shoot* me! I just got him before he got me is all, and now you guys want to kill me for it!"

"Nobody's going to kill anyone, Bob. I can promise you that. I'm really sorry that happened to you. I'm sorry that guy tried to be a hero or whatever. I'm sorry you're in the position you're in right now, but it doesn't have to get any worse. It's still salvageable. It's still something that you can get out of."

It was surreal negotiating with Beth like this. I've written and acted in dozens of training scenarios and this was no different, only this was no made-up scenario. This time, I was doing it for my life. The sense of déjà vu was like being on an episode of The Twilight Zone.

I sorted through the wallets until I found the reserve deputy's. I didn't know if the gal who'd escaped heard him identify himself or not. It was possible CNT and SERT didn't know the dead man was a cop. I don't struggle with issues of conscience, but in this case, I wanted someone to let the man's family know. Even though I knew the cops would go harder on me if they knew I'd killed one of their own, I decided to tell them. If things went my way, they wouldn't know that *I* had done it until I was long gone anyway.

"Beth, even though it don't look like it, I want you to know I'm not a violent guy. I didn't mean to kill that dude. I know that don't mean shit now, but I want you to understand that."

"I believe you, Bob. Thank you for that, and I'm sure you'll get to tell your side of it. If it's any consolation, I can tell you that, in the end, they're going to look at all angles of this. It's not just what you did, but what was going on in your mind at the time, and maybe what's most important to you—how you handled yourself afterward. Like right now."

"I ain't ready to talk about what I'm going to do sometime in the future. First, I want to give you that guy's name, and I want someone to let his wife and kids know he ain't coming home. I'd tell you to tell them I'm sorry, but they won't believe that."

"Well, I believe it, for what it's worth. I hope that makes you feel just a little better."

"Thanks, I guess. I got his driver's license here. His name is Horace Anderson, and he lives at 6583 SW Jefferson Avenue, down in Covallis."

"We can do that, Bob. Again, thank you for doing this. You're doing the right thing."

"Beth, he got ID that says he was a reserve Benton County sheriff's deputy. Tell his folks he died trying to do right by strangers."

She was unfazed. That's always been one of Beth's better qualities as a negotiator, her inability to get rattled. "I'll tell them that, Bob. And I'll tell them you said you were sorry."

"Won't do no good, but tell 'em anyway. I know they ain't gonna want to hear nothin' about me 'cept that I'm dead, but thanks for telling 'em."

"You're welcome, and thank you for telling me that, Bob."

"Ok, then. I'm gonna hang up now. I want you to call me back after you have someone talk to his people. I know you probably don't get it, but this means a lot to me."

"Wait a second, Bob. Before you go, can you promise me that you're not going to do anything to make this worse? Like hurt anyone?"

"Beth. I'm having you guys go down there to try to make this right by this guy, and you think I'm going to hurt someone else? Why in the hell would I do that? I thought you understood me."

She said quietly, "I meant you, Bob. I don't want you to hurt yourself."

Beth was awesome. She'll become the primary negotiator when the dust settles after this incident, and she deserves it. She's obviously ready for it.

"Oh, ok. Sorry I went off on you. I won't do nothing stupid. Will it take long to call me back?"

"Probably about ten minutes or so. We're on the phone with the Benton County Sheriff's Office now."

"Ok, I'll talk to you then," I said and hung up the phone.

So far, so good.

I gathered all the other wallets and laid out the IDs. I wanted to be ready the next time Beth called back. It was all going to be about good will and showing progress. I know that Darren, as the CNT team leader, would be giving regular progress reports to the command post on the state of negotiations. My plan was to make them feel full of hope—like they were making progress. I didn't want this to drag out long, so I began preparing myself for what was about to come.

The phone rang exactly ten minutes later.

"Bob?" said Beth when I answered it. "The Benton County S.O. is sending their chaplain and a couple officers to Deputy Anderson's house now."

"Who did you talk to down there?"

"We were put through to the sheriff himself."

"Did he know Anderson?"

There was a brief pause, "Yes. They were pretty close."

"Did you tell him I was sorry?"

"We did."

"And how did he take it?"

"Are you sure you want to know?"

"I asked you, didn't I?"

"Ok. But I don't want to lie to you, and I don't want you to lie to me. I think we've kind of established sort of an understanding, and I don't want us to break that."

"Just what did he say, Beth?"

Beth paused just long enough to let me know she didn't want to tell me. "He said he hopes we blow your fucking brains out."

"That's pretty much what I figured. That tells me you're being honest with me and not just jerkin' my chain. Ok, Beth, here's what I want to do next. I want to give you the names of everyone else in here. Go get a pen or something. I'll wait."

"I already have one, Bob. Go ahead."

"Ok. They're Eric Saunders, Crystal Manheim, Robert Stillwell, and James Halverson. You probably already talked to the red-haired girl who ran out earlier. She was with James Halverson. I figure she's either his wife or girlfriend."

"Thank you, Bob. We talked to her. They were married six months ago. But she said there were five others, and that's only four names."

"That's right. There's one more. I thought you might like to talk to him yourself. Hang on, and I'll put him on the phone."

I moved the phone away and said, "All right buddy, you're on." Then I jostled the handset and said in my own voice, "Hello, Beth. It's me, DJ."

"Oh, thank God! Are you ok? We found your car parked down the street when we ran all the plates parked nearby. When you didn't answer the call, we figured you were in there."

"I'm fine. Look, I'm really sorry. I fucked up bad, Beth. I gave up my gun. You *never* give up your gun. I fucked up really, really bad."

"Don't second-guess yourself, DJ. Please, don't do that. I'm sure you know what to do in there. Just keep cool and be reassuring to him. We're going to get you out of there; I promise you that."

"You already did. He's letting me go. I tried to get him to let the girl go. Christ, she's pissed herself, and she's just a kid. I don't want to come out of here and leave the others stuck inside, but he's making me. I don't think he wants a cop in here."

"No, DJ, that's good! You can give us intel the others couldn't. We'll use that to get everyone out. I have a good feeling about this. Can you tell me anything right now, like is anyone else hurt? What's his state of mind?"

"He's been straight with you, Beth. Nobody's hurt, and he really just wants this to end. He never planned on hurting anyone. Things went to shit real fast, and I believe all he wants to do now is fix it and get out. Maybe bargain for a lighter sentence or something. You can help him with that."

"This is going to end well, DJ. How does he—?"

"Beth? He wants me to give him the phone. I'm handing it to him now."

I did the handoff to myself again, saying in my country boy voice, "Ok, I'm lettin' him go first. Just him for now. The rest we'll do later. Like he said, I'm going to want a deal. No death penalty and a light sentence. This was your buddy's idea. I get a signed paper from a judge and a districk attorney. Then I'll let the others go. You start working on the judge and the DA. When you tell me they're on their way here, I'll let another one go. When we come up with an agreement, another one. Once it's signed by everyone, I'll give up."

"Fine, fine, Bob. I'm sure we can do that. Let me again say thanks for doing the right thing. Can you let him go now?"

"Yeah. I'm going to hang up, and then I'm going into the office with the others. I have three guns—mine, your cop buddy's, and Anderson's.

You know I don't want to hurt anyone, but if any cops come through that door when he comes out, I will. Please, Beth, give me your word that won't happen."

"I promise you nothing like that will happen. You hang up, and I'll tell everyone out there that the officer—his name is DJ, and he's a friend of mine—is coming out. I swear to you that nobody will try anything. We all want this to go smoothly, just the same as you."

"Ok, I believe you, Beth. He'll come walking out in one minute. Call me back ten minutes after he comes out, ok? And you better tell me you got a judge and a DA coming here. I'm going to want their signatures on paper."

"Sure, Bob. Thank you."

I hung up, walked back to the office, and opened the door. They were all quiet and calm. Nobody wanted be the one to get my attention.

"Ok. Here's what I want you to do. In about twenty minutes, I'm going to release one of you as a show of good faith. You guys are going to decide who it is. Talk among yourselves, and figure out the order you want to be released in. It doesn't matter to me."

Dr. Stillwell said, "It should be Crystal."

Eric said, "I agree."

I said, "I don't want to hear how or why. Just do it among yourselves. First, Doc, I need you to give me the PIN to your bank account."

"What? Why would you— "

"Just do it! And don't lie to me. What's a little bit of money? Besides, we all know I'm not getting out of here, so just give me the fucking number!"

"Ten forty-two. One, oh, four two."

"Ok. One of you be ready to go in twenty minutes. Do not open the door before then." With that, I closed them back in. I took the cash from their wallets, along with Stillwell's Wells Fargo card and put it all in my underwear. I had a hundred forty-seven bucks total, including the sixty-one I had in my own wallet when I came in here. I put the deputy's .380 in there too and stuffed my Glock in the front of my pants.

I unlocked the door, raised my hands over my head, and stepped into the street.

Chapter 5

"This way, DJ," shouted a voice just to the west of the front window. It was getting dark, and at first, the SERT officer was indistinguishable from the others. When I was close, I recognized him as David Woodrow, one of the night shifters I had relieved a few hours ago.

"Jesus, am I glad to see you," I said. "Where's the command post?"

"Around the corner, on Tillamook. I'll take you there."

"Don't worry about it. I'm not hurt or anything. I'm pretty sure I can find my way."

"Ok. They want you at the CNT van. They'll have someone there to debrief you."

I smiled at him. "I actually know that," I said.

"Yeah, I guess you do. Hey, I don't know what happened in there, but don't second-guess yourself. You're a good cop. I'm sure you did what you had to do. I'm just glad you got out."

"Thanks," I said. I was actually struggling with the fact that my brother officers were going to think I gave up my gun to a bad guy. I found myself concerned about them thinking badly of my officer safety tactics. No cop would ever give up his gun. If I wasn't terrified, I would have found the notion humorous, given that in a couple of hours, when they learned what really happened in Killer Burger, their opinion of me was probably going change a lot more than if I had given up my gun.

I rounded the corner, and there was the command post—two large vans and a white Sprinter parked next to each other, all with generators roaring. Additionally, there were no less than fifteen cars parked haphazardly around them. The blue and white van was a mobile command post, the dark blue one was the SERT van, and the Sprinter was the CNT van. The cars were a mix of marked and plainclothes units. Bright lights half a block to the east marked the press information area. Two news helicopters and a low-flying drone clattered overhead, no doubt hoping to film a juicy shootout in time for the ten o'clock news.

I wanted to go directly to my car and flee, but it was parked half a block to the west on Tillamook. Fortunately, it was outside the perimeter; unfortunately, I had to go through the perimeter to get to it.

Before I could get around the command post, the back door to the CNT van opened. Sandra Kowalski, a child sex abuse detective who was our intel officer, stepped out.

"Thank God, DJ. Perimeter guys giving out plates near the restaurant came up with yours almost right away. When you didn't answer the page, we all figured you were in there. Once we found that out, we made Menendez go back and check the body on the floor a second time to make sure it wasn't you. We all figured if he found out you were a cop, he'd take you out first."

"I don't blame you, Sandra. I would have thought the same thing. As it turns out, though, this guy isn't like that. I don't think he's gonna cap anyone. Maybe himself, though. I definitely picked up on some suicidal ideations when talking to him. But I think as long as you can keep him talking, you're going to get every one of those people out."

"What's he like? Is he scared?"

"He didn't mean for the robbery to go bad. He said when the guy with the gun stood up and started shooting, he just closed his eyes and pulled the trigger. I was in the bathroom, and had no idea what was going on. It didn't even sound like gunshots. I came out of the bathroom to see what the hell was happening and saw the dead guy. I started to draw my off-duty when the bad guy, who I didn't even see because he was behind me, stuck the barrel of his gun against my head. It was still warm from killing the guy. He . . . he grabbed my gun, and I just let go of it. Christ, Sandra, I don't even know why. I fuckin' pussied out . . . "

"Listen, DJ, no response is wrong if it works out. You talking to that guy probably saved the lives of all those hostages in there."

"Yeah. Still . . . "

"Dean, come into the van. We're going to need to formally debrief you."

"I know. Listen, my work phone is in my car of all places. He took my personal phone. Give me a minute to call my mother, ok? I'll be right in."

"No problem. DJ, did you know the guy he shot was a cop?"

"Yeah, we talked about brokering a deal with the DA. Release everyone for life instead of death."

"See," she said, "that was brilliant. That's why you being there probably saved all their lives. Don't worry about the gun thing. You're going to go down as a hero in this."

"Thanks, Sandra. I'll be back in two minutes." With my head hung low, I headed over to my car. Sandra went back into the van. I got in the car, but then I realized that not only half the cops in town know what I drive, but there would be a BOLO, or a be on the lookout broadcast for the car in ten minutes.

I set off on foot instead. Three blocks east on Sandy at 43rd was a Wells Fargo. For each account, I could only get $360 at a time, so after tapping both mine and Dr. Stillwell's, I had a grand total of $887 to go on the run with. From there, it was a short walk south to the Hollywood Transit Center light rail station.

Suddenly, it occurred to me that the police could track my phone. When I passed a convenience store, I placed it among the garbage in the bed of a broken-down pickup truck. Now they could follow it all they wanted.

Twenty-five minutes after slipping away from the SERT callout, I was seated on a westbound Max train heading downtown. I had no plan besides going downtown to blend in with the homeless crowd to buy time.

It was after ten when I got off at Skidmore Fountain, beneath the Burnside Bridge on the outskirts of downtown. It was still pouring, and the sheltered area under bridge was crowded. Welcome to Transient Central.

By now, the police must have surmised that, for whatever reason, I had decided I could not bring myself to face my peers and just wandered off. Maybe they were thinking the stress of having been taken hostage was too much for me, or I was too ashamed about giving up my gun.

I imagined their frustration when "Bob" never answered the phone. Since I was unable to lock my hostages up in the office, I figured they would eventually come out. When CNT called and I didn't answer, one among them would eventually venture forth to check. Or maybe CNT would loud-hail again. If that failed to get a hostage to pick up the phone, they would probably send in a robot to check on me. In any case, I didn't think it would be much more than an hour before they realized I was gone. Searching the building would take another hour or two, and then they'd realize exactly what had happened.

I would have loved to hear the radio traffic when hostages began wandering out into the dining room and eventually out the door. I expect there would be a warrant out for my arrest within two hours.

When the rain finally let up around 3 A.M. or so, I wandered south along the waterfront. The space under the Morrison bridge was a lot less crowded, so I staked out a spot and lay back. I was one of at least fifteen denizens camped out there.

Years ago, I worked this area on graveyards as a rookie, and I know the cops don't mess with the transients as long as they're not bothering anyone. I didn't sleep much, but at least I felt safely hidden from the police. I was sure that, by now, they were looking for me.

The night was uneventful and long, but when morning came, I was still free and had the beginning of a plan in my mind. I knew I would have to be extremely careful. I was by now probably the most wanted man in Bureau history, and I couldn't afford any mistakes.

I ate a deliciously greasy breakfast at one of Portland's famous food carts, and then I made my way to Pioneer Square, where I hung out for over an hour in a secluded corner of Starbucks until the Wells Fargo opened. I carefully weighed the risk of taking my money out and decided to chance it. I had another four thousand in savings, and on top of that, my paycheck would have been deposited in my checking account yesterday.

The way I figured it, if Wells Fargo had been notified that I was wanted, the teller would try to stall me while someone called the police. So, if anything unusual happened, my plan was to duck out and lay low.

How or where, I didn't know. They would flood the whole downtown area with cops, and every Max train would have officers looking for me. Eluding them might prove to be impossible.

The bank may not be such a good idea, but I'm a man who is known to take risks. If it pans out, I might stand a decent chance of getting away. It was a risk I was willing to take.

At precisely 9 A.M., I walked into Wells Fargo like I owned the place. I was the first customer, and the teller, an attractive young lady in her early twenties, never batted an eye when I presented my debit card and told her I wanted to close my accounts and take my money out in fifties and twenties. I thought she might need to get a supervisor's approval, but she didn't. Instead, she pulled a drawer, grabbed stacks of money, and started counting. At one point, she had to go to a different drawer, but she never spoke to anyone, and I never lost sight of her. I kept a sharp eye on all the other employees, and absolutely nothing unusual happened.

The girl handed me the contents of both my savings and checking account, just over six thousand dollars, and gave me a zippered cash bag, thanking me for my years of loyal business. And that was that.

On the way out, I turned to the little black globe containing the camera, held up my moneybag, and with a wink, I waved goodbye to the cops who would be reviewing the video. Like the hood rats say, "Fuck da police." It was immature, yes, but I couldn't resist.

Melting back onto the street, I returned to the waterfront and considered my plan. There were a couple of things I would need. In no particular order, I wanted a decent backpack, a water bottle, a couple changes of clothes, and some personal toiletries. I'd also love to have a smart phone and data plan, but that might just prove to be too dangerous. I'd have to check into how anonymous companies like Cricket actually were. Perhaps most important of all, though, I would need a legitimate vehicle with current tags and nothing illegal about it.

The gear I could purchase at any store. The car would be a little more difficult, but Craigslist would have a plethora to choose from. I had a windowless van in mind, to which I could add a foam pad and a sleeping bag, so I wouldn't have to spend any more nights outside. As long as the registration wasn't expired and it was street legal, I'd be good to go. I had nearly seven thousand dollars to work with, so I should be able to find something.

I headed to the library to use their free computers. Once there, I spent quite a while writing down phone numbers for potential cars before it occurred to me that I didn't have a phone to call or text with. I created a new Yahoo email account under a made-up name, which I used to email them, but only one guy got back to and his was the wrong kind of van.

Finally, I walked out with a long list of phone numbers. I'd have to change a ten into quarters and find a pay phone. I didn't know if payphones existed anymore.

As I walked down the stairs of the library, I noticed two cops walking a foot beat, which immediately set off alarm klaxons in my brain. There are no regular foot beats in this part of town.

The cops stopped a guy about my age and size and began shaking him down.

This did not look good to me. You don't get two officers on foot around here without a police car or two parked somewhere nearby. I ducked into a parking garage across the street a little north of the library and climbed to the top floor. Here, I got a nice elevated view of the area.

To my horror, there were cops everywhere. Two were on horseback, there was another pair a block east of me, and I saw two black-and-whites cruising slowly. One stopped to shake down a transient. He, too, was about my age and size.

I stood transfixed and watched for several minutes. Clearly, they were looking for me. When one of the squad cars pulled into the parking garage entrance beneath me, I ducked in front of a car and tried to hide against the wall. It took five minutes, but I finally saw the car cruise slowly past me. It kept going without stopping, but I waited another ten minutes just to be sure.

It was the bank. It had to be. I was there at nine, and nobody was interested in me at all. Now it was almost a quarter to one, and cops were all over the place, shaking down everyone who met my general description.

They must have contacted all the Wells Fargo branches within minutes after they opened. Going for my money had been a stupid move, and I'd been incredibly lucky to get in and out before the police got word to my branch.

I wouldn't last another night on the streets under this kind of pressure. I know the temperature of the Bureau. PPB had recently come under intense scrutiny for everything—from the way we handle the mentally ill, to a couple of inexplicable deaths of people in police custody, and questionable police shootings. The Department of Justice had recently concluded a scathing review of Portland police practices, and in response, the city manager and police chief put into place a civilian oversight committee to keep an eye on the police. I could easily see the city spending thousands of dollars on a huge manhunt for me. All the overtime you want, as long as you contact and identify anyone at all who could possibly be Officer Appleby. Find him, and bring him in, regardless of the cost.

I needed a way out of downtown, and I needed it now. At this point, stealing a car looked like an acceptable risk. I was in a parking garage full of them, but despite my years as a cop, I had no idea how to steal one. All I knew was it had something to do with ripping apart the steering column and twisting the ignition wires together, and I'd learned that from Hollywood. But how many wires were in there, and which ones were the ignition wires? If I got the wrong ones, might I start a fire or get electrocuted?

I had taken thousands of stolen car reports and recovered hundreds more stolen cars over the years, but I didn't think I could successfully steal one. Probably half of them had been hot-wired, but that didn't help me. What the hell kind of bad cop was I, anyway?

I was trapped in this garage, and I needed to get out of the city. Today. Now. I closed my eyes and made myself slow down. I tried to relax my racing mind. I didn't need to make any more stress mistakes, like locking the hostages into a small room with a bunch of phones.

Right now, for the moment, I was somewhat safe. There was a way out of here. All I had to do was find it.

I was afraid the owner of the car that I was hiding behind might return, and that's when it hit me. All of these cars were going to leave. Instead of stealing one, all I had to do was stow away in one. It was risky, but that's never stopped me before. It was better than my other alternative, which was catching someone getting into a car and jacking it, taking the owner along so he didn't call the police. Another kidnapping and robbery charge wouldn't hurt me since I was already looking at a capital crime, but I had no more stomach for committing crimes—at least not at the moment.

I decided to try the stowaway idea. If I could get in the back of a van, for example, and hide behind the backseat, the driver probably would have no clue that I was there. And if he did catch me, I would have to kidnap him.

The more I thought of that, the more it appealed to me. If I was caught, I could force the driver to take me to his home, where I could secure him and even hide out for a day or so.

I hoped that wouldn't happen though. It just wasn't clean, and something could easily go wrong. I might end up having to kill again, and I desperately didn't want to do that. I just wanted to get away.

There was a plethora of cars to choose from, but I was mainly interested in minivans. They would be easier to hide in, but I didn't want someone opening the rear door with an armload of packages only to discover me.

I tried several van doors, all of which were locked. I was a nervous wreck because trying door handles is a great way to get the police called on you.

There was nothing on the top level. I went down to the next level and immediately found a dirty white pickup with a canopy. Inside, there was a rake, a leaf blower, and other miscellaneous garden tools. Best of all, the bed was half-filled with leaves and a large canvas tarp.

I looked around to make sure I was alone. Smiling to myself, I immediately climbed inside, burrowed deep into the pile, covered myself with the tarp, and waited.

It was hot and uncomfortable, but I eventually dozed off. An hour-and-a-half later, I awoke when two men got in, both Hispanic males. The truck started and away we went. Once we were under way, I was able to peek out and follow our progress.

We drove our way right out of downtown and onto I-84, heading east. After that, we went south on the 205. So far, so good. We took an exit, though I couldn't tell which one. I knew it was still north of Sunnyside Road, where the Clackamas Town Center mall is located. We were probably on Foster Road or Johnston Creek Boulevard. From there, we went east into a confusion of side streets, and I lost track of where we were. Finally, we pulled into the driveway of a house sitting on a large piece of property. The occupants got out and disappeared.

I didn't wait. After hearing the door to the house close, I wormed my way out of the truck. A quick look around revealed that my good luck was holding. Not a soul to be seen. There wasn't even a child playing in sight. I just walked away in the direction we had come.

Eventually, I came to the intersection of SE 72nd and Tenino. I was on the northeastern edge of Milwaukie, and I knew how to get out of here. Heading south on 72nd, I eventually came to SE Harney, a street I'm familiar with. Harney crosses the Springwater Trail, which is a hiking and biking path that stretches from downtown Portland all the way out to the town of Boring, a distance of about twenty miles. The Springwater Trail is exactly where I wanted to go. And yes, there really is a town called Boring, Oregon.

Every cop is familiar with the Springwater Trail. It's like an interstate highway for much of Portland's homeless population, and I figured it would be the best place for me to lay low until dark. After that, I could probably make my way north on 82nd Avenue, which is full of cheap car lots, busy shopping plazas, strip clubs, and no-tell motels. I should be able to blend in perfectly with everyone else on the streets. The short plan was to get a room in one of the many cheap motels and lay low for a couple of days.

By this time, I was exhausted. I was tired of spending time outdoors, but I had to stay out of the public eye until dark, or at least until I could change my appearance. I longed for the comfort of a clean bed.

I had at least three or four more hours until dark. Once I got to the trail, I headed west. The next crossing, as far as I knew, would be 82nd. It wasn't long before I found a well-trodden foot path heading from the trail off into the woods. Following it, I eventually came to an unoccupied transient camp. From the look of the filthy blanket and sodden sleeping bag, it hadn't been used for a while.

I found the driest spot around and laid down. The ground was uncomfortable as hell, but I was so tired I fell asleep in minutes.

When I awoke, it was dark out. I had no idea what time it was, but I sensed it was still pretty early. I hung out for what I thought was an hour or so, then headed back to the trail. In about ten minutes, I came to

SE 82nd Avenue. I headed north, and in three blocks, I found exactly what I was looking for.

The Outside Inn looked perfect, and if it wasn't, there was always the El Rancho across the street. Both were located within feet of Area 69, a strip joint that looked as seedy as its name. I chose the Outside Inn.

This was nowhere I'd willingly go if I wasn't on the run from a capital crime, but as it happened, I was. The idea of actually getting into a bed here made my skin crawl. I wanted a decent night's sleep, but not at the price of a MRSA or scabies infection. Closing my eyes, I forced myself to rely on millions of years of evolution to give me what I needed to protect myself from a night in the Outside Inn.

The guy behind the counter looked as if he hadn't had a shower in a week. He was bald, greasy, overweight, and looked like the type of man who might have a heart attack at any given time. He didn't glance up at me when I walked in.

"Couple nights?"

He glanced up and was about to look back down, but then his eyes lingered on mine for a perceptible moment. I was hyper aware, almost to the point of paranoia, but I didn't imagine the slight widening of his eyes, or the hint of recognition in his expression, despite his attempt to cover it.

"Sorry. Full."

I pulled a wad of cash and said, "You sure there aren't any cancellations?"

His eyes lingered on the wad: "Maybe I do got a room. Oh, yeah, here's one. But it's a cash only room. This one's two hundred a night."

I don't know how much I'd been on the news, but I had no doubt he'd recognized me. I also got the impression he wouldn't have cared if I was wearing striped prison pajamas and was dragging an iron ball on a chain, as long as I had two hundred a night. Rooms were advertised at forty-five a night, so I figured I was getting the fugitive rate.

"Perfect," I said, peeling five hundred off the wad. He watched my every move and eyed the money hungrily. I handed the bills over and said, "Tonight and tomorrow. I would prefer to have no visitors, so the tip is for you to let me know if anyone shows interest in me."

He nodded, emitting a glottal noise that could have been either an acknowledgement or the onset of that heart attack. This was clearly a man accustomed to not always playing by the rules.

Our arrangement apparently did not include any paperwork. He handed me an old-fashioned key attached to a greasy blue plastic tag with the number four on it. Taking it, I said, "Maybe I could have a minute on your computer tomorrow morning?"

"Hundred bucks every thirty minutes."

"No problem," I said. The room was horrible, but it had a bed, a shower, a TV, and a phone. I could watch myself on the news and make all the Craigslist calls I wanted.

It was 10:45 when I closed the door and settled in. At 11:00, I turned on the local news. Needless to say, yesterday's SERT incident and its mysterious ending was still the lead story. From what I gathered, when it finally came to an end, the Bureau had initially stopped short of saying I had done it. I was listed only as missing and a "person of interest." A few hours after that, they had released the information that a material witness warrant had been issued for me, which alluded that I knew something the police wanted to know and was on the run from them. At a 5:00 P.M. press conference, they reluctantly admitted that I was now considered the only suspect, and the warrant had been changed to an arrest warrant.

I was out there somewhere, believed to still be in the Portland area. Citizens were being warned not to contact me if I was seen, but to call 911 immediately. I was armed and dangerous. I was also crafty; somehow, I'd slipped out of a SERT cordon after killing a fellow police officer. Efforts to find me have been concentrated in the downtown area, where it was speculated I might be staying in homeless shelters or hiding among street people.

Pretty much everything they said about me was true. Yes, I was armed. I had two pistols, though not much in the way of ammunition. I actually *was* dangerous because I had killed a man and was capable of killing again if I had to. As for my craftiness, well, they were partially right on that one. Negotiating my own release with my CNT partner had been a stroke of genius, but getting out of the downtown cordon was more luck than craftiness.

The good news was that, for the moment, my luck seemed to be holding.

I was torn as to what to do. My instincts were telling me to get as far away from Portland as I could as fast as possible. On the other hand, I was pretty sure I could trust the motel clerk as long as my money held out. I felt relatively safe here, and the Outside Inn was miles from downtown, where they were concentrating the search for me.

Buying a car from Craiglist was no longer viable with all the news coverage and my picture being broadcast regularly on TV and the Internet. I may be safe, but I was also trapped.

Trapped inside the Outside. If I ever wrote a book about my little crime spree, that's what I'd call it.

I revisited the idea of stealing a car. Some of the used car lots along 82nd Avenue wouldn't have building alarms, and many of the "offices" were merely flimsy trailers. It wouldn't be hard to get in one and break into the key box, where I would have my choice from among the lot's inventory. However, driving a stolen car around wasn't safe. I would have to get rid of it as soon as possible, and once it was discovered wherever I dumped it, the police would have an idea of the direction I was headed and a new place to start looking. Even if I were to drive it to another state and buy a car on Craigslist once I got there, the police would plaster my face all over the news there, and the seller would probably come forward.

I couldn't hitchhike out of Portland because of the news coverage. It was plain dumb luck that I hadn't been recognized and turned in already. What I really needed was outside help, but I didn't know anyone who I could trust. Contacting family was out of the question.

In desperation, I even considered stealing a canoe from somewhere and trying to paddle my way to some safe haven downriver on the Columbia.

The truth was, there were no viable options, and I was glad I had temporary shelter, so I didn't have to worry about it right at that moment. Regardless of how I was going to do it, my short-term goal was to get out of Portland and go someplace far away. I hadn't arrived at a final plan yet, but I was pretty sure it involved crossing illegally into Canada and living on the streets of one of the bigger cities. I'd heard that they had nice shelters, free medical care, and other social services up there. In any case, it was a predominantly white English speaking country where (hopefully) my fingerprints wouldn't come back with a warrant for my arrest.

I took a shower, but I didn't shave. I could grow a beard in about five days. It wasn't much, but at least it would alter my appearance to some degree. Finally, I screwed up my courage and crawled between the sheets. The seedy blanket was stained and had cigarette burns. I quickly shut the light off and tried not to think what would show up on a black light scan for evidence in this bed.

Sleep wouldn't come. I tried some background music from the cheap clock radio, but it was to no avail. Although my body was tired, my mind was racing. My life had turned a hundred eighty degrees in the past day-and-a-half. Yesterday morning, I wore a badge and a gun and patrolled my district as I had for the past eighteen years. A few hours after going off-duty, I was being ruthlessly hunted by my friends and colleagues after committing a capital crime.

The police, I knew, wouldn't hesitate to use deadly force on me if necessary. If I did survive the coming encounter with them, I would die in prison, either from natural causes, homicidal violence, or a hideous pharmaceutical cocktail while the world watched in eager anticipation.

It was no wonder I couldn't sleep. Instead, I thought of my past, which is something I don't like to do. My childhood wasn't easy, though I don't suppose it would help to blame it for who I eventually became.

Whenever I thought about my youth, I thought about Connie.

Chapter 6

October 31, 1982

Halloween was on Sunday this year. Last week, Mrs. Kaber let the class decide if we wanted to have our party on Friday afternoon before Halloween or on Monday morning after. As second graders, she said, we were old enough to make that decision ourselves. We voted and decided to have it on Monday, which was tomorrow, because then we could bring all our candy to share. That also meant I could wear my brand-new skeleton costume with the glow-in-the-dark bones to school tomorrow morning. I was more excited about that than wearing it tonight for trick-or-treat.

Mom didn't think Connie was going to be able to go trick-or-treating this year, and secretly, I was glad about that. Connie was my ten-year-old sister, two years older than me. She got sick six months ago, back in April, when I was in Miss Sarah's first grade class. Her sickness had been getting worse and worse, and that changed pretty much everything in our house.

My mom and dad used to laugh a lot and do things with us. On Saturdays in the summer, when Dad wasn't working, he used to take us down the Gorge in his convertible. Sometimes, we'd just go to the river and swim, other times we hiked, and other times we'd go to Hood River and have lunch. Once, we went all the way up to Timeberline, where people can ski even in the summer and rode the chairlift up the mountain. Mom brought a picnic lunch, and we hiked around all day, real high up on Mt. Hood.

I had really been looking forward to this summer because now that I was getting bigger, we could do more things. Dad was going to buy a canoe, and we were going to spend all summer canoeing and camping on lakes and rivers. I looked forward to that all winter long.

Then Connie got cancer.

Everything came to a stop in our house. Suddenly, Mom was crying all the time, and I even saw Dad cry sometimes. At the end of September, I won a citizenship award at school, and they didn't care. There was an assembly that parents were supposed to go to, but we didn't go because it was at night and Connie had to get a treatment that night, which they both wanted to attend. So instead of going to the assembly and getting my citizenship award, I went to the stupid hospital and watched Connie's medicine drip into her arm.

She got candy, and I didn't get anything.

Me and Connie have always been close. She always let me use her stuff when I wanted—play-doh, her Etch A Sketch when mine broke, and stuff that boys can play with that she had.

Even though she didn't really want to use my stuff, I'd let her if she wanted to, and she knew it. Ever since I was a little kid, if I had bad dreams, I'd go to her room, and we'd sleep in the same bed. That still hasn't changed now that I'm getting bigger, either. I knew it would someday. Last Christmas Eve, she wanted me to sleep with her, and I didn't want to, but I did anyway. We tried to stay up 'til midnight, but neither of us made it. We whispered all night long though, even after Mom told us we'd better go back to sleep because Santa knew when we were sleeping, and he knew when we were awake.

That's one of the things we talked about. She told me Santa wasn't really real, and I told her I didn't believe in him anyway because how could he go to everyone's house at the same time? But we tried to stay up anyway, just in case.

By Easter, Connie was sick. The Saturday night before Easter was the last time I slept in her bed. We got up in the morning, but she didn't feel well, and I gave her half of my eggs from the Easter egg hunt. I kept the one with the dollar though.

By the time school let out, Connie had to start taking the medicine. It made her even sicker, she got real thin, and her eyes got real big because she lost so much weight. I cried and cried right along with Mom and Dad when her hair started falling out. Everyone cried but Connie.

I never saw Connie cry about having cancer. Even when I could tell it hurt, she never cried. Not that I saw, but she had her own room, and I thought maybe she cried when nobody was around. I'd cry if my hair fell out, I'll tell you, and I'm a boy.

In the middle of the summer, there was a break from all the sadness. Connie was getting better. Mom and Dad bought her a Lhasa Apso—which sounds like a monster but is really a little dog—to celebrate her getting better. Connie named it Deeohgee. All that dog wanted to do was play, and Connie loved him more than anything.

To me, it was just another reason to be jealous of Connie. I wanted the dog to be mine, too, and I wanted a vote in naming him. I know there's no way I'd have named him Deeohgee. If it was up to me, that dog's name would have been something like Killer, or Spike, or Brutus, which would have been funny 'cause he was so little. But I didn't get to vote on his name. I think Deeohgee knew somehow that Connie was sick because he never left her side. He loved everyone in the family, but when Connie was around, all he saw was her.

The first couple weeks of that summer was a nice little island in all the sadness around Connie. As she got better, she started growing her hair back and gaining weight. We went to Fort Vancouver for the Fourth of July because Connie said she was feeling up to it. It was pretty boring, even though we had Kentucky Fried Chicken and Mom made brownies. It was forever before the fireworks started, and I fell asleep right after they finished. Connie was better, but she got tired walking back to the car, so I had to walk because Dad wanted to carry her. It was a real long way back to the car, too.

Not long after the Fourth of July, Deeohgee started acting different. He whined when he was around Connie, and he refused to leave her side. One night, he started barking and going crazy in the middle of the night and woke everyone up. He was running around in circles and barking at the foot of Connie's bed. When we got in there, he jumped up on the bed and started licking Connie's face, and that's how we learned that she was sick again. That night, we took her to the hospital and found out that her cancer was back.

Mom told me a bunch of times that summer that I was going to have to grow up and learn to do more stuff faster than if Connie wasn't sick because so much of their time was going to be spent helping her. Before Connie got sick, my mom always cleaned my room and made my bed, but that summer, probably two weeks after the fourth of July, she stopped making my bed. First, she said I had to do it every day, but whenever I made my bed, it wasn't very made. Pretty soon, she stopped making me, and I stopped doing it. I tried to keep my room at least a little clean, but just like the bed, it wasn't as clean as my mom used to keep it.

Before Connie got sick and her hair fell out, I was only allowed to ride my bike in our driveway, on the sidewalk down to Tommy Smith's house on one side, and to the green house on the other. But after she got sick, nobody cared where I rode my bike. They just quit noticing. I learned that I wasn't going to get in trouble if I did stuff like staying out too long, or going down to the woods by myself.

I started going to the woods every day. That's where I met Jason. Jason liked to get in trouble. I never heard a kid talk to grownups like Jason did. He cussed all the time, too. I know cuss words too, but boy, would Dad ever whip me if he heard me say them. I said them around Jason, though, a lot. Jason was a year older than me, but me and him got along real good. Once we rode to 7-11, and Jason stole a pack of gum. We chewed the whole thing ourselves that day.

I stayed out longer and longer, and my parents either didn't care or didn't notice. A couple of times, my mom yelled at me for missing lunch, but that didn't last too long. By this time, Connie's cancer had come back, and they said it was going all over her body. This was toward the end of summer before second grade started. She had to go to the doctor more and more.

Mom and Dad took really good care of her. They had to go into her room a lot at night when the pain got bad, and she called for them. I couldn't sleep when that happened. I'd be real tired the next day. She was up at night a lot, and that meant I was up, too. Pretty soon, I was getting just as mad as Mom and Dad always seemed to be.

They got madder and madder at everything—not just because Connie was sick. Dad was always mad about work. He was mad because Mom didn't cook like she used to. Mom was mad because Dad never talked to anyone anymore. He was quieter than I'd ever seen. They were both mad at the news on TV. Mom would get real mad and scream and cuss at other cars when she was driving. They both got mad at me, for nothing it seemed.

Even if I did something extra special—like the time I made them breakfast in bed (it was toast and orange juice because that's all I knew how to make, and they don't eat my kind of cereal)—they would smile and say thank you, but I could see that behind it, they were still mad. We quit going to church because they were mad at God for giving Connie cancer. That was the only good part of everyone being mad all the time, we didn't have to go to church any more.

It was the time of madness in our house. After a while, I learned to be like Mom and Dad, mad at everything. When Mom would cuss a driver out, I knew it wasn't really the driver. It was just everything. When everything gets you mad, you get mad at everything. I became like the cat in Tom and Jerry when Jerry stuck a bicycle pump in his mouth and started pumping air into him. There was nowhere for all the air to go, so he just blew up like a big balloon and floated away. That's how I felt with all the anger that was going into me. There wasn't any place for it to go, so it just filled me up, and I felt like I was floating away.

By this time, Connie couldn't do very much. She could just lie in bed with a book or the TV on, but I watched her, and she never read her book, and she didn't watch the TV. When she cried out at night and Mom or Dad went in there and it kept me up, I would get mad at her. I was doing things like making breakfast in bed and winning citizenship awards, and Connie didn't do anything but lie there, and she got all the attention. She didn't have to finish her dinner, and she still got desert. She got everything first. It wasn't fair. I was alive and well, and I should have mattered, but I didn't matter because Connie was sick and dying, and she took all the mattering.

Pretty soon, it was like I wasn't even there. People knew I was there, but it felt like nobody could really see me. I was like a piece of furniture. People sit in chairs, but they don't really see the chair. You sit down and you don't worry about it because you know it's there, and you know it's strong enough to hold your body while you're sitting, but when you get up, the most you remember is that you sat down a minute ago, but you don't remember what the chair looked like. It's there, and people know it's there, but really, it's pretty invisible. I became a chair.

And that's how I was on Halloween. My bones glowed in the dark, and my mask was a scary skull. We went trick-or-treating, but I was invisible because Connie felt good enough to go. Dad dressed her wheelchair up with painted cardboard and glitter to look like a princess carriage. They took tons of pictures of her and only one of me.

Mom told me I needed to understand that this was going to be Connie's last Halloween. I understood that meant she was going to die, but I wasn't really sure exactly what dying actually was. I knew she would be gone, buried in the ground, and it would be forever, but I didn't know where the life part of her would go or what would happen to her body in the ground. Whatever it meant, I knew that I would miss her, but I also knew that after she was gone, I would start mattering again, and the time of anger would finally be over. Secretly, I looked forward to that part.

In a way, I missed Connie already because, even though she was still here, she was so different from the Connie she'd been before. That Connie had long blond hair, was full of energy, and ran around singing and playing in the yard. This Connie was bald, and her eyes were sunk into her face like my skull mask, and all she did was lie around in bed all day.

Me and that Connie talked all the time and laughed about secret things that nobody else could understand. This Connie can't even talk without getting tired, and whenever we're together, she gets all the attention, and even though I'm there, I'm not really there. This Connie was still a little girl, but I had become a chair.

Sometimes I caught myself hoping Connie would just die and get it over with, so things could start getting back to normal, and that's how I knew that deep down inside of me, I was a rotten person.

Dad let me go trick-or-treating with Tommy and his parents. I was tired of being with my own family anyway because all I ever heard was people asking, "Who is that beautiful princess riding around in such a nice carriage?"

I only had less than half a pillowcase full of candy when Dad came running up and got me. We had to go right home because Connie took a turn for the worse, and we had to take her to the hospital immediately.

I told them I hardly got any candy at all, and why couldn't I stay out with Tommy and his folks? He said we didn't know how long this was going to take, and I wasn't old enough to stay at home by myself. As for my candy, he said I could share Connie's, but I knew that wasn't because I didn't get enough; it was because she'd never be able to eat it anyway. I didn't care anymore.

So I spent the rest of Halloween waiting around the hospital. We were there almost until two in the morning. Connie was worse than ever. She was so bad they wanted her to stay there where she would be most comfortable, but Mom and Dad refused, saying they wanted her to come home because that's where her family and all her stuff was, and that's where she'd be most comfortable. I could tell the doctor didn't agree, but he said that, in the end, it wouldn't really matter anyway. I knew exactly what this meant, but I didn't want to think about it.

When we got home, Dad said he wasn't going to work in the morning, and Mom said I didn't have to go to school. Wouldn't you know that this was the one day I really wanted to go to school? It was the day of our party, and I was going to wear my costume with the glow-in-the-dark bones. God damn!

When we got home, Connie was so tired that she went right to sleep. Mom said if I wanted to go to school, fine, but I was on my own. She wasn't going to get up and make my lunch or take me to the bus stop because she was going to sleep in. If I wanted to get up and use my allowance money for lunch and walk myself to the bus stop, then I could go to school.

I planned on doing just that. Before I went to sleep, I laid out my skeleton costume on my bed, so it wouldn't be wrinkled, and then I decided to sleep with Connie one last time. I thought maybe it would help her feel better.

That night, Deeohgee, who always slept with Connie, wouldn't let me get in bed. It was the first time he'd ever done anything like that before. Every time I tried, he growled at me. Finally, Connie, who could only talk in whispers, said to put him in the hallway, and I did. I was almost afraid to pick him up because he'd never acted like this before. He growled, but he didn't try to bite me when I moved him.

When I got in bed with her, Connie smiled at me, and I showed her some candy I'd snuck in with me. When I offered her some, she shook her head, and so I only ate one piece, so she wouldn't get jealous.

Connie woke me up sometime before it got light out with a bad coughing spell. Mom and Dad came running, but there wasn't anything they could do. They gave her some ice and wiped her face, but that was about it. They told me to go back to my room, but this time, I didn't want to and said no.

Mom yelled at me, and Dad got mad, but Connie quit coughing long enough to say, "Let him stay." It was obviously very hard for her to get that out, and it was just a whisper, but to my parents, it must have been like shouting because the moment she opened her mouth, they both shut the hell up and let me stay.

They stayed until she closed her eyes and fell asleep. But I knew she wasn't really sleeping—just because she was still my sister, and we understood each other better than anyone else in the world. She just wanted them to go away.

After they closed the door, she opened her eyes and smiled at me. It was obviously a very painful smile. I reached under the covers and brought out the candy, holding up a pack of Smarties, her favorite, and waved them in front of her face.

I offered her some, and she nodded, but she didn't even reach her hand out. I didn't think she could, so I held the Smarties up to her. She opened her mouth, and I put some on her tongue. She sucked them until they were gone, and then she fell asleep for real. When I knew she was sleeping, I fell asleep myself.

A while later, I woke up. It was starting to get light out. Connie was awake and watching me. Her face said she was in pain. I could barely keep my own eyes open, but I offered her some more Smarties, thinking they might make her feel better. She opened her mouth, and I put them on her tongue. When she closed her eyes, tears squeezed out of each eye and rolled down her face. It was the first time I'd ever seen her cry since she got cancer. It made me cry, too. I hadn't hugged her in a long time, so I did then, and that's how we both fell asleep.

I woke up late and barely had enough time to get to the bus stop. Connie was still sleeping. I ran to my room to get ready. I was in the bathroom when my mom knocked on the door and said that since she was up anyway, she could take me to school 'cause there wasn't enough time for me to make it to the bus stop.

I was putting on my costume when I heard my mom go into Connie's room. "Connie," she said. "Connie?" But Connie didn't answer. My mom yelled, "Jim! Oh, my God!"

Dad rushed in, and I followed him. Mom had thrown the covers off Connie and was sitting on the bed holding her. She was just a tiny little bag of bones. Deeohgee, who never left Connie's side, was nowhere to be found.

I know Connie better than anyone in the whole world, and all it took was one look at her to know she was gone. Mom and Dad were crying and wailing, and Mom was saying, "Why, God, why," but I knew it wasn't God's fault.

It was mine. Last night, when we had to cut Halloween short to take Connie to the hospital, I had practically wished that she would die sooner rather than later. Well, it looked like my wish had come true.

Dad heard me crying and got up to take me out of the room. As I left, I turned and took one more look at Connie. Mom was holding her head in her arms and rocking her back and forth, and I could see those three little Smarties still sitting on her tongue.

Chapter 7

Connie's funeral was very sad. There were lots of pictures of her, from the time she was a baby right up until Halloween with her in her princess carriage. The pictures, especially the ones of her with hair, laughing and running, made me miss her so much.

Three days after the funeral, we woke up in the morning and discovered that Deeohgee had died during the night. We found him on the floor outside Connie's room, where nobody was allowed in, not even him. The vet said he was a strong, healthy little puppy, and there was no reason he should have died. Deeohgee hadn't been sick a day in his life, but he had loved Connie the most, and I know what happened to him. The poor little guy had simply died of a broken heart.

I missed almost a week of school, but then things started getting back to their normal routine. I figured things would start getting better soon, but I was smart enough to know it wouldn't be right away. I knew it would take my parents longer to get used to Connie not being there than it did for me, so I just waited.

Days and weeks and months passed, and I thought things would get better, but they never did. Things got worse. Mom and Dad stayed mad like usual, only now they seemed to be more mad at each other and at me than at the world. They didn't talk very much, and they never laughed. A lot of the time, they were mad at me when I didn't do anything to deserve it. I wondered if maybe they were mad at me because Connie had died earlier than anyone thought. They didn't know that I had wished for it—nobody did but me—but maybe they thought I'd killed her by giving her the Smarties.

Who knows, maybe I did.

Any time I wanted to do something with my parents, there wasn't time, or they were feeling too sad, or just nobody felt like doing anything. I had a lot of time to myself—more than ever.

I wondered why my parents wanted two kids if they were only going to be interested in one of them. Now that one was gone, they didn't seem to want anything to do with the only one left. The one they wanted was the one that died.

I had been mad at Connie for having cancer and dying, and now she was gone. Things hadn't gotten better, they'd gotten worse. Now I was mad at my parents for not wanting me—for having me and acting like they didn't have me. I hated being mad, so when I started feeling that way, I forced it down like food I don't like, so I just swallow it fast to get rid of it. I did this knowing my parents would get along better if I wasn't being such a difficult child, if I could be more like Connie was. I made a place for all that anger so deep inside of me I couldn't feel it any more.

One night not long after Connie died, I snuck into her room when I couldn't sleep. It was a huge risk because if Mom and Dad ever caught me, I'd be in more trouble than I ever had been in my life. My parents treated Connie's room like a museum, and I wasn't allowed to be in it. I went to sleep in her bed, but I made sure to wake up before anyone else and snuck back into my room. They never found out.

I didn't worry about them finding her bed messed up. They didn't change anything in Connie's room after she died. Her dirty clothes were still in the hamper, and her bed was still unmade. I knew I'd never get caught, and I started sleeping in her room a lot.

Mom stopped taking care of the house. Dad came home from work later and later. Sometimes, he came home after I went to bed. And then one day, he took me out to Dairy Queen and made a really big deal of telling me how sometimes moms and dads love each other, but they can't stay together. He said that's the way our family was going to be now. He said I would always be their child, and they would both always love me, but things were too hard for them, and he felt like he couldn't breathe.

I know what he felt like because I couldn't breathe, either. I had been trying to be better for them, but obviously I hadn't tried hard enough. Maybe they knew I'd been sleeping in Connie's room after all.

Dad told me he was going to move out and get his own place, and I could come see him there. It would just be us two guys, and I could stay over for days at a time, and we'd have tons of fun.

I didn't say anything, but I knew what he was saying wasn't true. I knew from the way he said it—it wasn't going to be tons of fun. But I kept my mouth shut and enjoyed my ice cream.

After Dad moved out, Mom stayed in bed all the time. Now she didn't care what time I came home or where I went on Saturdays and Sundays. When she went to the store, she bought hot pockets, taquitos, and other things I could make in the microwave. I have to admit, I liked that part of it. I learned to make the stuff I like, and I could eat whenever I wanted to. I didn't even sit at the table; I could eat it in the living room with the TV on.

That was the only good part about it. Things like citizenship awards and doing good in school didn't matter anymore, so I quit trying to do them. My teacher kept asking me what was wrong, but I never told her I was alone all the time.

Once, a lady came to the door to check on my mom. When Mom answered the door and saw who it was, she smiled a lot and put her arm around me when she introduced me. She sounded nicer than usual, like the moms on TV, not like my mom at all. She showed the lady the house and yard and all the food we had in the fridge. They talked for a while, and the lady asked me if I could show her my room.

We went there, and I showed her my toys and things. She asked me what I liked to do and how much did I like being at home? I smiled and told her that I loved being here. I told her my mom plays with me and likes to make dinner, and on weekends, we do special stuff together.

The lady seemed happy about that. She told me she was so sad my older sister had died, and I told her how much I missed Connie. I don't know exactly why I said those things. None of them were true, except the missing Connie part, but somehow I just knew it was the right thing to say. It didn't bother me that it wasn't true. Ever since Connie had gotten sick, life sucked, but that's just the way it was, and I knew that there was nothing this lady could do to make it better. I didn't want anyone getting inside our lives and messing with things. Besides, lying was becoming easier and easier.

Even Mom said I was a good boy, and it made me feel really good to know that she knew I was lying, but she was proud and happy that I had done it. I thought that maybe things would get better after that, but they didn't.

Almost immediately after he moved out, Dad got a girlfriend, and I started seeing him less and less. Whenever we did see each other, Dana had to come along. Dana was pregnant, which meant she and my dad were going to have a baby. They got married in the springtime, and their new baby was supposed to come in June. By now, I knew not to be excited because once that baby got here, I'd be a chair again.

Not long after I found out my dad was going to have another baby, I got mad and blew up at my mom because I wanted her to cook dinner like she used to. I was tired of just putting stuff in the microwave for dinner.

We had a really big fight, and she called me a no good little shit and sent me to my room.

I slammed the door shut and hit the bed with my fists. I wanted to yell to my mom that I hated her, but I didn't. I ate that anger up, so I wouldn't feel it anymore, but it didn't go away; it just got worse and worse.

Finally, I was so mad I started a fire.

Chapter 8

Jason gave me the matches. He got them from his mother, who smokes cigarettes. He stole a cigarette, too, and we tried smoking it, but all I did was cough.

Curtains burn up to the top as soon as you light them at the bottom. Teddy bears and bedspreads go fast, too. The fire never went past my room, but most of our house was wrecked from all the smoke and the water the fire department used to put it out. I tried to lie about it at first, but the firemen said they could tell where the fire started and how, so I started crying and told them the truth. I had to talk to a cop who was there, too, and I was really scared that he was going to take me to jail.

We went to the Super 8 Motel, where we lived for a couple weeks while our house got fixed. It turned out that lighting the fire wasn't such a terrible thing because we got new carpet, a new couch, a new TV that was bigger than our old one, and a bunch of other new stuff.

The problem was that my mom made me start going to a child psychologist after the fire. His name was Dr. McNab. He didn't look old enough to be a doctor, which was one of the many things I complained about to my mom, but she said he was just starting out and wasn't as expensive as the other guys in town. He was fat, too, but I didn't really care—old or young, skinny or fat, I wasn't about to listen to anything he had to say. I figured he was on my mom's side from the beginning, and he would just tell me to listen to her and quit being such a little pyro.

Dr. McNab wasn't really so bad at first because all we did was talk. He had me draw pictures, and we played games and looked at shapes and things like that, too. Later, of course, we ended up doing other stuff.

When I first started going to him, Dr. McNab asked me if I knew why my mom wanted me to be there. I said it was because I lit our house on fire. But that wasn't good enough. He made me tell him about everything that was going on in my life. I started telling him about school, my dad and his new baby, and he asked me if I had any other brothers or sisters.

So we started talking about Connie, and suddenly that's all we talked about. I had to see him every two weeks, and we spent a lot of time talking about Connie. I was smart enough to know that the way I felt, and the way I had changed since Connie got sick, wasn't the way a nine-year-old kid should feel, and I was also smart enough to know that if Connie hadn't got cancer and died, all this stuff would't be happening now.

Sometimes Dr. McNab didn't want to talk about Connie and the way everything had changed after she died. Sometimes he asked me about what I wanted to be when I grew up or what kind of sports I liked. Once all we did was talk about football, and for the second half hour of our session, we tossed a little foam football around in his office.

He wanted to see if I could tackle him, so he took the ball and tried to run past me. I grabbed him, and we went down on the floor. He said roughhousing was good for boys my age. He tossed me the ball and told me to see if I could get past him, but of course I couldn't. He was a lot bigger than me, but when he tackled me, he protected me when we went down by keeping his arms around me. He said part of our therapy would be playing, but he still had the responsibility to make sure I didn't get hurt.

I guess I didn't mind going to see him. It was always something different for me to do. I hardly ever saw my dad anymore because they had their baby, and there just wasn't any room for another kid. I did see the baby, though, and I didn't like it. It was ugly and red and wrinkled; all it wanted to do was eat, sleep, cry, and poop. That baby got all Dana's attention, and I kind of figured that even my dad might be feeling like a chair around it. Now he would know how I felt.

They named the baby Clyde. The name reminded me of a monkey I saw in a movie once, which was actually pretty funny because the baby kind of looked like a little monkey. The day I met him, I told Dana I didn't like him because he looked like an ugly little monkey. When he dropped me off at Mom's that evening, Dad told me I wouldn't be coming back for a while.

It was the Fourth of July again, only this year we didn't do anything. Last year, we all went to Fort Vancouver. This year, things were way different. Connie was gone. Dad was gone, too, but he had a new baby to replace Connie, and there just wasn't a lot of room for me. Dana tried to be nice around me, but she couldn't hide the fact that she didn't like me. By the way, Mom told me Dad didn't really leave because of what happened to Connie. She said that while Connie was dying—and Mom was trying to take care of her and keep her family fed and trying not to kill herself—Dad was busy fucking Dana and making a new baby. She actually said it just like that, which made me feel grown up, but I was scared at the same time.

Anyway, on the Fourth of July, Mom didn't get up until two in the afternoon, and I ended up going to Jason's house, where everyone who lived on their street got together and lit off fireworks. Jason's parents let me light some of them.

For a kid who likes fire, I was pretty much in heaven.

After I'd been seeing Dr. McNab for a few months, he told me that a lot of my problems were because of shame—shame for the way I felt about Connie when she was dying. I admitted to him that I was really angry with her and said that even though I hated that she took all the attention, I didn't feel ashamed of it. But he said I did. He said there was a lot of shame in me. He thought I probably didn't feel good about myself and that a lot of kids who were small for their age tend to feel that way.

Dr. McNab said the way people get past the issues that give them problems is to confront them head-on. In my case, since I loved my sister and didn't ever show it, I needed to learn how to show love. And since I wasn't used to getting love from my parents after Connie died, I had to learn how to receive it because if my mom or dad tried to show me love, and I wasn't open to receiving it, I would only turn them away, and it would prove to them that there was no point in trying.

He came over to me and put his arms around me. It made me feel uncomfortable, but he said this was a breakthrough. He wanted me to put my arms around him, so I did. He held me tight and told me that if he could feel my stiffness, then so could my parents when I hugged them. He asked how someone hugging someone knows that person trusts them and is open to it, instead of resisting.

I said they hug them back, so he said to relax and lean on him and hug him back. So I did. We just sat there on his couch with our arms wrapped around each other, and after a few minutes, it wasn't so bad.

Dr. McNab didn't want to lose progress, so from then on, we started each session by hugging, and that's how we would end each session, too. In between, we talked about things. I opened up to him more and more, and sometimes I'd cry. When I did, he was always there to hug me.

Next, we started working on trust. He began by standing behind me, and I had to close my eyes, fall backwards, and trust that he was there to catch me. I did, and he always caught me.

Once we got trust done, we started working on shame. He already told me I was ashamed of the way I had treated Connie, and he asked if I was ashamed of my body, too, because I was smaller than other boys my age, and I said I wasn't. He said lots of people with different bodies get ashamed of them. He said because he was fat, he always felt ashamed of his body and asked me what I thought about that. I told him he didn't look any different than he did when I first started seeing him because he was fat then, and he was still fat now, so he just looks normal to me. After that, he said we were going to do something that worked on both trust and shame at the same time.

To show that we could look shame in the face at the same time as trusting each other, we had to take our clothes off in front of each other. I hadn't minded seeing Dr. McNab that much until then, but I didn't want to take my clothes off. I told him I wasn't going to do it, and he said they could send me to jail for lighting my room on fire if I didn't participate in therapy, and I didn't want to go to jail. He said we had been trusting each other, and this was another breakthrough. If I passed all the breakthroughs, he would write a report to the courts that said I was getting cured and wouldn't light more fires.

I really didn't want to go to jail, and he was my doctor, so I agreed, and we took our clothes off. Dr. McNab had red hair, which covered his entire body, and you could hardly see his thing because his stomach hung almost all the way over it. I was embarrassed to look at him and to be naked with him looking at me, so I covered my own privates with my hand.

Now we were getting somewhere, he said. Because I didn't want to look at him, he said that meant I was ashamed. To fix it, he made me look at him. Since I already knew what his face looked like, he made me look at the rest of him. He said people wear clothes so you can't see their private parts, and overcoming that was the key to fixing shame. He said to look at his penis, so I did, and then he made me take my hand away from mine.

I thought this was really stupid, but he was right about the shame thing. I guess I had felt shame about the way I treated Connie before she died, and I did feel ashamed to stand there naked in front of him. Maybe this would work.

He said my penis was a good part of my body, and I had no reason at all to feel shame about anything. He said it was a good penis for a boy my age.

To combine all the issues we'd been working on, he had me close my eyes and fall backwards again while I was naked. He caught me, and then he showed me that I was worth loving by hugging me, and I had to hug him back. Now we had combined trust, shame, and love all in one exercise.

I wasn't stupid, and I knew that this wasn't good therapy. I was very scared and uncomfortable and didn't know what to do. He could make me go to jail, or he could tell them I was cured. Finally, I told him this wasn't right, and I was done. I said maybe he should just tell them I needed to go to jail because this made me feel uncomfortable, and I wanted to stop doing it.

Dr. McNab said not to worry about it because we were now done with therapy. He said all we had to do now was end it like we ended all our sessions, by hugging one last time.

He hugged me, but since I was already done with therapy, I didn't hug him back. I was trying to be strong and brave and stand up to him, but really, I was very scared, and the inside of my head was very loud. I felt like my arms couldn't move, like they were too heavy, so I just stood there while he hugged me.

I could feel his thing on my stomach, and it got big and hard, like in the morning when you wake up. Dr. McNab said that happens to all boys and men when they feel love, and if it was happening to me, I was cured. He turned me around and put his arms around me from behind and took my penis in his fingers, but it didn't grow. He pressed me real hard from behind, and I could feel him pushing it against my butt, and that's when I struggled and tore away.

I began crying and ran to the corner. Dr. McNab rubbed and rubbed his thing, and I didn't want to watch him, so I turned around. While he was moaning, I got dressed as fast as I could. He was standing by the door, blocking my way, and when I tried to leave, he got all nice and said he was sorry. As he got dressed, he said I had done so well he would tell them I was all better. He told me that all of the lessons I learned were real. He said trust was the most important thing now, and we had to trust each other not to tell anyone about what went on in his office.

He said doctors aren't supposed to teach the lessons on love and trust and shame the way he did, but he did it because it was the fastest way to cure me. He said he did *not* want to see me in jail. He told me that I was now very, very powerful because if I told on him, he couldn't be a doctor anymore. He would get in a lot of trouble, but I would definitely go to jail for burning my house down. But we trusted each other, and by trusting each other, therapy worked itself out. I was cured, he was still a doctor, and I wouldn't be going to jail.

I know the way he cured me was wrong, but I didn't get hurt, and I wasn't going to jail, and I actually liked that I held power over him now. He held power over me, too, but as long as we both kept the secret, things would work out for everyone.

All I know is there was no way I was going back to see him, and that was good enough for me.

Chapter 9

Monday Night, March 17th, 2014, The Outside Inn Motel

Eventually, exhaustion overtook me, and I fell asleep, despite the filthy bed and the fact that I was being so ruthlessly hounded. My sleep was deep and dreamless, but at some point in the middle of the night, I became aware of a noise. It took me a moment to wake up and recognize it for what it was.

It was the ringing of the telephone.

Why would my phone be ringing? I wasn't here. As far as anyone in the world knew, I wasn't anywhere—anyone but the clerk, that is.

So, either it was the clerk, or it was CNT, after the clerk dimed me off.

I glanced at the clock. 4:32 A.M. I picked up the phone.

"What?"

"You still interested in potential visitors?"

I was awake now. "Yeah."

"Might they include about twenty cops, a big van, and an armored police tank?"

My heart sank. "Yeah, that would be them. Are they here?"

"Not yet. But a little birdie told me they're gatherin' in a parking lot at 82nd and Flavel. That's two blocks away. I was thinkin' you might want to cut your stay here a little short. No refunds though."

"Look, man, I can't just open the door and leave. They're gonna have someone out there watching, both the front and the back. I can't get out of here."

"You do what you need to do. I'm just telling you what I been told."

"I need some help! You need to sound a fire alarm or something, get everyone out of here at once, so I can mix into the crowd."

"Good plan. Except there ain't no fire alarm. And if there was, it wouldn't wake anyone up. Most of 'em are junkies already passed out. Even if it did, there ain't no crowd—unless four people is a crowd."

"Then if I were you, I'd stay away from the windows."

"How much money you got in that wad of yours?"

"Five grand." It was closer to seven.

"Really? Ain't that a coincidence, because five grand is exactly what I charge to escape someone from a SWAT team."

"And how do you do that?"

"I don't know yet. I'll call you back in a few minutes. Until then, just sit tight." He hung up.

Five minutes later, the phone rang.

"Hello?"

"Listen close. You're in a room that adjoins to another one. There's two doors between the rooms. Open your door, then stick your fingers under the other one and push up. Then lean into it with your shoulder and it'll open up. In five minutes, I'm gonna have a girl go in the room next to yours. You'll change into her clothes, then go outside and get in her car, a tan 96 Camry. There'll be a guy waitin' in the driver's seat, and he'll take you wherever you want to go. You pay him. When your visitors get here, they'll find the wrong person asleep in bed.

"What about that girl?"

"Does it matter?"

"No, I guess not."

"Go now. Hand the driver five large when you get in, or he turns you in."

"Don't worry about that. I'm going next door now."

I dressed and did as he said. The door between the rooms popped right open. Ten agonizing minutes later, I heard a key in the lock. The front door opened and a woman wearing a blue maid's outfit and a girl's parka came in. She immediately peeled off the maid's dress. Under it was a short skirt and tank top. She was a tweaker whore, but at that moment, I loved her.

"Put these on, then go out and get into the tan car parked by the door," she said, handing me the clothes.

"Thanks. Who are you?"

She stopped and locked her dead eyes on mine. "Who do you want me to be?"

"Some other time maybe. Anyway, thanks for doing this."

"I'm getting paid for it. So, what's gonna happen to me when they get here?"

"First, flush any dope you have on you, then get in bed. They'll call you on the phone. Just pretend not to know what they're talking about, and go out with your hands up when they ask you to. Swear that you have no idea what they're talking about, come up with some plausible story about how the manager lets you crash here for blowjobs or something. Tell them you got here last night at ten. Stick to your story without deviating from it. Make sure you refuse to take any polygraph tests, no matter what they say. Make a scene, demand to talk to a lawyer, call for a supervisor, complain that they felt you up when they searched you, whatever. You've probably done this dozens of times. They won't do anything. They can't. Whole thing will be over an hour after it gets started."

"Fuck you and your judgmental attitude, asshole. You don't know me."

"No offense, honey. Thanks again for doing this."

I dressed in drag, and am sure I looked ridiculous. I asked her, "How were you guys able to pull this off so fast? You can't tell me you've done this before."

She snorted. "My boyfriend's brother's the manager of this dump. He's done some serious time, and he isn't stupid, even if he works hard to make people think he is. He called my boyfriend five minutes after you got here and told him to turn on the eleven o'clock news. No offense, but I told them guys to give you your money back and turn you out. Anyways, when Gene got word the cops were coming, he called Mark, my boyfriend. This was mostly his idea."

"Don't forget to thank him for me."

"Yeah, well, money talks, and words ain't shit. If you hadn't flashed your wad, this wouldn't have ever happened."

I believed her. She went to the other room, and when the door closed, I opened the front door and walked out. Not looking around for the side one sniper/observer team was one of the hardest things I've ever done. But there was no wig or facial disguise, only a fur-lined hood on the jacket she brought. I had to look down to try to prevent them from seeing my face.

The car was actually three spaces away. Crossing those spaces was like walking the green mile. There was a guy in the driver's seat. He backed out as soon as I got in, and the moment of truth was at hand. If they knew it was me, police cars and the Bearcat would swoop out, and the shit would get very real.

But nothing happened. We drove out of the lot and turned left, heading south, away from the direction SERT would come. We drove for a few blocks down the deserted street, and then I began to smell a rat.

What if these people were jerking me around? What if SERT wasn't really staging anywhere?

"Turn left," I said. "Then turn left again. Drive north through the blocks until we get to Flavel. I want to see this for myself."

"Hey, it's your funeral," he said and made the turn. We finally turned west on Flavel back toward 82nd, and as we approached the intersection, there in a parking lot off to the south was the PPB SERT van, the CNT Sprinter, the Bearcat, a SERT Tahoe, and three police cars. They were just pulling out and making the left turn onto 82nd heading south. A police car with lights flashing was blocking the intersection of 82nd and Flavel, and we had to wait until the caravan was out of the intersection before we could make a right on 82nd to go north.

I turned around and watched them disappear into the lot of the Outside Inn.

"So, where we headin?" he asked.

I had absolutely no idea.

"Light rail started running at five," he said. "Want me to drop you off at a Max station?"

"No. What I need is a safe place to roost for a few days. Don't you guys know another motel that knows how to look the other way?"

"Not for you. Let me tell you something, pal. I told my brother not to fuck around with you. You're way too hot, and we got enough of our own shit to worry about without you, too. So, unless you got another wad like the one you showed him, you're better off on the Springwater Trail. I can take you down there if you want."

I couldn't think of a better idea, but I hate taking steps backward. Seven hours in a motel for fifty-two hundred dollars, and now I'm back to the trail? Not my idea of forward motion, but I was fresh out of options.

"Any chance I can borrow your car for a while?" I asked hopefully. "I can call you and tell you where I leave it."

"Nope. This is a one-way ride, pal. In ten minutes, I'm outta here and never saw you."

"Fine. Take me to the trail."

We drove down Foster until we came to the trail, and he pulled over. I reached in my pocket, and he produced a handgun.

"Only thing coming out of that pocket is your wad, right?"

"Relax, Sparky. I'm not going to stiff you. Put that thing away, or you'll be the second guy I killed in the past couple of days." I withdrew the money and counted out five thousand. Handing it to him, I said, "It's been real, my friend."

"Yeah, well, happy St. Paddy's day, tough guy."

I stopped half in and half out of the car. St. Patrick's Day?

He waved me forward with the gun. "Now ain't the time to do anything but leave, bud. Take off."

I got back in the car. "I know where I need to go."

He sighed. "Where?"

"You know where Mt. Tabor is?"

"Yep."

"Take me there. When we get there, I'll tell you where. It might take a second to find it."

"This is the last ride, partner. After that, we're through."

"Unless I got another wad."

He looked at me and smiled. "Hey, you learn real quick, dontcha?"

We went down Division until we got to 60th, and I had him turn right. When we got to Hawthorne, I had him turn left. I had him circle a few side streets for a moment, and then I had him take me to 60th and Hawthorne again, which is the entrance to Mt. Tabor.

"I bet you didn't know Mt. Tabor is an extinct volcano," he said.

"Spare me the tour guide info, and let me out here."

"Pleasure doing business with you," he said with a smile. I got out, and he drove away without another word.

Chapter 10

I walked west on Hawthorne to 55th, and then I headed south. It was just past 5:30, and nobody was stirring. About halfway down the block on the east side of the street, I cut into the driveway of a brick ranch. There was a fence around the yard, but it wasn't locked. I entered the backyard without a sound and breathed a sigh of relief. Nobody could see me here because of the arborvitae.

There appeared to be no easy way in, so I shouldered open the side door to the garage. It gave way with a crack that sounded like a shotgun in the still morning air. I didn't wait to see if lights came on next door; I immediately entered the garage and closed the door behind me. From there, it was easy. A swift boot to the interior door and I was in.

I already knew there was no alarm. I'd been in here New Year's Eve, and the homeowner, a friend of mine from East Precinct, had told me that after being charged for three false alarms, he had it disconnected.

That officer, Sean O'Rourke, along with his wife Peggy, were now in Chicago to participate in the St. Patrick's Day parade. He and a contingent of other Irish drinking buddies from the department went every year. I had been invited, but I politely declined, a decision I very much regretted at the moment. They left three days ago and wouldn't be home until the day after tomorrow.

I found Peggy's key ring in the dark on a peg by the front door. Her Honda Pilot was in the garage just waiting for me to decide where I was going to go and when I was going to leave.

By this time, I was ravenous. I made myself a bacon and eggs breakfast and even cleaned up the mess. When I was done, it was light out.

Next, I went shopping in Doug's closet. We both wore large shirts, so I chose a few and laid them out on the bed. He was taller and heavier than me, so his pants didn't fit, but I did find a nice pair of sweats I could use. While I was doing this, the phone rang. I froze. It rang three times, and when the answering machine picked up, it was just an automated message from Walgreens saying that Peggy's prescription was ready for pickup.

In the den, I found Sean's Macbook Air. I really wished I could take it with me, but I know those things are protected and can broadcast their location if stolen. I got online and started looking for the best way to get to Canada using smaller, rural routes rather than I-5. I made sure to just use the Maps app rather than do a Google search that would leave a trail of what I had looked at, just in case.

Since Sean wasn't coming home until the day after tomorrow, I knew I had the safe use of his car until tomorrow night. After that, it could be reported stolen any time. Since I was going to Canada, I could acquire a new vehicle via Craigslist anywhere between here and there. But I would need to dump the car somewhere, so I decided to go south, maybe to Salem, to buy a car, so as not to give them my true direction of travel. Now that I was down to a budget of about twelve hundred for wheels, I'd have to plan on a lot less car.

In the next couple of days, I was going to need more money. There was only one way for a guy in my boat to get quick cash. I'd done it before, and I could do it again. It wouldn't be anywhere near Portland, and I would definitely use a disguise—plus I'd need to plan on something with a large payoff. That was a day or so away and hundreds of miles down the road. I'd worry about it tomorrow.

After nine, I began calling the numbers I'd culled out of Craigslist in the Salem area. An hour later, I'd made two appointments for this evening and one for tomorrow morning, all in Salem. I would have liked a decent night's sleep first, but now I was wide awake and keyed up, so I decided there was no time like the present to get moving. After a night in the Outside Inn, a long, hot shower would do just fine. I took a shower, packed my new possessions into a fancy mountain backpack I found in the garage, and loaded it into the Pilot.

Then, through the garage door, I heard the sound of a vehicle pulling into the driveway. I froze and listened intently. It sounded like a hell of a big vehicle and just sat there idling loudly.

Just as I started running back into the house, the familiar voice of Darth Vader boomed over a loudspeaker. "DJ Appleby! This is Portland

SERT! We have the house surrounded. DJ, you know the drill. There's nowhere to go. Just come out with your hands up. Come on, DJ, you really need to do it this time. Don't make these guys gas you out. Don't make us destroy O'Rourke's place."

I felt lightheaded, dizzy. How the hell had they found me? I went into the living room, then ran to a bedroom, then back to the living room, which was the center of the house. My heart felt like it was going to claw its way out of my chest, and I was hyperventilating. When I realized I was completely trapped, I collapsed onto the floor. This was it. There would be no miraculous escapes from this one.

"DJ! Beth's going to give you a call. There's no point in not answering it."

A moment later, the phone rang. With no other choice, I picked it up.

"Hi, Beth."

"Hello, DJ."

We were both silent for a moment, as if neither of us had expected we'd ever be talking. In fact, neither of us knew what to say. Finally, I said, "Why don't you start by asking me how I'm doing? Tell me you're here to help; assure me that everything's gonna turn out ok?"

"You know what? *Fuck* you, DJ!"

"Whoa, that's a little unorthodox. Is this some kind of new negotiation style I don't know about?"

"You made me look like a fool, DJ. Not just me, but the whole team. Hell, you made the whole goddamn Bureau look bad, but I don't even care about that. You killed a *cop*, DJ—a police officer, who wasn't even getting paid. I hope you *don't* come out. You might have three minutes after we're off the phone before Russ gives the order to gas the living shit out of that place. You're going to come out of there one way or another—dead, or alive to be fried. You don't have any hostages to hide behind this time."

"Jesus, Beth, slow down. You're being recorded. You don't want my daughter suing the shit out of you after I'm dead, do you? Come on, chill out a little, and talk to me."

"I'm sorry, but Jesus, DJ. Ok, fine. Let's talk. What do you want to talk about?"

"Beth, listen. I hope you believe me, for what it's worth. I never intended to hurt anyone, *especially* a cop. You know me, Beth. I would have never shot that guy if I knew he was a cop. I just want you, and everyone else, to know that. Not that it makes a difference."

"No, it doesn't make a difference. And I *don't* know you. I thought I did. We all thought we did."

"I'm sorry, Beth. Sorry to you, to the Bureau, to all my friends there, but especially to Anderson's family. I know that doesn't mean anything, but I just wanted to put it out there.

Her voice softened, just a tad. "DJ, what I don't understand is, why? Let's say you never shot anyone. But armed robbery at a hamburger joint? I didn't believe it, even when the hostages all said it was you. Why would you do such a thing?"

"Trust me, Beth, it doesn't make any sense to me, either. I have a hard time understanding why myself. Do we have a few minutes before they do anything out there?"

"Yeah. They're finalizing the gas plan now."

"Good. Tell them they should start in the bedrooms, which are on the sides, and work their way in. Don't gas the back, which is the kitchen. The living room is the center of the house, and that's where I'm at. Drive me into the kitchen and eventually out the rear slider."

"I'll pass that along. So, this is your confessional. Why'd you do it?"

"It's hard to explain. I have this stupid thing I've been dealing with for years. It's a need in me that has to be fulfilled every now and then—a need to take risks. Real, actual risks, where everything's on the line. Lately, I've been filling it by doing robberies. That burger joint wasn't my first."

"You're right; that doesn't make any sense. If you want to take risks, why aren't you just a chronic gambler or something?"

"Trust me, I tried that. I've been dealing with this thing for a long time, ever since before I was a cop. It's why I joined the army, and it's why I got into special forces. None of that worked. As far as gambling went, the only risk there was financial, and that wasn't good enough. And gambling was just a game, not an actual risk. Special Forces was just an elite unit. It's not like there were enemy lines I could go behind on suicide missions all the time. That might have done it. And do you remember when a bunch of us went skydiving? That was an effort to fill it, too. I've learned over the years that there's a big difference between risk taking and thrill seeking. Cheap thrills don't do it for me. I've stood on one foot on a rocky precipice at the Grand Canyon with my eyes closed on a windy day, and it did nothing for me. I found out armed robberies helped because there was so much on the line. I never did it for the money. I did it for the risk."

"Maybe you should have done counseling instead of armed robbery."

"Next time we're in a standoff, I'll tell you a story about counseling. About a little boy and a . . . " It all caught up to me, and I started to cry. I forced myself to stop, but I couldn't speak.

She gave me a moment: "But you killed a man, DJ. A police officer."

Composing myself, I said, "You know how they say addicts don't think about the consequences when they do shit like pawning something they just stole, even though they know they'll get caught? It was kind of the same way with me. It never occurred to me that something might go wrong. The thrill was always in outsmarting the police—knowing that my friends are going over my crime scene looking for fingerprints and trace evidence, knowing that maybe I hadn't thought of everything. Maybe there was footage on a surveillance system I didn't know about. That kind of risk was intoxicating. But then that deputy came out of the bathroom with a gun. I didn't know he was a cop. I swear to God I didn't. I didn't think; I just acted. I just did what any officer would have done with a gun pointed at him, and I didn't think about it for a second. I just double-tapped him on instinct, like we've been trained for so many years to do. Poor guy wasn't ready for a gunfight. He wasn't mentally prepared, but I was. I didn't even think. I just did what I've been trained to do when I'm confronted with a gun. I'm so fucking sorry."

"I still don't get it. It doesn't make a damn bit of sense to me, but then again, neither does anything that people do. I don't get a junkie shooting that shit into his body. I don't get why the churchgoing politician who has a family cheats on his wife and throws it all away for a piece of ass. It's just so damn senseless. You know, if you hadn't ended up shooting that guy, you'd have probably gotten away with it. You'd probably be at work right now."

"I know. I've done it before."

"I'm still pissed as hell that you put one over on me with that cheesy hick voice, but I do have to admit, that was pretty damn clever."

"I tried to come up with one I haven't used in training before. Beth, tell me, how did it end? The callout."

"When you took off and never came back, we thought you might be sick, or just stressed, or something. Nobody guessed that it might've been you that did it. Then the "bad guy" never returned to the phone. We called and called. After about forty minutes, a hostage answered. Seems you had stuck them all in the office and scared them into staying there, but after a while, they needed to pee. They called out for you, and when nobody answered, they thought maybe we'd shot you, so they sent someone out to check. He heard the phone ringing, and he just picked it up. I had them all walk out. They all said there were no other hostages, so the person who was released had to have been the suspect. Even when SERT cleared the place, I still refused to believe it was you. There had to be another explanation. Of course, then we saw the video. So where did you go when you said you had to call your mother?"

"First, to the bank. Then I hopped Max and spent the night downtown, under the Morrison Bridge. I went back to the bank as soon as it opened, and it seems I got there before dicks got the word out. *That* was a hell of a risk."

"We found out moments after you left. You really pissed Carruthers off by winking at the camera, by the way. We flooded the downtown area after that. Stopped everything that moved. They made like a dozen warrant arrests and nineteen dope arrests. Downtown hasn't been so clean in years."

"I know. I sat up on the top deck of the parking garage by the library and watched it. You want to know how I made it out of there? I hid in a dude's pickup bed, and he drove me out. He never even knew it. But what I want to know is how the hell did you find me *here*?"

"I'll tell you if you come out."

"Beth, I might not come out. Remember my unofficial CNT motto, the one I could never say but always wanted to?"

"Yeah."

"Say it."

"No. This isn't a game, and we're not friends anymore."

"Come on, Beth. We *were* friends, for years. I trained you in this job. What's my CNT motto?"

She was silent for a moment, and then she said softly, "Sir, suicide is *always* an option."

"Yeah. Well, right now, it's my most attractive option. But as you well know, if I'm talking, I'm not killing myself. So tell me, how the hell did you know I was here?"

There was another moment of silence on the other end, and I knew someone was handing her a note. That's one of Beth's biggest faults as a negotiator. She can't carry on an active conversation and read a note at the same time.

"Is that Tom handing you a note?"

I could hear in her voice that she still liked me, but she didn't want to admit it. "DJ, you know me pretty well. Yeah, it was. He said I should tell you, so here's what happened. SERT's been scheduled to help the Drugs and Vice Division on a prostitution and drug warrant at the Outside Inn for about a week. They were just going to send a couple of entry guys to assist DVD, but then some confidential informant said he was in the owner's room, and he had a bunch of guns. It was right after your callout that DVD got with the brass and asked for SERT and CNT."

"I've been telling them for years that DVD has no business doing hot entries when you have a qualified SERT team that can do it for them, but do they ever listen to me?" I said. "So, anyway, go on."

"Well, as it turns out, the subject of their warrant was your good buddy Eugene Crowell."

"Sorry, but I don't know a Eugene Crowell."

"Yes, you do. He's the proprietor of the Outside Inn. Apparently, he's got informants all over the place. Someone saw us staging and tipped him off. He never even thought we were coming for him, probably because you just showed up a couple hours earlier."

I was amazed. SERT, gathering and armoring up a couple blocks away, had no idea I was even there. After all my good luck in escaping, I chose the one place in the world to hide where they were *scheduled* to do a SERT raid. How utterly ironic. "So, you're telling me SERT was staging to do a completely unrelated DVD door kick at the Outside Inn, which had absolutely nothing to do with me?"

"Exactly. Isn't karma a bitch? As we were staging, I heard the S/O team broadcast that a maid went into a room and came out a few minutes later. It was a quarter to five, and nobody thought anything of it. Well, when we hit the place, we secured S-1 right away. S-1 was Crowell. S-2, Crowell's brother Mark, wasn't there. In fact, he was out driving you here, but of course we didn't know that. S-3, Mark's girlfriend, Lisa something or another, was sleeping in one of the rooms. She's the maid that saved your ass, but dear old Crowell sure does like to talk. He said he had something to trade, and he wanted to make a deal. When they found out it was you, they agreed to give him everything he asked for, *if* it led to your arrest."

"I paid that guy five grand to get me out of there. Can I at least get that money back?"

"Fat chance. DVD took over twenty thousand in cash, plus four guns and a shitload of dope out of there. You know what happens to the cash."

"I guess it doesn't matter now."

"Anyway, Crowell called his brother and told him about the deal. This was right after Mark dropped you off. Captain Murl got a DA involved and worked out the particulars, and then the brother told us where he dropped you off.

"Half of us were at Sean's party on New Year's Eve, and Darren was invited to the St. Patrick's Day shindig in Chicago, so he knew that Sean was out of town. We called Sean in Chicago to confirm nobody was home, and he called the house. When he did, he got that ring with a blip at the end that said someone was using his phone, so we knew you were there. Right away, we got an eyeball on sides one and three, and the side three eye said the man-door to the garage had been kicked in. That's when we rolled."

"Fuck!"

"Yeah, I know. So, DJ, since it doesn't matter now, let me ask you something. What was your plan from here?"

"Yeah, I guess it doesn't matter now. I was going to leave in his Pilot. I was getting ready to go when you got here."

"Where were you gonna go?"

"To . . . Well, never mind where to—to someplace that's not here."

There was another pause while she read a note. "They're telling me to wrap it up, DJ. Are you going to come out, or are you going to eat your gun?"

"What the hell kind of question is that? That's not how you negotiate, Beth."

"Come on, DJ. This isn't a negotiation, and you know it. Pretty much, you have three choices. One, you come out now. Two, we gas the absolute shit out of you, and you come out that way. Three, you eat your gun. And if you choose the latter, Sean has asked me to direct you to use the downstairs bathtub and to make sure you close the shower door. If you don't want to do that, do it in the den. They're going to remodel that room anyway."

"Fuck you, Beth! God damn it!" Tears of frustration came to my eyes, and my voice cracked. I wasn't ready to give up. I was scared shitless. I wasn't ready for this to end. I wanted to kill myself, but I didn't have the courage. I was a chickenshit at heart. I'm sure Beth knew it, too. I was so scared I thought I might pee myself.

"Well?"

Trying not to sound like I was crying, I said, "I'll come out the front door. Can I have two minutes to compose myself?"

"Fine. They will gas exactly three minutes from now. I just want one promise from you, ok?"

"What's that?"

"Don't suicide by cop. You know these guys. Please don't make one of them do that. If you're going to suicide, do it now, not like that."

I hung up on her. I waited two solid minutes, but I couldn't stop crying. I hated myself more than anything during that time.

Then I opened the door and stepped out.

Chapter 11

June, 1989

Fourteen years old is a bad age. You're no longer a little kid, but you're still a long way from being an adult. At fourteen, I was old enough to understand that I was pretty messed up.

I didn't go to jail after the house fire because Dr. McNab's report said that through therapy, I had worked through all my issues and was cured. I would no longer light fires or do bad behaviors. In a way he was right because I planned to quit doing that kind of stuff, not because of his "therapy," but because I knew they'd lock me up if I didn't.

If they only knew what happened in that fucker's office, but I never told anyone. I knew I was messed up before going in there, and thanks to his report, I pretty much didn't have to do anything else but watch my behavior. But if I was messed up going into that office, I was way more messed up coming out. At least I was smart enough to know that if I did the things I was sometimes tempted to do, I'd have to go to a psycho ward where they'd tie me up in a straitjacket and throw me into a padded cell. I learned to control it on my own. I guess I could thank Dr. McGrab for that.

I believed that I was queer because of what he made me do. I didn't like being queer. I knew it wasn't my real nature, but I was very young and had no understanding, and I just assumed that once you did something like that, you were gay—a faggot, a fairy, a peter puffer, like it or not. I had no idea it was about desire and attraction, but I did know that just like anything else, I was a lousy at being a fag. I had no desire to puff anyone's peter.

Two years ago, I turned twelve and hit puberty. This was three years after Dr. McGrab had his way with me. Anyway, around that time, I suddenly became aware that being around girls made me feel different than I ever felt before. Prior to that, I just saw them as different from boys only because they liked more girly stuff and didn't like the stuff that boys did. Me and my friends sat around and played Nintendo when the weather was bad. When the weather was good, we rode dirt bikes and killed animals with our BB guns in the woods. No girls did that kind of stuff. We hung around girls sometimes at school, but there was never anything special about it.

But two years ago, being around girls suddenly started making me feel weird inside. I found myself acting different around them, like I wanted to impress them or something. I just liked being around them more. I became fascinated by their bodies, and I found myself staring at their tits and wondering what they felt like.

One day in seventh grade, we had a big tug-of-war in gym class. Of course we had separate locker rooms, but boys and girls still had gym together. It was eighth grade versus us seventh graders, and Angie Clifton was on the rope in front of me. The eighth graders kicked our asses, and someone at the front of our line tripped when they pulled all at once. We all fell forward on top of one another, and I landed right on Angie.

In the confusion, I had an opportunity to get my arms around her, and I made sure to put my hand right on her tit. It made me light-headed, and Angie didn't seem to mind at all. I had a big ass woody, and I was on top of her. I kind of pressed into her harder than I had to and lingered there as long as I could.

When we got up, she turned right around and looked at the front of my gym shorts. I mean, it was pretty damn obvious, and I turned every shade of red there is, but Angie smiled this big braces-toothed smile at me. I pulled my T-shirt out to cover it, and I made my way to the locker room without anyone saying anything.

That night, I couldn't get rid of my woody when I went to bed. I just kept thinking about her, and my mind went off in a million different directions. I kept replaying the tug-of-war, and I imagined her coming over when my mom wasn't home and us in my room, taking off our clothes . . .

Well, I'm sure it's pretty obvious what happened next. It was the first time I ever did it, and I was in awe about it. Let's just say I was a fast learner, and I'd found a new hobby.

Me and Angie started hanging around together at school. I think she was at about the same stage as I was in discovering the opposite sex. We were way too awkward to ever bring up the tug-of-war, but we really enjoyed just hanging together. She was a little intimidating because she was taller than me, but that didn't seem to matter to her, and after a while, to me either.

It lasted for a few months, and we never touched each other again, but the ice with girls had been broken. I knew I wasn't gay by choice, and even though Dr. McGrab had made a fag out of me, I wasn't going to do anything like that with a male ever again.

My dad and Dana didn't stay together. When Clyde, my half-brother was two, they got divorced. Carla took Clyde and moved back to Boston, and I never saw them again. It didn't matter because even though Clyde was my brother, he was more like a stranger to me than a brother. All he did was take my dad farther away from me, not that we were ever what you'd call "close" since Connie died. I only saw Clyde as a baby and a toddler, and I never felt any fondness for him. Dana never liked me, and I didn't like her, either, so it was no loss to me at all. In fact, I was glad when they moved away.

Dad was a bus driver for Tri-Met, and after Dana left, he got a promotion and started driving the Max train. But with all the money he had to pay her, there was never any left for him, which meant he could never do anything good with me, either.

My mom was uptight around me ever since the fire, and I could tell that she never trusted me, even though I never did anything like that again. About a year ago, she started dating a guy named Stu, who was actually an ok guy, but that meant there wasn't much time left for me. So I started hanging out with my friends every day after school, and during the summers, I was never home. I don't think my mom minded that too much.

My dad lived in a little apartment in Rockwood, which was close to the Ruby Junction light rail yard where he worked. Mom and Stu moved into Stu's house in east Portland. I could take the Max between their houses, and sometimes when I did, my dad was driving the train.

I started spending more and more time with my dad. His apartment had two bedrooms, so one of them was mine. Even though it was in a shitty neighborhood, it was more fun being there than it was at Mom and Stu's house.

Last summer, right before my first year of high school started, I talked my dad into taking me to a Bon Jovi concert. He actually saved up for it, and we rode the Max to the Memorial Coliseum for the show. It was my first concert.

I was a pretty big Bon Jovi fan. This was back when he had long hair, and so did I. Everyone wore mullets back then, and when I look at those old pictures, I crack myself up. I was way into hair bands; Bon Jovi, Guns-N-Roses, Van Halen, Def Leppard, and all the others.

I had an epiphany at the concert, and it came in the most unexpected way. My dad went to go take a leak and get us something to eat. Right after he got up, this lady who was sitting on the other side of him fired up a joint.

This wasn't anything new to me. I'd smoked weed before, but not a lot—mostly with this kid Tommy who lived two doors down. Weed was cool, and I liked getting high, but it really wasn't a big deal.

The lady turned to me and offered me the joint. I looked around, and my old man was nowhere to be seen. I took a hit and handed it back to her. I remember they were playing *You Give Love a Bad Name.* The lady was clearly loving the music and was pretty high. She was dancing and swaying and throwing her long hair around. I kept watching her. She was pretty, and she was sexy, and it turned me on to watch her. I remember thinking I hoped she stopped acting like this before my dad got back because I knew he would be interested in her, and then I'd be jealous. I know how stupid that sounds, but I felt like she was mine, and I didn't want him to take her from me.

She looked at me and caught me staring at her. She smiled and leaned in until her head was just about on my shoulder, and she put the joint between my lips. I took a big hit and held it, and then, believe it or not, she pulled her shirt out so I could see her tits. Oh, my God, what that did to me! I took another hit, and I felt like I was in heaven. My heart was hammering. She was an adult, and she'd just shown me her *tits*!

I was trying to screw up enough courage to touch her boobs because it was kind of like an invite—the way she showed them to me and then gave me a hit, but before I could do it, my dad came back with hot dogs. When she saw him coming down the row, she wet her fingertips and put the joint out, and she went back to being a regular woman. Several times throughout the rest of the concert, she glanced over at me. It was the coolest thing that ever happened to me and made me feel very grown up. Here was an adult woman, and she had shown me her tits. They were full and heavy, not little buds like Angie's, which were the only tits my hands had ever touched and just that one time. I swear to God, I fell in love with her right then and there. And it was during *You Give Love a Bad Name.*

She literally winked at me when she got up to leave when the concert was done. I lost track of her in the crowd almost immediately, and I got real depressed for a while because she was forever gone from my life. And that was it.

I had fallen in love, even if it was just for a real short time. With a *woman*. The epiphany I had was that I had been a *victim* of molestation by Dr. McNab, not a participant to homosexual behavior. It was something that happened *to* me, not something I *did*, and that didn't make me queer. Not in the slightest bit. I *wasn't* gay.

I know that seems like something I should have already known, and I suppose deep down I did, but this was the first time I ever completely got it, and knowing it made me free.

That summer, I moved in with my dad. There were a lot of gang kids and kids from bad homes around, and I never really found any friends there, but I liked living with him more than I did with my mom and Stu. I changed school districts and started at Reynolds High School in the fall. Reynolds was the largest high school in the whole state of Oregon.

Despite all the kids, I became a loner at school. Most kids hung together in cliques. There were punks and goths, which I didn't want to join, and there were the athletic preppies, which there was no way I could join. There were the gangs, and I sure as hell didn't join them. I didn't like doing things with groups, and I never considered myself a team player, which you kind of have to be if you're in a gang. There were also the nerds, but that wasn't me, either. So, I became a loner. Some of the loners grouped together, but that kind of defeated the purpose, didn't it? I called them the losers, and I'd much rather be a loner than a loser. I rather liked being a loner. It felt like who I really was.

I did pretty well in school. I knew kids who had no desire to graduate and just went to school either for the social aspect or maybe just to cause trouble. Most of the latter either dropped out or were kicked out by the second semester. I never got in trouble, and I never did any extracurricular activities. I did ok in all my classes and neither flunked, nor got A's. Basically, I was a chair again; only this time, it was by my own choice.

What I wanted out of school was to find a girlfriend. I didn't really want a deep relationship, but I did want someone to mess around with. I was fourteen years old, and I walked around in a constant state of horniness. I found a magazine in my dad's room one day called Barely Legal, and it was nothing but incredible pictures of naked girls—not just naked girls, but like, close-up pictures of right between their legs. Ho-ly shit! I had seen some pornography before, but when I found this magazine, I jerked off every time my dad left the apartment.

My goal was to get my hand down a girl's pants by the time I graduated. School meant nothing to me except for that.

I met girls and was friends with some of them, but there were no prospects for a girlfriend. I was determined to find someone though. It seemed that every time I had an opportunity to talk to one, either she was never interested, or I couldn't think of a way to get started. All the really pretty ones had boyfriends, and most of them were out of my league and showed no interest in me anyway.

That was the biggest problem with being a loner, the fact that girls tend to hook up with boys in their own social group, and a loner doesn't have a social group. But there were other problems with being a loner, too. One of them was that you tend to get picked on, and for me, this started the first day of high school.

My favorite class was art, which was followed immediately by my second favorite, photography. There was a bully who was a lot bigger than me, and he was in both of those classes. On the second day of art class, he made a comment under his breath to his buddies that they shouldn't allow fags in school. They all cracked up, but I just ignored it. His name was Billy Kunkle, but everyone called him Knuckles, which didn't bode well for me. He sat directly in front of me. Like a lot of bullies, Knuckles figured the smallest kid in class was the one who should get picked on most.

I'd dealt with this before by ignoring it, and eventually, the bullying stopped. I didn't think it was going to stop with this kid though. It really sucked having an asshole named Knuckles who had it out for me, and he was in two of my classes, one right after the other.

One day, the art teacher told us to draw a picture of something that was special to us and bring it in the next day. I drew a pretty good picture of my skateboard using perspective. That's where you make the lines non-perpendicular, which made it look really big. I shaded it, and I was particularly proud of my rendition of the skull logo. The next day, the teacher had us pass our pictures forward.

Well, Knuckles had drawn a crude picture of a hard dick and a big set of balls and put my name on it. He slipped my skateboard picture out of the pile and put the picture of the boner in its place and passed them forward.

When the bell rang, the teacher told me to stay. He was very pissed, and he said he was going to give me an incomplete and a demerit for my drawing. When he showed it to me, I told him I drew a skateboard, and Billy Kunkle, who hated me, must have put that in the pile when I passed it forward. Fortunately, the teacher believed me, so it was not really a big deal, but he said unless he could prove who did it, nothing would happen to Kunkle.

Kunkle was waiting for me in photography class with a couple of other friends of his. I wasn't surprised that these other kids would jump on the bandwagon of bullying me. It's surprising how many people have a mean streak in them. When I came in, they all started laughing and looking at me, so I knew this was going to be a tough class.

We'd spent all week learning about cameras; how to use them, all the different kinds of film, and some of the chemistry behind film development. On Friday, the teacher, Mrs. Albatross, gave everyone a 35-mm camera and a roll of film. She said to go home, shoot the entire roll, and on Monday, we'd learn how to develop our pictures in the darkroom in the back of the class. Knuckles piped up immediately and said she should talk to the art teacher because one of us already got in trouble for drawing personal body parts, and that person would probably take pictures of himself. He then turned and leered at me, and the whole class giggled.

I don't think he had the guts to try what he did with the drawing with actual photographs, but with a kid like that, you never knew. Him and his buddies kept making cracks about me all period long, and

Albatross told him to stop twice. Finally, when he didn't, she sent him to the office. After that, Kunkle really had it in for me.

I had put up with him doing shit like mashing my lunch, tripping me at every opportunity, and talking shit about me for a week, and I decided that I wasn't going to put up with it any more. But what could I do? Telling on him was out of the question. It would only make things worse.

I thought about vandalizing his house or paying someone older to kick his ass, but the first was revenge, which wouldn't stop the problem, and the second seemed like a demonstration of my own weakness. I thought about taking karate or jujitsu, but I didn't have months to waste.

The answer was to fight him myself. The problem was that I didn't know how to fight, and I was scared of him. Not only was he bigger than me, he was clearly tougher, too. I actually considered lighting his house on fire at night while he slept in it, but going to jail was not an option I would seriously consider.

That night, I talked to my dad about it. He didn't have a problem with me fighting him. He said he didn't expect me to just be somebody's door mat. He suggested I call his older brother, my uncle Phil.

Uncle Phil was the black sheep of the family. He had been a helicopter paramedic in Vietnam, but the war had screwed him up, and he couldn't hold a job after he came home. He wasn't what you'd call a good guy. After the war, he'd been arrested and sent to prison, more than once. I don't know exactly for what, but I know he did seven years for almost killing a guy the last time he was in.

I had only met him a couple of times, and he looked scary, but he was really nice to me. My dad gave me his number, and I called him and explained my situation to him.

"Boy, you sure you wanna fight this kid?" Uncle Phil said in his hillbilly voice. "Cuz you'll probably get your ass handed to you."

"I know," I said. "But I've never done anything to this kid. He doesn't have any reason to be on me like he is. I think he just picks on me because I'm small, and that's not right."

"No doubt about it. So you want some tips on how to fight, huh? Let me tell you a couple things. One, being small don't mean you're weak, or you can't fight. Toughness got more to do with attitude than about how big you are. Some of the toughest guys I ever saw in the can were small. Being tough is more about what you're willing to do and how much pain you're willing to take. Cuz fighting hurts. Personally, I don't know why some guys like to do it. I only do it when I have to, and it sounds like you have to. But what most folks don't get is that it only hurts for a while. A very little while, and it's usually worth the pain. So, lemme ask you something. You ever been punched before, kid?"

"No."

"It ain't exactly what you'd call fun. It hurts. If you get hit in the mouth, the inside of your lip'll get crushed up against your teeth and cut. I seen a guy's tooth go *through* his lip before, more than once. Usually, it hurts for a couple days, but then it stops hurting, and you forget about it. Same with a black eye, a busted nose, or whatever."

"But what if I lose the fight?"

"So what? Fighting ain't about winning or losing, 'specially if you're bein' bullied. It's about respect. That bully don't respect you 'cause you just sit there and take it. Fight him, and even if you lose, he'll respect you. Plus, he don't like pain any more than you do. Hell, most bullies are cowards anyway. That's why they pick fights with smaller kids who don't fight back. Chances are, even if he beats you, he'll leave you alone after you fight him."

"Not this kid. He's a real asshole."

"Yes, this kid, DJ. He wants a reputation. He wants to be a bully. So what he's really hoping is for everyone to see you chicken out of a fight. If you don't, if you actually fight him aggressively, he won't have a clue what to do. Most bullies will call you out in a real public place. They do this just in case. See, they know that a crowd'll gather, and before it gets too far, a teacher'll come and break it up. Then, everyone can talk about how bad he would have beat your ass if nobody stopped it. If you *really* want to fight someone, which he don't and you do, then do it where nobody will see. If he beats you up, he don't get bragging rights, and if you beat him up, he can lick his wounds in private, and he'll never touch you again. Either way, a fight in private won't end until it's over, and there won't be any question about what *would* have happened if someone hadn't stopped it."

"I want to do that, but I don't have any idea how to fight. I'm not a tough guy; he is. Can you give me any pointers?"

"Yeah, sure. First thing is, don't fold just because he rings your bell. Like I said, fighting hurts. You're gonna feel pain. Fight through it. I been in lots of fights, and for me, pain pisses me off. Getting pissed off is good, as long as you don't lose control. If you just get pissed and start swinging wildly, he will kick your ass. But if you get pissed and take your time to think, you might just beat his. And another thing—don't cry, no matter what. Never cry. If you cry, he wins. Remember those two things. One, losing is ok. Ain't no shame in losing, as long as you tried. Two, pain is temporary. Same with any injury you might get, like a black eye or bloody nose, it's just temporary. Just like pain."

"But *how* do I fight?"

"Use your instincts. If I threw something at you, you'd duck, right? So if you see a punch comin', get out of the way. Duck, sidestep it, whatever. Go on the attack instead of puttin' your dukes up like a gentleman waiting for the other guy to hit you. This is a fight, not a gentleman's duel. The only real rules are to keep it one on one, use what God gave you, not a brick you find on the street, don't cry no matter what, and when it's done, it's done. *You* should hit *him* first if you can. Some fights never make it past the first punch."

"I don't even know how to punch."

"Well, I'll tell ya. Close your fist as tight as you can—thumb on the outside, not inside, unless you want a broke thumb. Make sure you lock your wrist, so it don't fold up on you. And try to remember your follow through, kinda like a golf or baseball bat swing. Follow through is real important."

"What's follow through?"

"Well, best I can describe it is, punch through him. Don't just stop when you connect. Imagine he's a foot farther away than he really is, and your punches'll be a lot more effective."

"Wow, it seems there's a lot to remember."

"Not really. Most of this stuff will kinda just come to you. But here's another pointer. Remember, you're in a fight, not a wrestling match. Don't just grab him and roll around 'cause that ain't what he's going to do. Punch his ass, DJ. A lot. Even if he lands punches, you stay on the offensive, not on the defense. You can't win on defense. No matter what he does, attack him at every opportunity. Just do it smart, not flailing all over the place."

"How will I know it's over? Assuming it's not broken up first."

"You'll know. Whatever you do, don't puss out. Don't cry, don't say, "I give," and don't stop just 'cause you're tired. If you can't get to his nose, punch him in the throat. Punch hard. Just follow your instincts, and get it over with. Don't kill the guy; if he ain't fightin' back, it's probably over. And like I said, don't worry about winning or losing. You win in the end just because you're willing to fight. This kid's bigger and stronger than you, and he's bullying you. You'll win just by fighting him."

When I hung up, I felt like I was ready.

Chapter 12

The next day, I got to the art room as fast as I could. Kunkle and his friends were hanging out in the hallway outside. My heart was hammering, and I kept reviewing everything my uncle had told me. I was pumped up and already pissed off that Kunkle had put me in this situation.

In my mind, I kept replaying an incident from the year before when I totally biffed it on my skateboard. I had been bombing down a hill at light speed when I lost control. I went down hard, sliding and tumbling, and was covered in road rash. It was so painful that it was hard to walk afterward, and I couldn't move my left arm for a week without yelping in pain, but I powered my way through it, so I could get right back up on the board. Two weeks later, it was just scabs and a cool story. As I approached that art room, I kept telling myself that skateboard crash was way worse pain than this fight would be.

"You didn't take any pictures of your dick head, did you dickhead?" said Kunkle the moment he saw me. His friends laughed.

I stopped and gathered my wits. "Look, Kunkle, I don't know why you're always on my shit, but I'm asking you to stop it. Get off my back," I said. There was a tremor in my voice that betrayed my fear, but now the challenge was out there.

He looked at me, almost bewildered. "Did you just tell me to get off your back?" he asked, incredulous. "Or *what?*"

"Just get the fuck off my back, asshole," I said, sliding past him into the art room. There were a couple of girls in there chatting.

"Get out," I told them. There must have been something in the look on my face because they both got up and left.

Just as I knew he would, Kunkle followed me in. He turned to his buddies and said, "This will only take a second," and they all laughed. When he was inside, I closed the door.

"What the fuck is this shit? You a tough guy now?" he said, laughing. "What, are you gonna kick my ass?"

I looked at him and twisted the lock on the door.

His face took on a little expression of confusion. As soon as my hand came off the doorknob, I made a fist, locked my wrist, and lashed out with everything I had, aiming for that nose that was a foot behind its actual location.

He didn't have a chance to move. I connected on the bridge and heard the crack. He went straight to the floor. But Billy Kunkle wasn't a pussy. He got up and launched himself at me, hitting me in the waist with a football tackle, and we both went down, along with two desks and a trash can. There was shouting in the hall, and someone was pounding on the door.

At first, fear overtook me. I'd given him my best shot, and it only served to piss him off. Now, he was on top of me and really had the advantage. He popped me in the cheek hard, blurring my vision and bringing tears to my eyes. I was done and wanted to give up crying, but all I could think of was how my uncle said not to cry and to keep fighting.

Kunkle straddled me and got a knee up on my left bicep. He was a half-second away from pinning my right arm, too, when I threw my right hand up in his face. I didn't even close my fist, but I got him with my palm, right in the nose again. He howled in pain and showered me with blood, but he never pinned my other arm. I swung a wild roundhouse and hit him in the side of the head, knocking him off me. I scrabbled to my feet and kicked him, landing a pretty good punt to the stomach. I heard the air whoosh out of his lungs and hauled off to kick him again.

All he did was roll onto his back and hold his stomach. His eyes were wide, his face was covered in blood, and his mouth was open as he struggled to suck in air. His teeth were red with blood from his nose. He lay there trying to breathe. I had knocked the wind out of him, but good.

Suddenly, I realized the fight was over, just like Uncle Phil had said I would. I was standing over him panting when the door burst open. Mr. Petrelli, the art teacher, came in along with another teacher and the school security officer, whom I knew only as Jones. About ten kids flowed in behind them, including Kunkle's friends.

To my amazement, Jones ran up and grabbed *me*. I still viewed myself as the victim, but they were treating me like the aggressor. I liked that. It made me feel powerful. I even put on a brief show of struggling for a moment.

"Let's go," said Jones. "You're gonna need to see the nurse, but then you're going to the office. Fighting's gonna get you three days."

He dragged me off to the office. "I don't need the nurse," I said.

"You're gonna have a hell of a shiner. Your eye's already starting to shut," he replied. "But I gotta tell you, it looks like you gave Billy Kunkle the worst of it."

We got to the nurse's office, and she examined my eye. After telling me I was suffering from a "periorbital hematoma, commonly known as a black eye," and that I wasn't about to die, she gave me a frozen bag of goo to ice it with.

I didn't think I was "suffering" from anything. I thought I was sporting a war wound, a nice trophy that told other kids I wasn't going to be bullied anymore. I was proud of my periorbital hematoma. On my way out of her office, I caught a glimpse of Billy Kunkle in the other room. He was lying on his back holding a bloody rag to his face.

The eye hurt, but I was feeling pretty damn good about myself as I headed out the building for a three-day vacation.

Chapter 13

I noticed from the moment I returned to school that people treated me differently. Nobody teased me anymore. My eye was black and looked horrible, but both of Kunkle's were, and his nose was swollen and crooked, making him look even worse. My natural tendency was to avoid him, and I had to remind myself that not only had I stood up to him, but I had beaten him. He should be the one avoiding me.

Everything my uncle had said was true. The pain wasn't bad now, and it served to remind me that I didn't have to put up with bullying anymore. Kunkle ignored me in art class, but when we came face to face while taking our seats in photography, he said, "Hey man, I gotta admit, you have a good right hook. No hard feelings, ok?" he said, holding out his hand.

I looked at his hand and didn't know if I should shake it or not. I think he thought I was being a douche, but it didn't bother me. Finally, I said, "Just leave me the fuck alone, Kunkle." He held his hands up in front of himself. "Ok, man, whatever," and that was it.

When class let out, Mrs. Albatross asked me to stay a moment. Once everyone was gone, she said, "So tell me, Mr. Appleby. I heard you took care of a problem with Mr. Kunkle the other day. You want to talk about it?"

"Not really. He'd been bullying me since school started, for no reason. I just didn't want to put up with it all year long."

"Rumor has it you beat him up pretty good. And looking at you both, I'd say that's putting it mildly."

I liked Mrs. Albatross. She seemed like she'd be a good mother. She had remembered every kid's name the first day of class and had never forgotten one since. She was the kind of woman I wished I'd had for a mother.

"I've never been in a fight before," I confessed. "I was scared, but my uncle, who's been to prison, gave me some pointers."

"Well, you know, fighting is never the answer."

I just looked at her.

"At least, that's what we're supposed to say. I'll tell you a little secret. If you were my son, I would have told you to beat the shit out of him. There's not much else you can do with a kid like Billy Kunkle. I'm proud of you. That's what we're *not* supposed to say."

Did she just drop a curse word to a student like it was nothing? Awesome!

I smiled at her. "Thanks, Mrs. Albatross."

"Dean, I have some developing to do. Would you like to stay and help me?"

"Sure. If you can get me out of study hall."

"That's no problem, especially for study hall. I'll just write you a pass."

We went to the darkroom and developed a bunch of pictures. It was pretty nice hanging out with her. That was on Friday.

On Monday, I actually looked at Mrs. Albatross for the first time. She wasn't a bad looking woman, in a grown-up sort of way, except for some old acne scars. She had brown hair that was a little curly and fell down to her neck. She was short, just a little taller than me, and had very large brown eyes that were kind of pretty. She was thin, had smallish boobs, and small pretty hands.

I lingered in her class after the bell rang. Mrs. Albatross noticed and asked, "You want to stay and help again, Dean?"

"Sure," I said, as if this had just occurred to me. This time, there wasn't any developing to do, and we pretended to clean stuff up and spent some time sorting through student's pictures. Mostly, they just took photos of their pets and trees and stuff.

We chatted as we sorted, and I surprised myself by opening up more than I ever had before. She asked about my family life, and I suddenly just started talking about Connie.

"I find myself really missing her," I confessed. "One of my earliest memories is of her calling me her 'baby boo.' We were pretty close as kids.

I was eight when she got sick, and I was so selfish, all I could see was how bad her cancer affected *me*. My parents didn't have much time for me, just for her. We couldn't do the things I wanted to do, and nothing I did made them happy."

"I don't think that's selfish. I bet it's true. I'm sure they had to put all their resources into your sister. I don't think they meant to put you second, but she was dying, and they pretty much had to. It's so terribly sad, and I feel sorry for all of you."

I could tell she really felt it. Her eyes were wet like she was about to cry. I almost loved her for that, as silly as it sounds.

"Yeah, well, as bad as it was when she was sick, it was nothing compared to how bad it got after she died."

"In what way?" she asked.

"Well, it just totally fucked everyone up . . . "

Realizing what I said, my eyes got wide, and I trailed off. "Uh, sorry, Mrs. Albatross."

She giggled in a teenage sort of way. "Dean, that's ok. That word doesn't offend me."

I glanced at her, and she was still smiling. "Nothing much offends me. So, how did Connie's passing fuck up your family?"

I smiled back at her, and then the moment passed. "It just seemed like she took all the life out of everyone in the family with her," I said. "I was mad all the time. Mad at everyone, for no major reason. My dad moved out and had an affair with another woman. He ended up with another kid, and then they broke up, too. My mom just laid around in bed all day being depressed and not giving a shit about anyone else."

"And you? What did you do?"

"I tried to burn my house down."

She didn't move a muscle, and I didn't elaborate. After a moment, I started crying.

"Oh, Dean." She moved in and put her hand on top of my head, slipping it around so she was cradling the back of my head.

I was ashamed. "I gotta go," I said, heading for the door.

I didn't stay after class for the rest of the week. The following week, she asked me to stay again. She could use a hand with developing, even though we hadn't taken any pictures.

When we went in the darkroom, she said, "This is my own film. DJ, I like you. You opened up to me, and I appreciate that. Can I trust you?"

"Yeah, sure," I said. I had no idea what she was talking about, but there really wasn't any other answer.

"These are pictures my husband and I took. I'm not supposed to use the school facilities for personal use, and uh, I can't take them to the drugstore to get developed. I feel I can trust you not to say anything. I could get in trouble."

Mrs. Albatross was breaking the rules. She just went up a notch in my book. It was kind of cool sharing a secret like that, and I smiled at her. "I won't tell."

She smiled back, and we got to work. The pictures were from their summer activities. Mostly, they were of her and her husband in the gorge—hiking by a waterfall, standing on a trail high above the Columbia River, hanging out on a sandy river beach in bathing suits. I lingered on one of her lying on her back, her stomach flat, her navel far above the top of her bikini bottoms. It was a very sexy photo.

"You like that bathing suit?" she asked.

I felt myself blushing and was embarrassed, even though it was too dark for her to see. "Yeah," I said.

"Good," she said cheerily. She paused and took one off the line I hadn't seen yet. Without a word, she handed it to me. It was her naked, lying on her back with her eyes closed to the sunshine.

I sucked in a ton of air and looked at her. Even in the low light, I could see her blushing.

"Do you like that one?" she said.

Not trusting myself to speak, I just nodded. I looked at the picture again. In it, her whole body was wet like she just got out of the river. Her boobs were small, but very full, and her nipples, small and pink, were standing out. Her legs were slightly parted, but I couldn't see down between them because of the angle and shadow. She had a triangle of light brown hair there, which I could see. It glistened with droplets of water in the sunlight. I was mesmerized by the photo, especially that triangle with the water drops that looked like jewels, and I just stared at it.

After a moment, she took it back. I couldn't bring myself to look at her. She moved in very close to me and whispered, "You think about that picture later tonight when you're all alone in bed." Her lips brushed my ear ever so slightly. I shuddered, and she slipped out of the room.

The next day, she didn't even glance at me in class, but I knew she was thinking about me. I sure as hell knew I was thinking about her. Mrs. Albatross had gone from a regular woman old enough to be my mother to a hot babe. Suddenly, she was beautiful. I knew what she looked like naked!

After class, she glanced at me and let her eyes linger just a moment before disappearing into the darkroom. I waited until the last kid had left, and then I went in after her. Even though it was dark, I still faced away from her.

"Did you think about me last night?" she asked quietly.

I swallowed and nodded. There was enough light for her to see.

"What did you think about?"

I couldn't believe we were doing this. I was scared, but I was exhilarated at the same time. I didn't fully trust my voice. "I . . . I imagined I was there with you on that beach—instead of your husband."

"Is that all?" she asked coyly.

I shook my head. "Huh-uh. I . . . we . . . well, I took my clothes off, too."

"Good, Dean, good. I knew you'd know what to think about. I thought about you too last night. I knew you were thinking about me. I thought about you when I was in the bathtub. When you thought about me, did you . . . touch yourself?"

How could she ask me that? But, I figured, it wasn't any crazier than everything else. She was definitely in control, and as weird and scary as it was, this was the most intensely horny I could ever remember being. I knew I was going to go wherever she took me. I wondered how far that would be.

"Yes," I whispered.

She took me by the shoulders and turned me to face her. I was so glad for the darkness because I had a giant-ass woody. "So did I," she whispered to my face. "I was *so* wet. I wanted you because I knew you were touching yourself. I knew you were hard. You were real hard, weren't you?"

I could feel my Adam's apple bobbing up and down. I nodded.

"I'm wet now," she breathed.

I thought I was going to come in my pants. I'd heard the term 'getting wet' before but I didn't know exactly what it meant. We were so close that I could have put my arms around her and kissed her. In fact I wanted to do just that, but there's no way I could have moved.

As it turned out I didn't have to. She moved right in to me and crushed her body against mine. I felt my hard-on digging into her crotch and I know she could feel it, too. She kissed me, pushing her tongue into my mouth. It felt like heaven. She moaned just like they do in movies when they kiss like that.

I don't want to go into all the details of everything happened between us, but I can attest that Mrs. Albatross—Julie, for she insisted that when we alone I should call her by her first name—tutored me in a subject other than photography for the next twenty or thirty minutes, right there in the darkroom, and I was an eager learner.

We didn't go all the way, not that first time, but we didn't have to, either. Let's just say that the one goal I had set for myself in high school was fulfilled in a way I hadn't dreamed possible. And Julie wasn't some scared little fourteen-year-old zitface who smelled like pizza and bubblegum either. She was a mature, very sensuous woman who knew how to take care of herself—and knew how to take care of me.

As if this whole thing weren't surreal enough, it got even weirder when we reached the height of our passion. Her jeans were open and I was doing exactly what she'd shown me. My pants were still on, but her hand was working the front of them like a pump, and when she sensed I could take no more, Julie, with her lips and tongue just barely brushing my ear, whispered between gasps that if we got caught, she would lose everything. Her job, her marriage, her home, her reputation—everything. This caused me to think, but I was way too into what we were doing for it dampen my passion even a little, and as I began shooting the biggest load of my life, she kept repeating, "But it's worth it. Oh dear God, it is *so* worth it!"

And how right she was, too. On both counts.

This was by far the weirdest, yet most wonderfully fulfilling experience of my young life—at least up to that point. It didn't just end there, either. In the coming weeks, it only got better.

When we finally emerged from the darkroom that day, Julie went to her desk and pulled out a pass to excuse my absence from study hall. She handed it to me with a smile, and I turned and left, feeling a mix of guilt, pride, and maybe just a touch of shame, but at the same time, more grown-up and more satisfied than ever.

Later that day as my mind endlessly turned over and minutely examined every detail of what we had done, it occurred to me Julie had never filled the pass out. Obviously, she'd made it out before class even started. I knew that was a significant detail, but I didn't know why. And to be honest, I didn't care. I only knew I would go wherever she led me, and I couldn't wait to find out where that might be.

Chapter 14

March 17, 2014

The front of the house was bathed in bright light from the Bearcat's powerful spotlights. I stood in the open door for a moment, feeling as vulnerable as I ever had in my life. I knew I was in the sights of at least ten guns, two of which were high-powered sniper rifles. In a way, I wished someone would just shoot.

Suicide by cop. It's the chicken's way out. You can't do it yourself, so you have them do it for you. It's the ultimate passive-aggressive move. All I'd have to do is reach behind me like I was pulling a gun from my waistband. Once my hand started forward, I would just . . . end. I knew a lot about ballistics, and I'd gone to a sniper school when I was on SERT. Their point of aim would be between the tip of my nose and my upper lip. I would not hear the shot because the rounds our snipers use—Federal match-grade 175-grain boat tailed hollow points—are supersonic. I would feel no pain because the bullet would be traveling faster than my nerves could carry the signal, and the distance from its point of entry to my brainstem was just too damn short.

The bullet would sever my spinal column from my brainstem, and my death would be instantaneous. Death would occur before my legs collapsed under me, and there would be an odd moment where I was still standing on my own, but I would be dead. Nobody would actually see that because I would crumple and fall where I stood before the sound of the shot reached most people's ears, but it would happen, even though it could only be measured in milliseconds.

No pain, no knowledge of it, nothing. The perfect way to go. All I'd have to do is put my hand behind my back. The officer, probably Tom Aikins or Everett Harrison, would be entirely justified in the shooting.

Both of those guys are good cops. I'm not off-duty friends with either of them, but that isn't to say we're not friends at work. Beth begged me not to put them through the heartache and anguish they would suffer if they had to shoot me, but that's not why I didn't pull my imaginary gun. I didn't do it because I still didn't want to die. I wanted to live, even if that meant going to prison.

Plus, I'm a coward. I neither fear death nor afterlife, but I was just too damn chicken to do it—at least, right now. If prison proved as bad as I imagined it might, especially because I'm a cop, then I could always find a way there.

Suicide is *always* an option.

I couldn't see anything but the Bearcat's lights.

"DJ, walk straight toward the Bearcat!"

I stood there a moment longer. I wasn't ready to walk straight toward the Bearcat. But if I didn't, they would beanbag me. I sniffled and wiped my eyes on my shoulders, hating that I was being such a little pussy and crying in front of these men, of all people. In an effort to sound stronger, I barked, "I know what to do, Leon!"

"Then do it. Last warning before you get less-lethaled."

I nodded and walked toward the Bearcat. Two unrecognizable forms stepped out and handcuffed me. It was probably the first time that I know of where they didn't knock the bad guy to the ground.

They hustled me to the back of the Bearcat where Sandra Kowalski was waiting for me. "Anyone else in there with you, DJ?" she asked.

"No, I was there by myself. The guns, mine and the one I took from Anderson, are on the kitchen table."

She keyed her lapel mike. "Intel to CP, he says he's alone, and he left two weapons on the kitchen table," she announced.

"CP, copy. Entry, clear the house."

"Code red," announced Everett Harrison. It meant there were good guys in the target. They could take care of themselves no matter what they encountered in the house, and the announcement was made to let the entire perimeter know not to shoot into the structure, no matter what.

A moment later, the entry team announced the house was clear.

I was loaded into the Bearcat and immediately driven to Central Precinct where I was led up to an interrogation room in Detectives on the thirteenth floor. At least they spared me the indignity of being stuffed into a holding cell. I was uncuffed and told to sit at the little table. They reminded me that the room was being constantly monitored by both audio and visual recording equipment. They were required to tell me, as if I didn't know.

I sat there alone for nearly half an hour, wondering over and over how I'd come to be here. Three days ago, I worked East Precinct. I was supposed to testify before the grand jury tomorrow in a felony domestic violence case. I had a locker filled with gear back at the precinct. My passwords to half a dozen law-enforcement computer systems were still good. Yet here I was, under arrest, on my way to jail, court, and prison—for the rest of my miserable life.

I wished at that moment that I had stuck my hand behind my back.

The door opened up, and Jeff Haley, the president of the Portland Police Association, came in. I was so guilty that I didn't even expect them to make a show. The PPA provides legal services to any member accused of a crime, and a PPA representative is the first person to talk to an officer involved in a shooting.

"Hi, DJ," he said. "I'm not here as a cop; I'm here as your PPA rep. Let me first say that all recording equipment is off for our conversation. Of course, it'll go back on the moment I leave, but for now, anything said in this room is just between you and me."

"Hey Jeff. I guess I didn't expect to see you here."

"Until I'm told otherwise, you're still in the union. So as your rep, I'm telling you that you don't have to say a word to anyone. I just got off the phone with Walter Humphrey, the lawyer we keep on retainer. He said . . . Uh, well, as you know, since your current legal situation isn't related to work, he won't be coming out here. He suggests you retain a guy named Deacon Summerville. He's represented a lot of cops before. Of course, this falls outside the umbrella of union protection, so that's your call. I'm just here to represent you to the city. Because what you're accused of doing can result in criminal charges, you're not required to answer their questions. Any internal investigation will be delayed until any criminal proceedings you face are concluded."

"You're telling me I'm still employed by the City of Portland?"

"Nobody's told me anything to the contrary, DJ. Until they do, you fall under union protection, at least with regards to the city."

I smiled wryly. "Thanks for coming here, Jeff. I know you want to just get the hell out of here. So go, I officially decline union representation. But first, I want you to know I never intended to shoot anyone, let alone a cop."

"I don't want to hear it, DJ. Between you and me and the lamppost, you need a priest, not a union rep or a lawyer. And I'm not your priest."

"Right. Well, anyway, I meant it. I've enjoyed working with everyone here. Please pass that along. Hell, I know you won't. But remember, for the last eighteen years, I was there any time someone called for cover. I always gave my best. I never dumped shit on other officers, and nobody ever had to cover for me because I screwed anything up. Roger Slidell is still alive and working because I saved his life, and he'll still tell you that. I've had a good career here. I . . . I just don't want people to lose sight of that . . . Anyway, thanks, Jeff."

I stuck my hand out. Jeff just looked at it and without another word, he turned and left.

Moments later, Robin Garibaldi, a homicide detective came in. I knew him only by name. I'd never worked with him directly before.

"Hi, DJ."

"Rob."

"DJ, you know everything going on in here is being recorded, right?"

"Yes."

"Ok. For the record, it's fourteen hundred hours on Monday, March 17th, 2014. I am Detective Robin Garibaldi of the Portland Police Bureau, and I'm here in Interrogation One with Officer Dean J. Appleby, date of birth December 14th, 1974. It should be noted that Dean Appleby goes by the name of DJ, and that's what I'll be calling him throughout this interview.

"DJ, I'm here to interview you regarding an incident that occurred at the Killer Burger restaurant on March 15th of this year, the day before yesterday, and related events that have taken place in the days since. Before I get to the interview, though, I want you to be aware of your Miranda rights. Now DJ, I know you're already familiar with them and have, in fact, informed suspects of them thousands of times, but just for the record, please listen up. You have the right to remain silent. Anything you say can and will be used against you in court. You have the right to talk to an attorney and to have him or her present while you are being questioned. If you cannot afford to hire an attorney, one will be appointed to represent you at no expense. Do you understand your rights?"

"Yes."

"Ok, DJ, thanks for that. Look, can I get you anything? Cup of coffee? Something to eat maybe?"

"No thanks, Rob."

"Ok. You good as far as the bathroom goes—that kind of stuff?"

"Yeah, I'm fine."

"Ok. I know this sucks, DJ. It sucks for everyone. I know you've been through a hell of a lot the past few days. I don't suspect you intended for any of this to go down this way."

I just sat there and didn't say anything. Interrogation 101 teaches you to throw something like that out there and then lapse into silence. Pretty soon, the person being interrogated feels the need to fill the void and starts talking. But I was fine with the silence.

I knew all I had to do was say those magic words, and he couldn't ask me anything: "I want to talk to a lawyer." It's called invoking or lawyering up. Once a suspect does that, the cop can't ask any more questions related to the crime without the approval of the suspect's lawyer. That, of course, never happens.

I could have invoked, but I didn't. Part of me wanted to talk. Hell, I'd already freely admitted to Beth and Jeff both that I killed Horace Anderson. That was no doubt on tape and would be used against me. Beth, a police officer, had expressed disbelief that I had killed a man before I admitted to doing it, so that would probably be construed by the courts as questioning. Of course, she had given no Miranda warning and any lawyer would claim I was under duress and could therefore probably get the confession rendered inadmissible at trial. Still, though, I talked to her because I *wanted* to talk about it to someone.

I knew what kind of evidence they would have against me. First and foremost was the video of my crime. There was the murder weapon, which I had left on Doug O'Rourke's kitchen table along with Anderson's .380.

The two spent brass casings were gone, but they wouldn't need them; ballistics would easily match the rounds that killed Anderson to my gun. There were also five eyewitnesses to my initial crime, and they presumably either saw, or heard, me shoot Anderson.

None of the other charges were important. Aggravated homicide was the only one that mattered—the death penalty charge.

It was the only chip I had to play. Offer a guilty plea on anything they wanted in exchange for life without the possibility of parole instead of death by lethal injection. They might be interested in saving the cost of a trial, and I'm sure the Bureau would be interested in keeping as much of this out of the media as possible. A trial would spotlight PPB for months.

That's the reason I said those words: "Rob, I think I better talk to an attorney first."

"Fine. This interview is terminated until you can acquire representation. The time is fourteen thirteen hours. I'm turning off the recorder." Garibaldi got up and left the room.

A moment later, Jeff Haley came back in. He had two cups of steaming coffee and gave me one of them. Garibaldi returned with an evidence tech. They made me strip to my underwear and gave me a paper suit. They took my clothes as evidence, which is standard procedure. The clothes would be examined for blood or trace evidence linking me to my crimes. The evidence tech left with them, and Garibaldi told me he'd be back in a moment, but first, someone wanted to talk to me. He got up and left the room.

I looked at Haley quizzically, and he said, "I'm sorry, DJ, but this should come as no surprise."

Chief Waller came in. She didn't sit down. She was a detective when I first got here and had been promoted quickly after that. I'd never worked closely with her and had only met her a handful of times. She was a stern looking woman, and she stared at me for five full seconds before saying a word.

"DJ, I don't know what to say. I'm not even going to try to understand you. I checked your record with the Bureau, which is, as you know, pretty much unblemished. How the hell could you . . . Well, never mind. Don't answer that. DJ, I'm terminating your employment with the city. All your city equipment will be repossessed by the detectives executing the search warrant at your residence. I've already spoken with Jeff, and as I'm sure you've already figured out for yourself, the union will not be taking up your cause."

I looked at Haley. "You can't have expected us to stand for you. I'm sorry you've done this to yourself, DJ. I don't get it, man. Eighteen fuckin' years down the tubes."

There was nothing left to say. They left, and Garibaldi came back in. He escorted me down the interminably slow elevator to the lower level, through the parking lot and over to the county jail intake, which was right next door, for booking. There, I was surprised to see a wall of cameras and TV lights waiting for me. I guess I shouldn't be surprised. I was quite the antihero. Given the temperature of the city, I and my crimes would no doubt be hot news for weeks.

Ignoring the cameras, I stood at a counter that I'd stood at hundreds of times in the past, only now I was on the other side of it. I was asked all of the booking questions I'd listened to all those other times by a deputy whose face I recognized, but I had never before bothered to ask his name. Finally, I was shepherded into the next room to be fingerprinted and photographed. There, I was issued a pair of county jail blue jeans, a blue INMATE shirt, socks, and sandals. Socks and sandals—Portland all the way.

Finally, at 2:30 P.M., I was ushered into an isolation cell away from the general population.

Welcome home.

Chapter 15

"Hey, DJ. I thought you might like to see this." The speaker was Russ, a dayshift corrections deputy for Multnomah County. He was essentially my handler. He shoved the morning edition of The Oregonian, Oregon's largest newspaper, through the food tray slot into my cell.

He was right. I did want to see it. I wanted to see what my friends, my folks, and especially my daughter would be waking up to this morning. "Thanks, Russ," I said.

The headline was big and bold. "PPB's 'Bad Apple' Falls from the Tree."

I had to admit, it was clever. They justified the tongue-in-cheek headline with a first sentence quote: "Portland Police Bureau Officer Dean J. Appleby, now being referred to as a rare 'bad apple' by his peers, was arrested last night in Portland for aggravated murder, robbery, kidnapping, burglary, and a host of lesser charges. Aggravated murder is the only crime in Oregon punishable by the death penalty.

"The arrest culminates a city-wide manhunt following a takeover robbery of the Killer Burger restaurant in the 4600 block of NE Sandy Boulevard Saturday, in which off-duty Benton County Sheriff's reserve deputy Horace Anderson was murdered while trying to arrest the perpetrator . . ."

The article was laced with juicy quotes from the police chief and the mayor about how I, as an officer gone bad, was an anomaly within an otherwise stellar Police Bureau, and how the Bureau would always swiftly and thoroughly investigate and, if necessary, arrest and prosecute any of its employees who were accused of wrongdoing.

Everyone who was interviewed expressed shock and surprise that a highly decorated officer with an otherwise spotless record could have gone bad. The term "bad apple" was used several times, both intentionally as a play on my name and unconsciously by those who could think of no other way to describe me. The article was very long and continued on two more pages.

My history with the Bureau was laid out, starting with a photo of me being sworn in eighteen years earlier by then-Chief Moose and listing my assignments as patrol officer, field training officer, SERT operator, and CNT negotiator. The contents of my personnel file were minimal—four unfounded citizen complaints, eight letters of commendation from superiors, a Lifesaving Award, a unit citation for CNT, a Purple Heart, and the departmental medal of valor for disarming a suspect who was attacking another officer with a machete (I had been cut on the hand and received eleven stitches as a result). All of my evaluations were listed. In none of them had I received any marks less than "meets or exceeds standards."

There was a long description of the Killer Burger incident, an entire column of which was dedicated to Deputy Anderson. There was accurate speculation from the hostages that I had negotiated my own release, and the paper made no bones about how stupid I made CNT look in this. Finally, there was an account of my breaking into the home of an officer whom I knew to be on vacation, and the subsequent SERT incident that culminated in my arrest.

All in all, it wasn't a bad article. It begged the question on everyone's mind: how could an exemplary police officer such as this resort to committing an armed robbery in which hostages were taken and a man was killed?

Related articles listed the types of psychological tests police officer candidates have to undergo, as well as other high profile cases of officers gone bad. None of them came close to answering the question.

Later that day, I asked Russ for an opportunity to call a lawyer. I was given a phone and a telephone book. I found the number to The Law Offices of Deacon Summerville and gave him a call. Once I got Deacon on the line, he told me that he'd been advised by the union that I might be interested in calling him. He agreed to talk to me and made an appointment later in the day to meet me in the jail.

I was taken to a secure interview room for the meeting. Summerville came in, and we talked about money. His retainer was fifteen thousand, and his hourly rate was three hundred. I told him I couldn't afford that, and he pointed out that between my deferred compensation account and my city retirement account, I had a lot more than that. There would be no pension, but they still had to give me the money in my retirement account.

"Deacon, that's all I have to leave my daughter," I said. "You won't have to do very much on my behalf. All I want to do is negotiate away the death penalty."

"You can kiss that money goodbye, DJ, if you want representation. You don't qualify for court-appointed council with assets like that. You're either going to have to pay an attorney, or take a chance representing yourself."

"My life is at stake here! I can't risk representing myself."

"Then hire someone."

"Can't you give me some kind of a break on your fee?"

"Look, DJ, I'm the guy your union calls to represent cops that don't fall under the blanket of union protection. Usually, that means for drunk driving, or domestics, or cases when some bad guy wearing cuffs gets a fat lip after the arrest. I've had a couple of assault cases, but the worst thing I've ever had to represent was an officer arrested for embezzling from the union. I don't like representing cops who've gone bad. I happen to be a fan of the police department, even if I am a defense attorney. But a death penalty agg murder case? I don't like it. And, I don't like *you*. Trust me, I don't want this case, but I'll take it if you want me, so I can keep up my reputation with the union. If you decide to retain me, I'll fight as hard as I can for you, like it or not. But I'd sure as hell be happier if you don't."

"*Can* you swing a deal? Guilty on all counts in exchange for life instead of death?"

"I don't know. I can try. The DA's office may not want to deal you away. You're a poster boy for promotion over there. Everyone's going to want to see you swinging from a low-hanging bough."

"Would you try?"

"Of course."

"Then I'll retain you."

"Fine." He pulled out a contract and a pen. I signed it without reading it and handed it back to him.

"Ok," he said, "as to robbing Killer Burger and killing Deputy Anderson, I assume you did it?"

"Well, I can't really deny it, can I?"

"Sure you can, and you will. It's called pleading not guilty. You'll do that at arraignment in about an hour."

"What then?"

"This is a capital case, and as you've already surmised, they're going to go for the death penalty. I have an ear in the DA's office, and I already know that. So we're going to have to prepare a defense in case they don't want to deal. And even if they are willing to make the deal, the court doesn't have to accept it."

"Why wouldn't they?"

"Any one of a dozen different reasons, not the least of which is that whatever DA prosecutes you and whatever judge hears the case gets instant fame, recognition, and a shorter path to promotion. Someone's gonna get a book deal. And I have to tell you up front—when and if all this happens, you don't have enough money to cover it from your retirement accounts. You're going to have to liquidate. Your house, cars, investments, everything. There won't be anything left over for your daughter."

"And if they do deal?"

"Depending on what you have, there will be some left. A couple thousand and whatever assets you have. It won't be much."

"Fuck it then. If they don't take the deal, I'll just change my plea and let them kill me. At least Grace will get something that way."

"Why don't we cross that bridge when we come to it? Arraignment first. It's going to take all of three minutes. The DA will read the charges, the judge will ask how you plea, and you'll say, 'Not guilty.' That's it. I'll be there with you. Any questions?"

"I guess not."

An hour and thirty minutes later, a Kevlar vest was placed over my shoulders, and I was led to Room 3 in the Justice Center. This room was, like the booking area in jail, filled with cameras and reporters. Deacon Summerville had already instructed me not to say a word to them, not even a terse "no comment."

There was no avoiding the spotlight, and I hated every moment of being in there. I kept thinking of how all this would look on TV, and I imagined Grace having to watch it. I had not yet had the opportunity to call her, but knowing her as well as I do, I doubted she'd even take my call. Both she and her mother would look at this as some sort of personal insult—something for which there couldn't possibly be an excuse.

They're right about that, actually. There isn't. There's an *explanation*, but that's not the same as an excuse. Though I understand the explanation, I seriously doubt I could make anyone else understand it. When a judge asks me why I gunned down a fellow police officer while committing an armed robbery, 'I have a compulsion to put everything dear to me at risk' wasn't going to cut it.

The judge, a stern, older man whom I did not recognize, was named Bernard Katz. Finally, he called my case. "Case number 14-27792, State of Oregon vs Dean J. Appleby. Mr. Appleby, you have the right to remain silent through all proceedings. You also have the right to council and to have council appointed for you by the court if you qualify. However, it appears you are already represented. Counselor?"

Deacon stood up. "Deacon Summerville, Your Honor. Bar number 111859. Retained as council for the defense."

"Thank you, Mr. Summerville. Is the state ready to proceed?"

A young looking, bookish man of in his mid-fifties stood at the other table and said, "Ben Johnston, Multnomah County DA's office, Your Honor. The state is ready."

"Very well," said the judge. "Mr. Appleby, this is your initial court appearance. I have before me an instrument from the Multnomah County District Attorney's office listing the charges against you, beginning with Aggravated Murder. Would you like me to read them all?"

Deacon stood again. "We waive the reading of the charges and would like to enter a plea."

"Mr. Appleby, are you aware of all the charges against you?"

"I am, Your Honor," I said.

"And you've had a chance to confer with your council about this?"

"Yes, sir."

"Then how do you plead to the charges?"

"Not guilty, sir. On all counts."

"Very well. Mr. Johnston, how do you wish to proceed?"

The assistant DA stood and said, "I would like this case bound over to the grand jury, Judge."

"Very well. As to the matter of bail, this is a potential death penalty case, so there will be no bail. Adjourned." With a flourish of his black robe, Judge Katz stood up and disappeared into his chambers.

And that was that. I was returned forthwith to my isolation cell, where I would languish for twenty-three hours a day for the foreseeable future.

Time doesn't seem to pass when you're in a room by yourself without human interaction. It took days, weeks maybe, before I fully realized that this wasn't a game or a temporary problem for me. I was stuck in prison. I was being isolated from the other inmates because I was a police officer, and as such, I was at risk of being killed by them. There were people in this very building that I had personally arrested and transported here. Virtually all of them would love to see me bleeding on the floor from dozens of little holes.

About two weeks after I arrived, a deep, suffocating depression settled over me. I became indifferent to my plight. Remaining in my cell all day was just fine with me. I had no motivation even to get out of my rack. I wasn't eating, and I began losing weight.

During this time, I spoke to my daughter exactly once. At the beginning of our conversation, Grace asked me if I actually robbed that place and killed the deputy. I told her yes and tried to offer my weak and meager explanation, but she hung up on me.

During this time, I had a few meetings with Deacon Summerville about the case. He was in negotiations with the DA's office to save the county and the city hundreds of thousands of dollars and all the embarrassment of a trial by allowing me to barter my death for my life. Also during this time, the Multnomah County grand jury met in closed-door sessions, and in a detailed presentation by the DA's office lasting more than a week, they indicted me on all counts.

Finally, I was taken next door to the Justice Center for a second arraignment.

This one lasted a little longer than the first. In it, the same judge read the indictment from the grand jury. The list of charges was longer than I thought it would be, but the only one I really heard was aggravated murder.

Judge Katz allowed Ben Johnston of the DA's office to lay out the deal he'd come to with Deacon Summerville. Essentially, it was an agreement that I would change my plea to guilty on all counts in exchange for a sentence of life in prison without the possibility of parole. There was nothing else to bargain for. Either way, it was a death sentence. One way would just take a little longer than the other.

"Mr. Appleby, how would you plead to the charges against you in view of this agreement?" asked Katz.

"Guilty on all counts, Your Honor," I said.

"Before I accept your plea, Mr. Appleby, do you understand that by pleading guilty, you are condemning yourself to die in prison?"

"Yes I do, Your Honor."

"Do you understand that if you plead not guilty and stand trial, and if you are in fact acquitted, you would be set free? In other words, that by changing your plea, you are closing the only possible door to freedom that remains open to you?"

"I do."

"Do you further understand that if you opt to plead not guilty and stand trial, and if you are convicted, this court could still sentence you to life in prison without the possibility of parole? That the court is not required to sentence you to death by lethal injection?"

"Yes."

"And it is still your wish to plead guilty?"

"Yes, sir."

Katz removed his glasses and leaned forward in his chair. "Mr. Appleby, I am inclined to not accept your guilty plea. I'm of a mind to have you stand trial. You of all people, a police officer with an exemplary record, are accused of gunning down another police officer who, while off-duty, was trying to stop you from committing armed robbery and kidnapping. I believe you should have to account for your actions."

"I don't know how to answer that, Your Honor."

"You could answer it by testifying at your trial. Beyond my desire to hear your answer, you should know that I—as an outspoken proponent of capital punishment and a strong supporter of law enforcement—believe that if you are guilty, you should die for your crimes. Therefore, I would not shy from sentencing you to death if you are convicted. No, Mr. Appleby, I do not believe I will accept your guilty plea."

Deacon Summerville stood.

"Your Honor, if it would please the court, it's obviously in my client's best interest to strike this deal. Beyond that, though, I believe it is also in the state's best interest to stick to the terms of the agreement. Additionally, I think it's in the best interest of the City of Portland as well."

"Your client is the least of my worries right now, Counselor, and neither are the City of Portland or even the State of Oregon. Right now, the people I'm most concerned with are the family of the slain deputy. They may very well have an interest in watching Dean Appleby die for his crimes if he did in fact commit them. I believe they are entitled to his day in court."

Ben Johnston stood. "Your Honor, if I may? I've been in contact with the Anderson family a lot over the past three months. I've gone over all the potential outcomes of this case with them. They know the defendant stands to either spend the rest of his natural life in prison or be executed. They also know he could be exonerated, or that this case might somehow end up in a mistrial.

"In response to the question of his sentence if found guilty, the Anderson family collaborated together and wrote a letter, with the request that I read it into the record if the matter came up. I'd like to read that now if I may."

Katz looked at Summerville who just shrugged and nodded.

"Very well."

"Thank you," Johnston said. "It says, 'To whom it may concern: in the eyes of his family, Horace Anderson wasn't just a husband, a father, a son, and a brother. He was one of the most caring and considerate people God ever blessed this Earth with. He was a man who dedicated his life to following his Lord and Savior Jesus Christ; to helping others, both as a teacher, which was his profession, and as a reserve sheriff's deputy, which was his passion.

"'We will never understand why he was taken from us, but as Christians, we have a deep, abiding faith in God. His ways are not always our ways, and it is not up to us to question him. In keeping with our faith, we just want everyone to know that whereas we hate what Dean Appleby has done in taking Horace from us, we don't hate him as a human being. As the Bible teaches, we forgive him for killing Horace. The Bible teaches us to abide by the laws of both man and God, and there are penalties for breaking those laws. It is our hope and prayer that Dean Appleby goes to jail for the rest of his life, and that while there, he finds peace and salvation through Jesus Christ. However, if we, as the family of Horace Anderson, have any say in his fate, we would respectfully ask that he not be put to death for this terrible crime. We would not want his family to go through what we are going through. Thank you.'" Johnston sat down solemnly.

After a respectful moment, Summerville stood and said, "So, Your Honor, the family has requested that, upon his conviction, my client *not* be put to death. I agree with the court that their interest ought to be placed higher than that of the state and the city. It seems, Your Honor, that this deal is in everyone's best interest, and therefore, the defense asks you to reconsider accepting my client's plea based on the agreement with the state as to his sentencing." He sat.

"Mr. Johnston?"

Ben Johnston stood. "We agreed to the deal, Your Honor. Saves everyone a lot of time, effort, and heartache."

Judge Katz sighed, clearly disappointed that he was not going to be able to put me to death. "Very well," he said. "Mr. Appleby, knowing all the potential outcomes of this case, do you still plead guilty, pursuant to the arrangement we've discussed?"

I stood. "I do, Judge."

"All right then. I will accept your guilty plea and render a finding of guilty on all charges. Per the aforementioned agreement, I sentence you to life in prison without the possibility of parole." He leaned forward again. "You will die within those walls, Mr. Appleby, just not as soon as I would have liked. Case closed!"

Three days later, I was shackled, placed aboard a prison bus, and driven an hour-and-a-half south to the Oregon State Penitentiary in Salem. There, during my in-processing, I was told that because I had been a police officer, I was considered a high-risk prisoner. As such, I would be incarcerated in a solitary confinement cell in the Administrative Segregation Unit for my own protection. When no other inmates were present, they would try to give me sixty minutes a day out of my cell in a two-hundred square foot chain-link cage within the yard. Sometimes, it would only be a couple of times per week. Other than my handlers and on rare occasions, my lawyer, I would have no contact with anyone else for the rest of my life.

I was taken deep within the prison, where I was unceremoniously shepherded into a seven-by-twelve foot isolation cell. The corrections officer unchained my legs, stepped back, and the door slid shut with a metallic bang that reverberated inside my head long after the sound died away.

I turned around and offered him my manacled hands through the meal slot in the steel door. He unlocked them and disappeared without a word.

My father died at age ninety-one of kidney failure. They say if your father died of natural causes, his longevity serves as a decent indicator of how long you will live. I was forty, so if that was true, I had another fifty-one years left.

Twenty-three hours a day in my cell, every day. An hour a day outside in a twenty-by-twenty cage. For the next fifty-one years.

I did some quick calculations in my head. I would listen to that awful banging of the cell door almost nineteen thousand more times.

I now wished I hadn't agreed to the deal.

Chapter 16

October, 1989

I was head over heels in love with Mrs. Albatross—with *Julie*. What fourteen-year-old wouldn't be? Usually, all it takes at this age is for a girl to smile and flash her braces and we fall in love. Julie had done so much more than that, and I could not help but fall in love with her despite our age difference.

She was way into me, that much was plain as day. I have no idea why. I was no different than any other freshman boy. I was smaller and skinnier than most, and in my opinion, no better looking than any other kid. At least I didn't have acne, that was a plus. But for whatever reason she was into me, and that was all I needed to know.

All day long after our little extra-curricular session in the darkroom, I walked around with a smile (and my fingers) plastered to my face. As soon as I got home, I wanted to jerk off, but I denied myself this pleasure in the hopes that I might perform better for her tomorrow. I slept soundly that night, but found myself wide awake at five the next morning.

I left class with everyone else, but immediately returned after I was sure all the other kids were gone. Julie looked as eager as I did, and we went right into the darkroom, where she turned on the red light.

Without saying anything she kissed me, then reached up under her skirt and wiggled out of her panties. That little hip wiggle, with her hands under her skirt pulling her panties down, was the sexiest move I had ever seen a woman make. Then she sat me down on the stool while she hopped up onto the developing table in front of me. She opened her legs and. . .

Well, the specifics of what happened aren't really necessary, and even at fourteen years old I know that gentlemen don't speak of such things in detail.

Obviously, we had sex. Of a sort anyway; not yet full-on, you know, sexual intercourse. Julie was a teacher and that's exactly what she did. She taught me. Just like in school, some lessons are written in books and others are oral, and so it was with Julie. Today's lesson was of the latter variety.

She taught me what she, as woman, likes. It was actually kinda technical in a way. She gave me actual lessons on how to do it—where she likes to be touched, how she likes to be touched there, and how to read her reactions to it. I learned her anatomy; how the female body is constructed down there, how it reacts to stimulus, and how to provide that stimulus several different ways. She said that all women—even girls my own age—are physically constructed the same basic way despite little differences in size and shape, and these lessons generally apply to them all. I learned a lot, and by the time we were done I was sure I could teach a sex-ed class—and I could speak from my own experience.

Then we switched roles as to who was doing what to whom. She was still the teacher, only now she was teaching me what men like women to do to them. She said a boy and a girl who have never done this before eventually figure it out on their own, but she was saving me from all the fumbling frustrations of having it done unsatisfactorily the first few times. Instead, we went right to me learning from a pro. And trust me, Julie Albatross was an absolute pro.

I will say this much: As an inexperienced boy, I had virtually no control, and things didn't last very long the first time. When I was at the crucial moment, Julie was experienced enough to know it. Suddenly, she said, "Oh my God, here comes Mr. Vogel!"

Mr. Vogel is the school principal. Julie had already told me many times what would happen if we got caught. She would get fired and charged with a crime. She would never be able to teach anywhere again and would probably be labeled as a sexual predator. Additionally, she would lose her career and marriage in one fell swoop. Everybody in school would eventually learn what we'd been doing. As much as it might seem like I'd be worshipped by the other boys, the truth is it would be extremely embarrassing and humiliating for me. My folks would hit the roof. There would be all kinds of publicity, and in order for me to escape it, we would probably have to move. Basically, Julie and I were risking everything by doing this.

Well, suddenly the worst was happening. That definitely brought me back from the edge, and as I began to shrink, she just laughed and said she was kidding. There I was, a kid getting my first BJ, and now I was just standing there with my junk hanging out and her laughing at me. But even this was a lesson. She told me to recognize when I was getting close, and then imagine something terrible happening, and it would help me learn to last longer.

Well, like I said, Julie was very good and it it didn't take long before we were right back where we were before the Mr. Vogel scare.

Over the next several minutes, I imagined my parents catching us, her husband catching us, her dying of a heart attack while we were having sex, and many other terrible things. All of these were horrible circumstances, and they definitely served to slow me down some, but I was a horny-ass kid and none of them held me off for too long.

In the end, Julie took me to a whole new level of sex that day in the darkroom, and I fell utterly and hopelessly in love with her. Needless to say, I was in absolute heaven.

Julie had brought a box of baby wipes, which she'd strategically placed in the darkroom before we even got started. We used these to clean ourselves up, and rather than put them in the trash, she put them in a plastic sandwich bag in her purse. She had thought of everything, and that made me pause for a second. It almost seemed like she was using me, rather than the other way around, but even if that was the case, it didn't really matter as long as we kept doing what we were doing.

"Next time," Julie promised, "we're going to go all the way. And, we're going to be naked when we do it."

I walked out of there the happiest boy on the planet.

We didn't do anything for the rest of the week. I lingered after class each day, but there were other kids around, or she just smiled and said she couldn't today. Then, on Friday, she told me to stay after class.

Once everyone left, Julie told me that her husband, who was a cop in Gresham, was flying to Chicago to visit his mother for a few days. He was leaving in the morning, and he wouldn't be back until Thursday. She handed me a slip of paper with her address on it.

"Be there at noon," she said. "I'll be back from the airport by then. And make sure you take a shower first."

Well, the next day was the day I really became a man. I won't get into all the details, but I will say this: Julie was a married woman. She wasn't some fumbling high school girl. I couldn't imagine that sex with an inexperienced girl could come anywhere close to sex with a mature, experienced woman.

I had never met her husband, but I saw pictures of him all over their house. Many of those were of him in his police uniform, with his gun and everything. It was scary, with him being a cop, but it was exciting, too. Being in his bed with his wife, with his things all around me, was a strange, exhilarating experience. At first, it was very intimidating, but then I realized something huge. Julie's husband, a fully grown man, was in a competition with me, a skinny teenager, for his wife, and *I* was the winner. And to the victor goes the spoils, as they say. Being there like this made me feel more powerful than I had ever felt before. I liked it very much.

We made love the real way, and it was better than I ever thought it could be. Julie knew everything there was to know about sex, and she was eager to teach me. So, I know the sex was better than with any fumbling teenage girl, despite that she was closer to my mom's age than my own.

Julie told me not only was I a good lover, but sex with me gave her a thrill she couldn't get from her husband. She said that knowing that we could get caught made it better. She told me sometimes she and her husband liked to have sex outside, like when they took the picture she'd shown me. The reason she liked it so much was the possibility that someone might catch them. She said sex is like a fine cut of meat, and the right element of risk is the spice that makes it even tastier. I loved Julie's analogies, and from the things we'd done so far, I wholeheartedly agreed.

We began seeing each other two or three times a week, mostly in the darkroom. Once, we even went to a motel in Vancouver. We checked in as a mother and son in the afternoon and just left the key in the room when we left that evening.

Two weeks before Halloween, we made plans to go on a picnic in the Columbia River Gorge. I told my dad I was going to spend the day with my friend and his family hiking. He didn't question me, and I rode my bike to the library. By that time, I could disappear all day long without saying a word, and he'd never mention it as long as I was home by dark. Julie arrived a few minutes after I locked my bike up.

We drove for over an hour into the Gorge to a place called Mosier. There was an abandoned highway there, which was closed to cars and used only for hiking and biking now. She had packed a lunch and a blanket, which we carried in backpacks. It was a beautiful, warm Autumn day, and the leaves were at the height of their fall colors. One of the reasons Julie wanted to come here was to get some fall pictures for the photography class.

The road goes for about fifteen miles from where we had parked, all the way to Hood River. It was high up on the south wall of the Columbia River Gorge and was lined with a white picket fence. The land to our left was heavily wooded and very steep, almost straight up in places, to the top of the gorge wall. To our right was a spectacular view of the Columbia River far below us. The river was deep, wide, and very blue. White, puffy clouds floated lazily overhead in a sky the same color as the river. The trees were old oaks, birch, and maples, and the leaves were in brilliant, flaming color. The oak leaves were the biggest I'd ever seen, the size of basketballs in some cases. Julie shot almost two rolls of film along the way, and each photo would look like a postcard.

About a mile and a half down the road, we came to a place where the land flattened out a little to our left and was thick with trees before becoming a sheer rock wall. There, we found a deer trail leading into the small wooded area. We followed it to a secluded little clearing and spread the blanket. We ate and lay down in each other's arms, and we made love until the shadows got long, and it started getting cooler. Julie still had some film in the camera, and I begged her to take some pictures like the one she'd initially shown me.

After hesitating, we used the rest of the film in her camera to take naked pictures of ourselves. We didn't do any real porno ones, just tasteful nudes, including one of us both after she set the camera up on a log with the timer on. In it, her head was on my chest, and we both had our legs pointed to the camera, which was positioned by our feet. Our legs were open, but we were strategically covering each other's privates with our hands, and my arm was around her with my hand cupping her right breast and her hand cupping her left, so you really couldn't even see her boobs. We were gazing into each other's eyes when the shutter clicked. Just taking the pictures got me hard again simply because it was so sexy. Julie called it erotic art. We both had a great time doing it.

Afterwards, it was time to pack everything up and head back to the car. The walk to our spot had seemed to take forever, but the walk back only seemed to take a moment. We tossed everything inside and reluctantly drove down the hill toward the freeway.

All day, I had wanted to tell Julie that I loved her, but I was afraid that it would ruin our day or maybe even chase her away. As good as we were together, I knew it couldn't last, and this made me sad and depressed. I'd had more fun today than ever in my life, but now it was over.

As we passed through the little town of Mosier, the Halloween decorations reminded me of Connie's passing, and this only added to my melancholy. Before we got on the freeway, I asked her to pull over. After she stopped, I slid over to her and leaned in close, putting my arms around her and resting my head on her breast. I sighed deep, and for a moment, I thought I might cry. Julie sensed this and held me tight.

"Honey, what's the matter?" she asked.

"I don't know," I said. "I just don't want this day to end. I had such a good time today, and I have ever since we've been . . . you know, together. And now, the best day of my life is over, and it's Halloween, and that always reminds me of my sister . . . "

Julie already knew about Connie. She looked at me with sadness and what almost looked like love, and she snuggled me close. I just couldn't help how I felt about her. I knew she didn't love me, and that she was married, and there was no way we could really be together, but I couldn't help but love her. I looked up and a tear fell down my face, but I wasn't embarrassed. She actually kissed it away.

Pretty soon, we were making out. Even this made me sad because at that moment, I would have traded a month's worth of sex for her to just tell me she loved me. But I was also horny, and she had definitely gotten my motor started.

I had just slipped a hand under her top when the inside of the car was suddenly bathed in brilliant light. We jumped like we were electrified, and as we slid apart, there was a tap at the driver's window.

It was the police.

Chapter 17

Julie rolled down the window, and I scrambled over to the other side.

"Ma'am, please step out of the car," said a gruff voice. Julie, obviously terrified, tried to tuck her shirt in and button her jeans as she got out. The cop shined his flashlight on me, and I could see his eyes widen when he saw how old I was.

"What's going on here?" he asked.

"I . . . Well, he's my, uh . . . " she said.

"How old are you, kid?" he said, keeping his light on my face. I turned away and didn't say anything, and the light swung back to Julie.

"You're gonna have to break out some ID, lady," he said.

"It . . . It's in my purse. Can he get it for me?"

"Hey kid, gimme her purse," he said, leaning into the car and shining the flashlight on me again.

This was really bad. He'd caught us making out. Julie had told me she was risking everything, but it never occurred to me just exactly what that meant. Now we were busted. Once they found out she was a teacher and I was her student, she'd get fired, probably even arrested. They'd call my parents, and my dad would have to drive out here and pick me up from the police station. Everybody would find out, and maybe we'd even have to move or something.

"I said gimme her purse, kid. I didn't just say it to hear myself talk."

I began to yell incoherently and wildly slapped my hands against my head. I rocked violently back and forth in the seat, acting like this retarded kid I'd seen in a store over the summer. The mother had been unable to calm him, and she finally had to leave their shopping cart full of groceries in the store and take him outside. I'd always been good at imitations, and I really played this up.

"Jesus Christ, kid, slow down!" he said. "What the hell's wrong with this kid?" the officer shouted desperately above my yelling. The more he tried to calm me, the more agitated I acted. Finally, I jumped out of the car and ran up to Julie, putting my arms around her and burying my face in her chest. "Mom, mom, mom, mom, mom!" I yelled.

She immediately caught on and wrapped her arms around me. "I'm sorry, Officer, but my son is severely autistic. He gets very upset at nothing sometimes. When he gets like this, all I can do is hold him tight and soothe him. That's what we were doing when you knocked on the window. I had just gotten him calmed down."

I kept yelling, and the officer literally backed away like if he didn't, he'd catch my retardidity or something.

"Look, it's ok, don't worry about it," he said, getting back into his car. "Just get him calmed down, and take him home."

With that, he drove away.

"Oh, my God, did you see that?" I said excitedly. "I just thought of it right then! Oh, man, we were *so* busted! I can't *believe* we pulled that off!"

Julie didn't say anything. She was clearly shaken by the encounter. When she got back in the car, she was literally shaking. She immediately pulled out and got onto the freeway.

"DJ, do you realize how close I just came to losing everything? If you hadn't pulled that little stunt, I would have gotten arrested. They would have called your parents, and I'd have been fired, and my husband would have left me and . . . everyone at work would know, and . . . oh, my God."

"But none of that happened, Julie! We faked him out, big time. I have no idea how I even thought of that, but wasn't it the coolest thing?"

"Well, it *was* brilliant, DJ, but we should have never—oh, my God, when I think of what would have happened if you hadn't thought of it . . ."

She quieted and said nothing for a long time. She really seemed to be freaked out. As for me, I was incredibly proud of myself, keyed up and excited. Julie remained quiet and reserved all the way home, and she wouldn't even kiss me when she dropped me off. She said she was afraid someone might be watching.

After photography class on Monday, Julie took me into the darkroom and said, "Dean, we're going to have to slow down. That incident in the gorge really scared me. I just can't afford to get caught. I just *can't*."

My heart was already breaking because I knew what was coming. "We can be more careful," I said. "And we can maybe just see each other once a week for a while, can't we?" I desperately didn't want her to break up with me.

She grabbed my face and looked me in the eyes. "Oh, Dean, the past two months have been a lot of fun, and I've come to love you in a very special way. But that encounter made me realize that there's just too much on the line for us to keep going. I've never cheated on my husband before, but I've always imagined myself with a student for some reason. I don't know why; maybe it's just the excitement of it. I've been looking for someone like you for a long time—someone who is sensitive and not overly confident, someone who needs someone, someone attractive but shy and lonely, without friends. You're the most handsome student I've ever had, and you meet all the other criteria. At first, I just thought I'd want to flirt or maybe even mess around some, but it just turned me on so much to flirt, I had to go farther. But then I started having feelings for you, too, which I knew was wrong, but I couldn't help it."

"What kind of feelings," I asked, hopeful.

"Well, I thought it might be love. But don't you see how this could never work? Don't you see how it will destroy us both?"

"No, Julie, I don't. It *could* work!" I said, crying. "I love you, and you're starting to love me. I know we could *make* it work somehow, if you wanted it to."

"No, we couldn't. We're like the bird and fish who fall in love. They may love each other, but where will they make their home?"

"No, Julie, we're *not* like them. You're just older than me is all."

"Oh, Dean, don't you see? We couldn't let anyone know about us until you were eighteen, and that's four years. And by then, I'll be forty-two. Why, when you're twenty-five, I'll be almost fifty years old! You won't be attracted to me by then. You need someone your own age. And I still want to have a baby someday. You can't be fifteen years older than your own child. It *can't* work."

"Julie, don't do this. Please, Julie, don't break up with me!"

She put her arms around me and said, "I'm sorry, Dean. I should have known better than to even start this. We can't keep seeing each other. What we had was special, and I know that as you grow, for many, many years, you'll always look back and treasure the times we shared together. I know I will for the rest of my life. But you'll soon see that we *had* to end it. And you're a lot more grown up than you were at the beginning of school, too. That will really help you in your relationships with girls your own age. You can teach them the stuff I've taught you. You'll soon see that what I'm saying is right. I know you will."

"Please, Julie . . ."

"I developed our pictures before school, Dean. I want you to have them," she said, handing me an envelope. Ever since we'd come in here, she'd been calling me Dean instead of DJ, and this had a terrible ring of finality to it. "They're our private ones. Hide them very well, and don't look at them for a long time after today. And when you do, a long time from now, you will see that we shared something very, very special. A special kind of love, but the kind of love that's doomed from the beginning, like Romeo and Juliet. You'll treasure what we had."

I took the envelope and leafed through the prints. In addition to our special ones, there was one of us sitting on a stone wall looking into each other's eyes, the Columbia River far below us. The picture was very innocent if you didn't know what was in our hearts, but to me, the look on our faces just screamed love. Out of all of them, it was the only one I wanted to keep. But I knew she'd just destroy the other ones, so I took all of them. Maybe I'd do what she suggested and not look at them for years, but the innocent one I would keep close and look at often.

She pulled me in and wiped my tears with her thumb. It was such an intimate gesture that I knew she still loved me. I knew that she was just scared, and that we really weren't over.

"I copied the one of us on the wall. That one I'm going to keep, too, Dean, to always remind me of you. I think it's my favorite picture." She kissed me on the forehead and lightly on the lips. It was the kind of kiss a mother would give her son if he was going to camp for two weeks. Then she turned off the red light and walked out, leaving me alone in the empty, dark room.

Chapter 18

Over time, I realized that Julie had been serious when she let me go. I thought her love for me would eventually win out, but Julie's head was apparently stronger than her heart. Starting the following day, she either locked the room and left after class, or she had a girl stay afterward to help her.

She wouldn't even look at me for a solid week. Not even a glance. And then, when she did, our eyes would linger on each other for a moment, and then she would look away. Once, in a tiny gesture that only I could detect, she sadly shook her head, as if telling me no. It was like being dumped all over again.

All of this hurt me very much. I had never really had a crush on a girl before, but now I knew why they called it that. Now I knew what all those sappy songs were about, and I knew why Romeo felt he had to do what he did after seeing Juliette die.

Over the past two months with Julie, I fantasized about us endlessly. I created numerous scenarios in my mind in which she divorced her husband, and we got together. I had looked up the laws about minors marrying, and I found that in Washington, all you needed was permission from both your parents and the family court. Making the most common version of my fantasy as real as possible, I had us wait until her divorce was final before we made our relationship public, and by then, I was fifteen. Then, together, we talked to my folks and explained everything. My parents, recognizing the love we shared, agreed to give their consent for us to marry.

One day in my fantasy, Julie took a vacation day, and my folks excused me from school, and we drove across the river to Vancouver. We just went to the courthouse, found a judge that wasn't busy, and got him to marry us. We drove home to her house in Gresham as a married couple (her husband was now living a sad life in a crappy apartment, envying me and writing checks to Julie, which we used for stuff like vacations and new cars), and it was all perfectly legal.

I fantasized about every aspect of married life and decided I would love it. I changed schools to Gresham High because it would have been too awkward to have us both in the same school. No other girls could turn my head, and all the boys looked up to me. I was everyone's hero, and they all knew that Julie and I either had wild sex or made passionate love every night after school. It was awesome.

But that was just fantasy. The reality of it was that Julie and I were over. It was as if we'd never happened. I treated the picture of us on the wall no differently than the erotic photos. I put them all away, folded into the thick cardboard on the bottom of a box that held an old, unused weight set in the back of my closet. I never even opened the envelope after putting them there the day Julie gave them to me.

When we had parent-teacher conferences, Julie sat at the other end of a table from me and my dad, and she blankly talked about my progress like I was any other kid. I wanted to cry. I wanted to bolt from the room, but I just sat there. When she told my dad I was a pleasure to have in class, I wanted to ask her about the pleasures I had given her outside of class, but of course I just sat there silently dying inside.

I don't know how I wanted her to treat me, but it hurt a lot to have her treat me the same as everyone else. There wasn't a wink, a little coded phrase, or even an understanding glance shared between us. It was just a report of the facts and a display of photos I had personally taken and developed. She talked to my father and totally ignored me.

But I had power in that meeting, and I felt it. Julie had to feel it, too. If I wanted to be a prick, I could have said something. I could have pulled out another photo I had taken. I could have ended the career of Mrs. Julie Albatross. She must have known it, been thinking about it. I was hurt, but I was strong and powerful and had the ultimate weapon at my fingertips.

I thought about using my photos to blackmail her into having sex with me again, but that seemed like an abuse of my power. Part of having great power was *not* using it. That's where the power actually existed—like a hornet who had great power over a scared human. To use it was to lose it. The bee could sting him, making his greatest fear come true, but once it did, it would die. I could use my power, but then I would lose it, and then I'd be nothing again. I had already been nothing, and I didn't like it much. But the power . . . *That*, I liked. A lot.

Besides, I didn't want sex from Julie. I wanted love. Sex would come naturally with love. I wanted it all, or I wanted none of it. And I didn't want to hurt her. I couldn't, no matter what she did. I simply couldn't hurt her.

Toward the end of the summer that year, my mother took me out to dinner. It was nothing fancy, just Shari's, but as we were eating, Julie came in with her husband. They passed right by our table, and our eyes just happened to meet at the same time.

Before I could think about what to do, I said, "Hi, Mrs. Albatross."

She was walking ahead of her husband and had to stop. "Hello," she said. She paused for a moment, as if trying to recall my name, and I saw a momentary flicker of panic: "Dean, right? Dean Appleby?"

"Yeah," I said. I wasn't even disappointed with the charade by this time.

My mother said, "Hello. I'm Ruth Appleby, DJ's mother."

"Pleased to meet you. I'm Julie Albatross. I was Dean's photography teacher last year. I think I met your husband at parent conferences."

"That would be my ex."

"Yes. Uh, this is my husband, Frank."

I actually stood up and shook his hand. "Pleased to meet you, sir," I said, trying to sound mature.

"Well, I'm pleased to meet you, too, son," he said.

Son? Really? How about Your Highness? And I bet he was pleased to meet me. I wondered how pleased he'd be if he knew how often I'd fucked his wife.

Smiling, I called up the image of my face between Julie's legs—how wet she was, how the taste of her lingered for the rest of the day. I called up images about me in his bed, using his washcloth to clean up, about how his wife laid his picture facedown on the night table before we had sex. Mostly, I thought of the intimate things about her only he should know, like the little moans and gasps she made that sounded like a kitten when she came, or the two little freckles on the inside of her upper right thigh, right where things started getting good. While shaking his hand,

I exacted mental revenge on him for being the winner. I hated him because he possessed her, and I didn't.

I glanced at Julie before I let go. *She* knew what was in my mind.

That night, I formed a different opinion of Julie. Rather than be pissed at her, I came to feel sorry for her. She was kind of a lost soul running around, not truly knowing what she wanted out of life. She had seen something in me that struck her deep inside. Maybe we were like kindred spirits, both alone and searching, our only misfortune having been born into the wrong generation. She knew in her head that we couldn't really make it, but getting that notion into her heart had taken a lot longer. She'd tried to resist it, but she hadn't been able to. Only when the prospect of getting caught slapped her in the face did she finally realize that it simply couldn't work. But she had loved me, and had I been even ten years older, it might have lasted. I couldn't hate her for breaking it off. She was right; being together was, unfortunately, impossible for us.

Running into her had only served to demonstrate that I was really, actually done with her. I had gotten over her.

Our time together had been good for me. She had found me a boy and made me a man. She'd taught me things other boys wouldn't learn for ten or maybe even twenty years. Through her, I'd known love, and sex, and satisfaction, and had an early glimpse into the world of adulthood. I'd experienced fulfillment and rejection, triumph and tragedy. But I had survived it all and come out better in the end.

That night, as I lay in the dark, I closed the book entitled Mature Sexual Relations and the Pitfalls of Falling in Love with Your Teacher, and I began living my life as a normal kid again.

I'd lived as an adult long enough.

Chapter 19

It felt good to be a fifteen-year-old kid again. After I got over the initial heartbreak of losing Julie, I was able to see things from a different perspective. A piece of me would always love her, but I no longer needed her.

I saw her occasionally at school in my sophomore year, and she even looked different to me. She looked old and not nearly as attractive as I remembered. You could see the little lines around her eyes and the age of her pitted skin, and when I compared her body to the girls in my class, she was saggy and jiggly. None of that had mattered when her clothes were off, but I sure admired the tight butts and perky tits of my classmates in comparison.

As for the other areas of my life, things were pretty good on all fronts. My dad and I were getting along, and we had moved from our crappy Rockwood apartment to a little house in Fairview. I was seeing my mother more often, and we were getting along better, and after my fight the previous year, no bullies had tried to bother me. In school, I was doing well and making mostly B's with a few C's and the occasional A.

The biggest thing that happened to me in my sophomore year was a growth spurt. I finally began catching up to the rest of the kids in the class. I never became a giant, but I hit 5'8 by the end of the year. I actually got on the JV basketball team, which I enjoyed.

I had always been fast, and that year, I kept up with drills after the season ended. I continued working out through the summer, and I went out for football in August. I wanted to play tackle and tried to bulk up, but I just wasn't built that way. Since I was fast, I made a good running back. I wasn't that great of a receiver, but the coach said we could work on that. But my ground game was pretty good, and in my junior year, I got a lot of field time. By the end of the season, I was getting almost as much time as the first stringers.

Football became about as big a distraction for me as Julie had, only in a more positive way. Even though I played, I was never what you would call a sports guy, but for the first time in my life, I felt like I had a place where I belonged. I had friends on the team, and I began hanging around with them after school and on weekends.

I started in varsity football in my senior year, and I only went two games without scoring a touchdown. I even dated a cheerleader, which was very weird because my only experiences with a female had been so advanced.

Christine was a chubby redhead, but she was cute as a button, and we dated pretty solid for about four months. She was a virgin when I met her and a woman when we broke up. I got to do what Julie had suggested, which was teach her some of the things I had learned. Christine knew I wasn't a virgin, but she didn't ask who I slept with, and I didn't tell her. She was awkward and timid sexually, and to my amazement, so was I. I remembered all my experiences with Julie, but all that went out the window when we started messing around. I was actually glad of this because I wanted to experience sex with a girl my own age as any normal kid would.

Despite her youthful body, when we finally made love, the sex with Christine was lacking in comparison. Part of it was her inexperience. Tearful, nervous sex with a scared teenager just couldn't compare with the confident experience of a sexually charged woman.

When Christine and I did it, it was in the safety of my house when my dad was gone, and I knew he wouldn't be back because he was driving the Max train. Her folks didn't even know where I lived, so we had no chance of getting caught. We were using a condom, so we didn't have to worry about getting pregnant. In short, it was a fine cut of meat, but it was without spices, and that made a noticeable difference in the taste. Sex with Christine was ok, but without the risk of having everything on the line like with Julie, the excitement just wasn't the same.

We didn't last long. We broke up in February, and after her, my life was as uneventful as any other kid's. For the first time that I could remember, my life was at peace. I had no dying siblings, my family wasn't in turmoil, depression wasn't destroying anyone I loved, I wasn't burning my house down, no perverts were trying to molest me, and I wasn't sneaking around with a sex-crazed teacher. Instead, I'd had made friends, had an age-appropriate relationship with a girl, and I was actually enjoying school. Even more than that, I actually enjoyed my life.

My senior year was my best year by far. Though we didn't have a winning season, I played well and was the Raiders' second highest scorer. After Christine, I began seeing a new girl, Susan, and things were looking promising. My mother was on a new medication and was happier and more alive than I'd see her in years. My dad and I were getting along, and he was even trying to get me a part-time weekend job at Tri-Met.

One day in March, I happened to be walking down the same hall as the photography lab. It was just after fourth period started, and I was on my way to my locker, having decided to skip Government, my last class of the day. I was still at the far end of the hall when I saw a freshman boy, who looked like he should be in seventh grade instead of ninth, coming down the hall from the opposite direction.

When he got to the photography lab, he stopped, looked furtively around, quickly opened the door and went in, quietly closing the door behind him.

Chapter 20

To anyone else, it would hardly have been noticeable, but I knew right away what was going on. I recognized myself and my own behavior in that kid's eager, nervous apprehension. He was even built like I had been at the time—small, thin, young looking.

I went to the photography lab and peeked in the door. Of course, the classroom was empty, and the little light was on over the darkroom door. I snuck into the classroom and sat down behind Julie's desk. I was going to wait them out, get rid of the kid, and front Julie off.

After fifteen minutes, I went over and put my ear to the door. I could hear her moaning in there, and it brought back every memory of what I had believed to be our unique and special relationship. I was enraged, and almost burst in, but then I thought better of it. Instead, I left the lab, gently closing the door behind me.

Julie had told me she had never cheated on her husband before. She had made me feel special by telling me that she had never felt like this about any other student and never would again. It had only been natural that I fell in love with her, but she had made me believe, quite intentionally, that she was in love with me as well.

Now, all of that went out the window. The truth was, Julie had a problem. She was a pervert. For whatever reason, she didn't like age-appropriate sex. Whatever her husband was doing for her wasn't enough. Maybe she couldn't really get off if there wasn't some kind of major risk involved.

I was probably somewhere in the middle of a long line of kids who thought they were her one-and-only. The truth was, there had been nothing special about me. All I had been to Julie Albatross was easy prey, another target. A weak, skinny kid who lacked self-confidence. A kid who was not likely to have a girlfriend or any friends for that matter. A kid who would embrace an older woman who showed him a little love and gave him a lot of sex. A kid who would never tell, no matter what.

But now I was older and bigger. Now I was more confident. I didn't fit her profile any longer. She wouldn't give me a second glance now. How many had there been before me? How many since? That kid in the darkroom probably thought he was the luckiest boy in school. He probably thought this was the greatest thing in the world for him, but the truth of it was, she wasn't just fucking him, she was fucking him up. She was using him for her own perverted fetish, and when he realized that, he would be worse off than he was before he'd ever met her. He probably wouldn't be lucky enough to grow big, be fast, and become a Raiders football star. When he found out, he'd sulk and hide and become depressed and withdrawn.

She shouldn't be allowed to get away with this.

That night, I dug out the old, unused weight set from the back of my closet. There, folded into the bottom of the heavy cardboard, among my old journals, was the envelope of pictures Julie had given me three years ago—Julie, naked in the sunlight by the river, a beautiful, but forbidden photo taken by her husband; Julie and I in the woods in Mosier, lying naked on a red and black blanket, her legs wrapped around my waist, her ass facing the camera; one of us both standing up fully nude, facing the camera and making funny faces; us lying with our legs open, strategically covering each other's privates with our hands; us together on the wall, fully clothed, gazing lovingly into each other's eyes.

Using an X-Acto knife, I cut my face out of all the pictures. There was no doubt that the person pictured with Julie was a small boy, but without my face visible, nobody could possibly guess it was me. I put the picture her husband had taken, along with the one of us standing up making faces, into one envelope, and I put the ones with us lying on the blanket and sitting on the wall in a different envelope.

I wrote two simple notes in blocky handwriting. The first one said, "Isn't it illegal for an adult to have sex with a minor? Mrs. Julie Albatross, 'teaching' an unnamed Reynolds High School Freshman." This I put into the first envelope, which I addressed to Chief of Police, Gresham Police Department, which happened to be the department her husband worked for. The second note simply said, "Photography is a favorite subject of a *lot* of boys." This one went into the second envelope, addressed to Principal Vogel.

I went to the Gresham Police Department, which was closed because it was night time and slipped the first under the door to the business office. The second went right into the large mailbox located just outside the main office doors at Reynolds High School.

The drama room at school was situated almost directly across the hallway from the photography room and wouldn't be used until after lunch. I skipped my early classes and hung out in there the following morning. A few minutes after second period started, I watched as the principal and vice-principal disappeared into the photography room. Seconds later, the principal emerged leading Julie out, and together, they headed in the direction of the office.

I followed surreptitiously and watched them disappear into Mr. Vogel's office. Then, I joined several other kids hanging around in the commons outside the main office area, which serves as a popular gathering place between classes. I could see two police cars parked out front.

Thirty minutes later, the principal's office door opened, and two officers led a crying Julie Albatross into the hallway. Her hands were cuffed behind her back, and she was clearly mortified.

The hallway fell into stunned silence as everyone stopped what they were doing and stared at her in wide-eyed wonder. Mrs. Albatross, head of the pep club. Faculty chairman of the yearbook committee. Beloved photography teacher. Friend of all students. Arrested? Nobody could believe it.

Mrs. Albatross, Molester of Young Boys.

Julie's eyes darted nervously from face to face, but she stopped and locked onto mine just before she walked out the main doors. The running mascara made her eyes look decidedly raccoon-like.

I saw no anger in them, just a crushing hurt and an expression of shocked disbelief at my merciless betrayal. I tried to make my eyes blank and flat like a shark's, but I couldn't hold her stare and was the first to turn away.

That night, as I lay awake in bed, I tried not to think of what might become of her.

Chapter 21

The Oregon State Penitentiary

Shortly after the bus arrived, I realized things at the Oregon State Penitentiary would be no better than they were at the Multnomah County Jail. The food was crappy, and there was nothing to do but read books that held no interest for me, nothing to look forward to but my daily hour in a cage outside.

Funny how even in a place like this, a man's reputation will follow him. By the evening of my first day in the state pen, the corrections officers were calling me Bad Apple. But apparently, that was too much of a mouthful, and within a day or so, it had been shortened to just Bad. I guess if I was going to have a prison nickname, Bad is better than some of the alternatives.

I can't describe how I longed for human contact. Since my case had been adjudicated, I had seen nothing more of Deacon Summerville. Grace wouldn't take my calls, and I hadn't had any visitors. I wasn't allowed contact with the other inmates because I was an ex-police officer, and it would be too difficult for the staff to protect me, so that left only silent encounters with the few correctional officers (oh, how they hate to be called guards!) who delivered my meals and let me out of my cell for my daily hour in the yard. Those guys didn't like me because I was a cop killer, and they tend to think of themselves in the same genus as cops.

The isolation was killing me. Never before had I experienced loneliness or desolation like this. I'd been bored lots of times, but in retrospect, that wasn't boredom at all. That was lack of motivation to do any of the myriads of things I could have done.

Protective segregation distorted my entire sense of being. Hours, days, and weeks all ran together, and soon, it made no difference if I slept during the day or during the night. After a while, I quit keeping track of time altogether. What difference did it make if I popped awake at 2 A.M. and didn't go back to sleep? Nothing changed. When I was awake, I did nothing but sit and wait to be allowed out of my cell. All I wanted to do was sleep and get out for my hour in the yard. Wakefulness held nothing for me but that which I could manufacture or recall inside my head, and the inside of my head was not always a healthy place to spend every waking moment.

Probably the thing I missed the most was a routine. When I was a free man, I did the same things the same way day after day, and I liked it. I had more routines than I was aware of. They changed some if I was working, or off-duty, or traveling, or had plans for the day, but I had a routine for everything, and it was all healthy.

On days off, for example, I would get up, brew myself a latte using my fancy espresso machine and spend a quiet hour reading the news on the internet, catching up on Facebook (always a watcher, never a poster), and doing my email. After that, I'd take Brutus, my Maltese, for a walk. Following that, I'd work out, take a shower, and I'd be ready to start my day. That was my morning routine.

Here, I wake up, get off my cot, and if I feel motivated, I work out in my cell. Then I sit on my cot for the rest of the day until my yard time.

When you're in prison, you realize the value of everything you used to take for granted, no matter how small or insignificant it was. My first waking moments were filled with things I never once considered to be nice or luxurious, but in comparison, they were.

My master bedroom was a large suite, with his and her walk-in closets (even though there was no her) and a spacious bathroom. I had a large, comfortable bed with a warm, thick comforter. For some reason, I was in the habit of putting on a pair of slippers for the short walk through the closet area into the bathroom.

I'd unconsciously hit a bank of switches, which could change the bathroom lighting from soft to brilliant, illuminate the tile and stone shower, and control a quietly effective exhaust fan. There was a nice sink, a mirrored medicine cabinet filled with anything I might need, and a pump bottle of lavender hand soap. Beneath my feet was a soft, plush rug. These are things I took so much for granted that that they faded into the background to the point where I wasn't even aware of them anymore.

I would bluetooth my iPhone over to a portable Bose sound system and listen to any kind of music I was in the mood for. Believe it or not, I favored classical. Classic rock and old-school delta blues were my favorite alternatives.

I would close the door to take a dump even though I was the only one in the house. The softly purring fan kept the room well ventilated for me. The toilet paper was thick and soft. I never considered any of this stuff until it was time to change the roll or refill the soap bottle.

Here in prison, things are a lot simpler. My bed is a concrete bunk covered with a thin mattress. My linens are a heavily starched sheet and a scratchy woolen blanket. I have prison-issue clogs to protect my feet from the cold of the bare cement floor. The stainless steel toilet is three feet from my bed, the smell from a morning sit-down becomes my faithful companion for the next hour, and the sandpapery toilet paper shreds when used, giving me the only piece of ass I hope I ever get in this Godforsaken place.

Morning coffee used to be a big part of my day. I liked the routine of preparing a home-brewed latte, and I had the procedure fine-tuned for the perfect taste and consistency. Sometimes, I would forego that routine and take my iPad to a Starbucks, just to change things up a little. I liked to watch the people coming and going while I caught up on Fox News and local news websites. I could wile away hours there. The women that came in were beautiful, and Brutus was responsible for me snagging more than one phone number.

Here, brown water is delivered with the morning's gummy eggs on a stainless steel tray. As for the beautiful girls, it is doubtful that I will ever see another living female for the remainder of my life, other than the frumpy nurse and geeky social worker, both of whom I've only glimpsed from a distance.

When I'd get bored, I could get in my car and go anywhere I wanted or do anything I felt like. How many times did I drive into the Columbia River Gorge and either go hiking or just sit someplace pretty and eat a sandwich? Several times a year, I'd drive to the coast and take a cheap room for the night, just so I could take a morning walk on a chilly, windy beach. Not being able to ever smell the sea air again has become a tragic loss. I'd give my left nut just to breathe a lungful of sea breeze now.

The isolation of protective custody quickly became a fate worse than death. I was a trapped and dying animal. I kept thinking how, if my sister Connie had lived, she might have understood me and what I've done to my life, but I can't say if this was really true. Her imagined presence with me in my cell saw me through some very dark times.

One of the only bright things I had going for me was Pedro, a small Hispanic hack, built like a fireplug, who seemed to have taken a liking to me. Pedro worked nights, and rather than treat me with utter disdain like all the others, he often hung out and chatted through the food tray slot.

Pedro was my only real human contact. Sometimes he hung out for twenty minutes, just chatting about nothing. We talked two or three times a week, and though that may not seem like very much, to me, it was what kept me alive. I craved his visits more than I craved pacing the cage in the yard. Pedro was nonjudgmental. He kept me up to date with what was going on in the world.

One day, rather than talk about the news, he said, "You know, I've been thinking about trying to roll over to a law enforcement job. You got any pointers for me?"

"Where do you want to work?"

"Probably Salem. It's the biggest agency around where I live. I'd like to work for Portland, but I don't want to move."

"You probably wouldn't have any trouble getting on. You should apply now, though. The process can take a long time. Eight months to a year even."

"Yeah, that's what I figure. So, did you like being a cop? Before all this happened, I mean."

"Yeah, I did. I loved being a cop. And I want you know that I never was a bad cop. I never even had a founded complaint—no excessive force issues, no I.A.s, no accusations of wrongdoing of any kind. Hell, I even arrested a guy who tried to bribe me for fifty bucks to get out of a ticket once."

"I can believe that, just from the little I know about you."

"Everyone liked me. I had a good arrest record and a good reputation with the DA's office. I always got good evals, and other cops wanted me to cover them when the shit hit the fan. That's the real test of whether you're a good cop or not, what your brothers think about you. Guys thought I was a good cop. Nobody could believe it when I got busted. Hell, even *I* couldn't believe it."

"So, why, man? What made you do it?"

"It's a long story, Pedro. It's gonna sound stupid, and you won't buy it, but since you asked, I don't mind telling. Basically, I have this unreasonable urge to take risks. Not like thrill seeking, but to take actual risks, where everything is on the line. It's not something where I'm out of control, like some zombie or anything, but I get a physical rush from it, like a drug addict's high. After years of it, the cravings were probably as bad as a drug addict's, too. Anyway, one day when I was really feeling it, I was eating in a Shari's. This was a couple weeks before Christmas two years ago, so it was cold out, and I had on a turtleneck and a black watch cap. I was carrying, and when I paid the bill, I had this crazy idea to pull out my gun and clean out the till. I remember thinking I could unfold the turtleneck, cover my face up to my nose with it, and pull the watch cap down, leaving only my eyes exposed, so the waitress would never even see what I looked like. Talk about putting it all on the line!

"Well, I didn't do it, but the idea wouldn't leave me alone. I thought about it continually for a solid week. I remember driving around on patrol, scoping out what would be easy targets to rob. Convenience stores and the like. I remember studying the surveillance cameras when I'd take reports of robberies, looking at the bad guy's mistakes and such. Our clearance rate for stickups is surprisingly low.

"Well, the following week when I was off duty, I made the decision to do it. Up until that time, the worst thing I'd ever done as a cop was lie once on the witness stand when I forgot to read a guy his rights before getting a confession from him. The defense attorney asked me point blank if I read them, and I answered 'yes.' I didn't care about losing the case; I just didn't want to look like an idiot to my peers. I felt horrible about it for months, for years afterwards, and I never did it again.

"Well, that day, I put on my black turtleneck and watch cap. It was cloudy, but I brought dark sunglasses, and I went to a porno bookstore. This meth skel was working there, and I stuck my gun in his face and demanded the money. I'll never forget how sketched out he got, shaking and stuttering. He even dropped some of the cash while handing it over.

The whole time I kept thinking what would happen if I got caught. The thrill it gave me was like shooting meth right into my veins. The high lasted for days afterward. It filled me up, but I swore to myself I'd never do anything like that again."

"But obviously, you did."

"Yeah. Like five more times. I never once did it for the money, though. In fact, that first time, I dropped the two hundred bucks I got into a Salvation Army kettle in Fred Meyers on the way home."

"Damn, Bad. We ought to change your name to Robin Hood."

"Don't. I like Bad better. Besides, I kept the take from the rest of the robberies."

"How come you killed the cop?" he asked earnestly. "I mean, I almost get why you were doing it, but killing a cop seems like, incongruous or something."

"I know. I didn't think; I just acted. I never heard him identify himself. All I saw was a man pointing a gun at me. I'd been a cop for eighteen years, and before that, I was in a Special Forces unconventional warfare unit, and I reacted according to my training. One of the things we're taught is that action is faster than reaction, which means I could shoot him before he shot me, even if he intended to shoot me. But that guy wasn't ready for a fight, and he didn't intend to shoot. He was just hoping I'd put my hands up and surrender. He shouldn't have tried to save the day unless he was mentally prepared for a fight."

"Come on, you can't blame *him*, Bad. That's not fair, and you sound like too much of a stand-up guy to put this on him."

"Don't get me wrong, Pedro; I'm not blaming him at all. I'm just saying, for your own benefit, he made a fatal error. He pulled a gun on a man without the mental preparedness to use it. I don't think he was trying to play hero; I just think he felt he had to act. What he should have done in his frame of mind is, rather than try to be a hero, simply be a good witness. I never searched the people I took hostage. If he wanted to pull his piece after I took him into custody, he could have won the day. He would have had numerous opportunities to either shoot me or at least try to take me down at gunpoint. Or, I suppose he could have changed his frame of mind in the first place and have been prepared for a fight when he pulled his gun."

"Well, the way I hear it, you didn't give him any chance. You shot him in cold blood. The word out there," he said, indicating beyond the confines of the protective segregation unit, "is that you were willing to kill any cops that stood in your way."

"Is that what they're saying?"

"Yeah. You already got a rep for badassery."

I snorted. "The truth is, I didn't even think. I just acted. I shot before I realized it, and of course, by then it was too late. At that point, I lost control of the situation, and a hostage escaped, and the rest is history. What it really proves is that I'm a lousy criminal. Hardly a badass."

"If I were you, I wouldn't try to talk down my rep. Not in here. So let me ask you something. What would you have done if you *had* heard him? If you knew he was a cop?"

I thought about that question for a moment: "I honestly don't know. I wouldn't have shot him; that's for sure. If I had time to think, I suppose I could have disappeared into the back room. There was an exterior door back there, and I could have gone out and just disappeared. That deputy was a reserve, and he was fat and out of shape. He wouldn't have chased me, and if he did, he couldn't have caught me."

"Think you would have gotten away with it?"

"Naw. They would have had the whole thing on video, and I wasn't wearing a mask or disguise."

"Why weren't you wearing a mask?"

"I was going to take the computer that records the surveillance video. It's all part of the risk. If I planned everything out perfectly and made the robberies as foolproof as possible, the risk factor just wouldn't be there, and I would be defeating the whole purpose."

"I guess I can see that," he said. "I've heard of lots of different kind of addictions, but not being addicted to risk. Why do you think you had that?"

"It's going to sound like Freudian bullshit, but the truth is, I think it's sexual in nature."

"You get off doing robberies?"

I considered my response. I decided to tell him about Julie Albatross, but not Dr. McNab. The feelings of shame I felt whenever I thought about him were still too strong.

"No," I said laughing, "or I'd have done it a hell of a lot more than five or six times. When I was a freshman in high school, I had a sexual relationship with a teacher. She constantly drilled into my head what a risk we were taking every time we made it. I was only fourteen years old and hadn't developed any real concepts of sex or relationships, but I knew she was married, and I knew in my heart that sex between an adult and a kid was wrong. She was married to a cop, by the way."

"Ouch! What agency?"

"Gresham."

"No shit? Jesus, is that department cursed or what? Remember that deal they had a couple years ago where that one sniper shot the shit out of the other one who kidnapped his family?"

"Yeah, I do. So I guess maybe you shouldn't apply with them, huh. Anyway, like I said, I've thought about this and researched it for years online. I've concluded that the natural feelings of guilt and dishonesty about the nature of our relationship became entangled with the positive feelings of sexual gratification and the power I held over her. I held her entire life in my hands. Simply by telling someone, I could end her marriage, cause her to get fired, and maybe even send her to jail. I knew this because she told me all the time. Sometimes she talked about it even while we were doing it, before I would finish. I think *she* got off on that part to some extent, too. In fact, when she gave me my first BJ, she made me stop and think of what would happen if we got caught as a way of training me to hold off."

"Damn, Bad, you gotta be kidding me."

"Well, trust me, I wish it had never happened. See, she was always stressing the need for absolute secrecy and giving me dire warnings of the consequences we'd face if we were ever caught. Over time, I came to associate the positive feelings of having such a special relationship—especially the biological response from sexual pleasure and orgasm, you know, endorphin release and such—with secrecy and risk-taking. Like I said, I was so young and impressionable that those associations took root inside my psyche. When I matured and developed normal sexual relationships, they were ultimately unfulfilling."

"You ever try doing married women? You know, for the risk involved."

"Yeah, once, but it kind of went against my moral code. Even with the married woman, sex was never as good as it was with the teacher, and it's because the association with risk was no longer present. Doing the married woman had consequences, but not for me, and they weren't dire, so it was ultimately unfulfilling. Eventually, I subconsciously had to find a way to get that satisfaction, and taking risks did it. Doing dangerous things didn't do it. I needed something that combined the need for secrecy with real, measurable risk, and the more I put on the line, the better. So, eventually I started doing the armed robberies. Right away, I'd get the same sort of immediate endorphin kick that sex gives, only it lasts so much longer."

"God damn, Bad, that's a hell of a story. What if doing robberies got old and didn't do it for you anymore?"

"You're a perceptive guy, Pedro. That was already starting to happen. I was thinking of other crimes I might start pulling. I was actually kicking around the idea of killing someone—a bad guy. Someone who's done something really heinous and gotten away with it. I don't know if I could have brought myself to actually kill a man, but I'd be lying if I said I wasn't considering it."

"Do you think getting busted was good for you? Like, you'd have ended up doing something really bad?"

"Well, I'm pretty sure killing people, even bad people, would be considered really bad. So yes, otherwise, I'm not sure where I would have eventually gone. Trust me, I'm no saint. I'm just a guy who got fucked up as a kid."

"Yeah, well, I wish I had your teacher when I was a freshman."

"I know. I always smile to myself when I hear people say that about female teachers who molest their male students. I would have laughed at the idea of me being a victim, but look at me now."

"Good point. Still, you got a hell of a story."

"Now I'm in a place where talking to you is the only thing in my life that's keeping me sane. I'm not sure how much of this isolation I can take."

"You should consider petitioning the prison board to get out of protective segregation. I don't think you'd be in much danger in general pop. They already know about you over there. You already got status as a cop killer. I think that overcomes the negative stigma of you being a cop any day."

"You think so?"

"Yeah, I do."

"How would I do that?"

"You make a request to the prison board. You start by telling someone about it, like me. I could put your request in and get the ball rolling if you want."

"Yeah, I think I'm ready for that. You'd do that for me, Pedro?"

"Sure, I'll write a memo and email it up the chain. I can do it tonight."

Chapter 22

He did, and three months after entering Oregon State Pen, I was unceremoniously transferred into the general population. The difference between protective segregation and general pop was almost overwhelming at first. I went from virtually no human contact to constant human contact. On the face of it, this might seem like what I needed, and it was, but in reality, these weren't my "kind" of humans at all. Not yet, anyway.

I hadn't yet been conditioned to my new role of inmate. In my head, I knew I was a con, a bad guy, but in my heart, I was still a cop, a good guy. For the past eighteen years, I had lived in an "us versus them" world. I'd spent the majority of my life walking backwards around people like those who now occupied my every waking moment.

I learned right away that I could mistrust these people all I wanted, but I could never get away from them. I might avoid direct self-initiated contact with them, but this only made them more confrontational with me. I could only sit with my back against the wall for so long. And the more I viewed them as "them," the more I realized that there was no longer an "us." Here, it was only "me." And "me versus them" was a situation I could never win. Not in the joint.

My cellmate was a guy called Roach. He was a heavyset, hairy-armed bear of a man who kept his head shaved and had a long biker's chin beard. Roach was a hardcore con, but he was also a very intelligent man. He kept books by Sun Tzu and Patrick Buchanon in the cell, and he was the leader of the European Kindred, a violent white supremacist prison gang. He didn't seem like a bad guy on the face of it, but I knew he could be big trouble for me if I wasn't careful. The only other thing I knew about him was that he was here because he'd killed someone.

Roach would never fully trust me because he knew I was a cop, and I certainly would never trust him because he was a hardcore bad guy. But we shared a cell and a common bond—murder—so there was at least some mutual respect.

Roach didn't say a word to me the entire first day I spent in general pop. There, as opposed to protective custody, the cell doors remained open during daylight hours, and inmates were free to either stay in their cells or congregate in the day room, which is a common area with stainless steel tables bolted to the floor that serves as both dining room and gathering place. We had free access to the yard and its exercise equipment. There was still little to do, so many of the prisoners took to working out every day, which is why they got so buff during their prison sentences.

Those first few days, I was pretty much terrified. I was overwhelmed by the amount of human contact and fearful that I would be assaulted the moment I set foot outside my cell. I stayed in my cell all day long, which necessitated me skipping lunch. Finally, motivated by hunger, I ventured out to the day room shortly before dinner. I ate alone and in silence, and nobody bothered me.

Afterwards, rather than head directly back to my cell, I decided to stay out and see what happened. I got a lot of stares from people, but nobody tried to contact me. Twice, the word "pig" was said loud enough for me to hear it. I sat with a group watching TV, but I couldn't tell you what show was on because all my attention was on those around me. At lights out, I headed back to my cell with a sigh of relief.

After lights out, Roach spoke for the first time. "You can't hide forever, man. Sooner or later, you're going to have to talk to someone. Right now, people are keeping their distance 'til they get to know you. So far, all they know is that you're the enemy because you were a cop. Some guys are gonna want to get up in your grill 'cause of that, but on the other hand, you carry a certain amount of street cred because the dude you smoked was a cop, too. And Bad *is* a cool name. So they're holdin' off. For now. At least, that's the way I see it. But sooner or later, you're going to have to get out there and prove yourself. Whatever's gonna happen is gonna happen, man. If it's bad, you might as well get it over with. Hell, you could always transfer back to Ad Seg."

"I'm not going back there," I said. "You ever spent time there?"

"I've done some stints in the hole. Can't say I like it much."

"Well, imagine you couldn't get out and had to do the rest of your time there. I can't take that kind of isolation. It was driving me nuts."

"It could be worse. I hear you damn near got the needle, Bad. You ought to be glad you dodged that bullet. Appeals and shit'd take ten years, and during that time, you don't talk to nobody but a hack or two. Maybe a lawyer twice a year."

"I couldn't handle that. So, Roach, you seem to know a lot about me. What about you? What brings a nice guy like you to a place like this?"

"I beat a nigger to death with a crowbar."

"Shit. Glad I'm not black. He do something to you first?"

"Wasn't a 'he.' It was a bitch. And yes, she shanked my buddy. Killed him. We were doing a dope rip, and she was the dude we were ripping off's old lady. She stabbed my buddy with a steak knife after he shot her old man, so I beat her face with a crowbar—not with the side of it, but the end. I rammed the end of it right through the side of her head and left it sticking out of her temple for the cops to find."

"Jesus Christ."

"Fuck, I don't like niggers anyway. None of your darker types. My buddy died in the car, and I was tryin' to drag his body out near a park when a cop rolled up on me. I was gone by the time he got there, but they called in a dog and eventually caught me."

"That was what, maybe three years ago? Somewhere by Ventura Park?" I asked. I had been on the perimeter, but I wasn't involved in the capture.

His eyes narrowed, and I remembered this was his world, not mine. Just because we shared a cell and were talking didn't mean I was safe with him. I was, after all, the enemy.

"Yeah, I was tryin' to get him to Portland Adventist before he bled out. Why? Were you there?" His tone changed, became more menacing. "There were like twenty cops swarmin' everywhere lookin' for me. Were you one of 'em?"

My threat radar was going nuts with his tone.

"No, man, but I heard about it. One of my buddies was there."

"See, man, that's why nobody's gonna like you here. It ain't so much what you did to bring you here, it's the fact that you're one of *them*."

"Not anymore," I said, going for a conspiring tone like we were now buddies on the same side sharing a laugh at the irony of my situation. He didn't go for it.

"Is that right. Since you're not one of them anymore, why don't you tell me how it is you fucks catch us so quick on something like that? I saw that cop coming, and I was three blocks away by the time he got turned around and found my buddy in the backseat. How'd something like that happen?"

"I don't know. He probably called for everyone to just start looking around the area or something. I wasn't there."

Roach got out of his bunk and stood up. He was a very big man, and standing there, he was eye to eye with me as I lay on the top bunk. "No, man, I don't mean give me some bullshit answer. In case you didn't hear me, I asked you a legit question. I want to hear details, fuckface. Tell me cop procedure. You see something suspicious, and you turn around and roll up on a dead fuckin' body, and the dude who was there a second ago ain't there now. Exactly what do you do?"

I hadn't been in general pop for an entire day, and now I was being told to snitch on the police or face getting murdered by my cellmate. If I disclosed police practices to this man, I would be putting officers' lives at risk. Guys I know. If I didn't, I would probably get my ass kicked, which would set a precedent others would follow. If they didn't kill me, I'd wind up back in protective custody. I couldn't figure out a way to handle this.

Apparently, my hesitation didn't please him. Roach grabbed me by my shirt and dragged me off the bunk. I fell to the floor and jammed my left wrist trying to break my fall. It hurt so bad I thought it might be broken.

"You want to find out what happens to pigs in this place, asshole? You think it's *them* you gotta worry about?" he asked, sweeping his hand toward the dayroom. "Half those dickheads out there take their cue from me!"

I could feel my wrist beginning to swell, and it was already stiff and hard to move. I was terrified, but I knew if I showed fear, I was done for.

"Get your fuckin' paws off me, asshole. I got no loyalty to anyone right now. You asked the question. You want an answer? What's in it for me?"

"I could break your fuckin' neck right now, cheesedick. Your life's in it for you. I don't have to even touch you. One word from me, and you'll be a dead fuckin' cop by lunchtime tomorrow, and I won't have nothin' to do with it. That enough incentive for you?"

I stood up, and it took every ounce of guts in me, but I turned my back to him and started climbing back up to my rack. My left wrist was entirely out of play, and I had to do it all with my right hand. He didn't touch me.

When I finally made it up there, I was panting and sweating. I said, "Guess what? I lied to you. I *was* there, you big fucking gorilla. So I can tell you exactly how we do it. I can tell you a *lot* of shit. Like how to get out of a perimeter like that."

"Well, start talking, Officer."

"You guys make it so fucking simple. Everybody goes to ground. We call in a dog, and he can follow your trail from the last place we saw you, and that's all there is to it."

"Fine. Is that your final answer? Because if it is, sleep well tonight. Tomorrow, you'll be a dead man. Nighty night." He smiled at me and got in his rack.

I waited a minute, not sure what to do. I did not want to betray my fellow officers, but it wasn't a principle I was ready to die for, either. This wasn't a day camp I could just leave at will; it was a state penitentiary. I made the decision that some of the rules have to go out the window when you're in prison. I'd have to do whatever it took to survive.

"Fine," I said. "I guess I'm not a cop anymore, anyway. I don't suppose I owe them anything. All the officer said was he had a suspicious vehicle in the parking lot of the medical clinic on Stark across from Ventura Park, and a large white male ran from it when he turned on it. When he got there, he said he had a fifty-five in the backseat."

"What's a fifty-five?"

"A dead guy."

"Go on. I want to know exactly how they caught me."

"He didn't see which way you ran. He described you as being big. I think he said six-two or three and bald. He called right away for a perimeter. Every unit in East responded."

"How many cops are on at any given time?"

I felt like shit, giving away this confidential info, but if it bought me my survival, it was a good enough bargain. What did it matter, anyway? To the cops, I was no longer one of "us." I was now one of "them." The enemy. It's funny, because in here, I was the enemy as well. I was a man without a country, a "me" without a "them."

"Fifteen during the day, twenty-five on swing shift. The primary officer calls out the perimeter. I remember in your case it was all of Ventura Park, something like Burnside to the north, 113th to the west, 117th to the east, and Alder to the south. I remember I was at Alder and 115th, in the middle on the south side of the perimeter."

"How do they know how big to make it?"

"Depends on a lot of stuff. Are you on foot, on a bike, in a car? How much of a head start do you have? They usually start big and narrow it down as needed. If the officer's unfamiliar with the area or too busy, the dispatcher can pull up a map and do it, or the on-duty supervisor can. They adjust the perimeter bigger or smaller based on information that comes in. Cops drive to their positions code-three, with lights and sirens, to get there. That's supposed to scare you into hiding and allows them to get there as quickly as possible, so you don't escape the perimeter."

"Soon's I saw the cop turn around, I ran across Stark, into the park. I know he didn't see me 'cause he went into a parking lot and out of sight for a few seconds to make the turn. They still caught me in about a half-hour, man. What I want to know is how."

"We concentrated on the park because it was the most likely place you'd run. We got a canine coming right away, and while the dog was en-route, we buttoned up the perimeter. Most bad guys go right to ground. Find a decent, hard-to-get-to hiding spot and lay low, which is exactly the wrong thing to do. It's what the cops hope you'll do because the dog'll track right to you."

"How do they do the dog, man? They just let him go or what?"

"No, the dog handler and at least one other cop go with him. Usually, they let the dog go on a long leash and just follow him. He—"

"How's the dog know where to go?"

"He follows the scent. Fear, adrenaline, sweat . . . it all leaves a trail he can follow on freshly matted grass, shrubs and trees you bump into, that sort of thing. The dogs are trained to follow that scent. They'll track you right to the door of an apartment. I've seen it happen a hundred times."

"Why two cops? So one watches the other, who's watching the dog?"

This was some sort of test. Roach would protect me if he trusted me. Anyway, I was a bad guy now. I had to face that sooner or later. Might as well be now. "Exactly. So let me ask you something. Where'd you hide?"

"In some arborvitaes on the edge of the park, next to some dude's back yard. Dog came right to me, it seemed."

"How come you didn't try to get out of there before he found you?"

"I could see a cop car with its lights flashing about half a block away."

"That's why we do that. The guys on the perimeter keep their overheads on, so the bad guy can see them to discourage him from coming out of hiding. We put 'em on the corners of the perimeter and then fill in the gaps along the way. Then, while you're hiding, they let the dog take them right to you."

"See, that's good shit we need to know. Now tell me what's the best way out of something like that?"

"Don't stop running. Don't go to the ground and hide. Stay off major streets. Go through the yards if you can, from house to house, not in the street. If you gotta use streets, head into the middle of a neighborhood. Keep moving though. Chances are, you'll make it out of the perimeter. Watch for rovers. We—*they*—like to have extra guys cruising outside the perimeter looking for people on foot. The farther you get from the scene, the better your chances are of getting away. Once you've gone to ground like you did, they're probably going to find you. If you're hiding and you see a car with its lights flashing somewhere on the perimeter, see if you can get a look at the officer. Half the time they're dicking around on their phones or something. If he's not out of the car scanning the area, I'd think about taking my chances. Run across a street in the opposite direction from the crime and go to ground again a block away if you can. Your chances'll be better going to ground if you're outside the defined lines of the perimeter."

"So what if I can't get out of the perimeter?"

"It usually takes maybe ten minutes to get it pretty buttoned up. If you think you can't get out in time, steal a car and drive out. Be careful about calling your buddy to come pick you up though. They're always looking for someone driving aimlessly around while talking on the phone. Caught a lot of guys like that. Get creative, man. Think outside the box. I know of one guy who stole a dog from a backyard and walked it out, just like some area resident out taking his dog for a walk. He even stopped to chat with a cop on the perimeter about what was going on. If it's during the day, find a house that looks like nobody's home and start watering the yard or doing gardening or something. Hide in plain sight. Change clothes if you can, but don't take off your shirt. They always take off their shirt. Anything to make them think it's not you."

"What if it's at night, and I can't do that shit?"

"I don't know, man. I'd climb a tree, I guess. The higher the better. Hard to see, and it'll confuse the dog."

"How long'll they stay there?"

"Half-hour, forty-five minutes. You can't keep that many cops tied up too long. But just 'cause you see perimeter cars clearing doesn't mean you're out of the woods. The dog and the guy running with him will probably keep working, even after the perimeter is broken down. And another thing, it really stirs up a neighborhood when we set a perimeter. The whole neighborhood knows we're after someone, and it makes them edgy. Everyone and their mother calls the police every time they hear a dog bark, so stay low 'til dark if you can. People are looking, and when you crawl out from under someone's deck, they'll see you and call 911 right away."

Roach didn't have any more questions. He lay there for a while, and I thought he was sleeping, but then he said, "How's that wrist, Bad? Think it's broke?"

I massaged it, wriggled my fingers: "No. It's swelling a little. Probably just sprained."

"Anyone gives you shit tomorrow, let me know." And that was that. We didn't say anything else. A few minutes later, he was snoring.

I had passed. I had no doubt Roach could be my worst enemy or my best friend in here. I should have felt better about my situation, and I did to some degree, but when I thought of the betrayal to my badge, I felt like a real piece of shit. To me, snitching on the cops was worse than committing armed robberies. My immediate worry was surviving this place, and I knew my chances of that had just gone up.

Finally, after what felt like more than an hour, I drifted off to sleep.

Chapter 23

In the following days, I began to notice a distinct change. It was subtle at first, but Roach's buddies, other EK members, began acting different around me. Gone were the glares that could freeze water, replaced instead by grunts and head nods when we passed. They weren't exactly friendly, but they weren't menacing, either. A week after entering general population, I was feeling more relaxed than I had since my arrest.

One day, while I was in the line for chow, a black guy who was dishing out the food shorted me on mashed potatoes. He was using a big scoop for everyone, but when it was my turn, he used a tablespoon. I stood there holding up the line, looking at him, not quite sure what to do with the obvious dis.

"How about a fair share there, buddy?" I said.

"Whatchooo gonna do, bitch, arrest me?" he sneered.

"Look man, I haven't done shit to you. All I want to do is eat my dinner and mind my own business. Why do you have to start shit when there's no reason to?"

"Aw gee, you're right officer. Ain't no cause to make you feel unwelcome. Here, man, have some extra, on the house." With that, he peeled off his latex glove and scooped a handful of potatoes with his bare hand. He flung them at me, half hitting my plate, half covering my hand and arm.

"God damn it," I said, stepping back, and having no idea what to do to regain face. Before I had the chance to say or do anything, though, a hardcore con of about forty with a shaved head stepped in front of me. He had a big swastika tatted on his arm, and I recognized him as being an associate of Roach's called Panhead, another member of the European Kindred.

"Bad move, Sambo. I been looking for a chance to fuck you up for quite a while. Now make this right, or that time has come."

The black guy looked around but found himself without friends close enough to bail him out. I could see the wheels turning as he considered his options. Finally, he gave a slight nod and said, "Yeah, my mistake, Officer." He then scooped out a normal portion into a bowl and set it on the counter. The skinhead muttered something and disappeared into the crowd.

As I picked up the bowl, the black guy said, "You gonna need to grow another pair of eyes, pig, 'cause you gonna die in general pop. Biggest mistake you ever made, comin' out of Ad Seg. Same goes for them cracker EK bitches you sleeping with. I got friends in this place, too, motherfucker."

My heart was racing, but I tried to keep a straight poker face. "I'm sure they'll be interested to know you said that, *Sambo*," I replied.

That night, after lights out, Roach said, "Today was free, Bad, with Panhead savin' your bacon, so to speak. But if you want to live longer than a month in this place, you're gonna need our protection. Them spades, and most everyone else in here, are gonna exploit you. And I gotta be straight with you. You ain't the kinda guy that's gonna do well in here. Maybe if you didn't have the rep of being a cop, you could just keep to yourself and fly under the radar, but you got a big ass target painted all over you. They're gonna push you to see what you're made of."

"Guess I'll just do what I have to," I said. The words were a lot bigger than the feeling behind them.

"As for me, I don't think you're a straight-up pussy so to speak, but I can see you still think like a good guy. What you gotta learn, and the sooner you learn this the better, is you *aint* a good guy no more. None of that shit matters—good guy, bad guy, right, wrong. It's all meaningless in here. You're in the joint, and you're gonna have to do what you have to do to survive. So quit trying to play by the rules. There ain't no rules. Like they say, it's dog eat dog in here."

I knew that Roach was saying the truth, but it was hard to change my way of thinking. Even though my risk-taking had led to my incarceration, I was unable to quash my natural instinct to play by the rules and do the right thing. But as he said, in here, there are no rules. You can't fight fair, and you can't do the right thing. You have to fight to win, and if that means doing the wrong thing, you do it. Like calling the black guy Sambo. On the outside, I'd never say a thing like that, but here, on the inside, it felt like something I needed to do to prove that I wasn't going to be intimidated.

I was starting to hate this place. "I can't say that I'd like to go my whole stretch without friends in here," I said. "And I suppose I could do a lot worse than you guys. Yeah, I guess I'd be pretty interested in something like that."

The following afternoon, Roach kicked me out of the cell. I saw Panhead and several others go in after I left. None of them were savory types, and all of them were guys I'd have stopped to shake down on the street just a short time ago, but only after calling for cover. Most had tattoos that included a shield with the letters EK in it.

I hung out in the day room and kept to myself. Nobody bothered me. After about an hour, a skinny kid of about twenty-five approached me.

"Roach says he wants to see you." Without another word, he turned and headed toward my cell. I got up and followed him.

There were only three guys left in the room. Roach, Panhead, and somebody I didn't know. The kid made four, and I made five. In a prison cell, this was a crowd.

"Get lost, Billy," said Panhead, and the kid disappeared.

"Bad, this is Semper. I think you know Panhead already. We were just discussing your situation."

"Yeah," said Semper. "We were talking about how it's too bad you're gonna get wasted sooner or later. Roach floated the idea of us giving you some protection, but Panhead thinks you gotta be, what, at least a quarter Jew from that nose of yours."

"At least," echoed Panhead. "Too bad, too, cuz I was looking for an excuse to kick a dent in the side of that fuckin' jig's skull."

"I don't know what you're talking about, Panhead, I'm not Jewish at all."

"Bullshit. At least one of your grandparents is Jewish. I can smell a kike a mile away."

"Yeah, well, think what you want. My grandparents all came from the UK, except my dad's mother, who was from Sweden. But I don't give a shit. I don't have anything against the Jews."

"Neither do I," said Panhead. "I just don't go out of my way for them. They sure as hell don't go out of their way for me."

"What part of the UK?" asked Roach.

"My mother's family is from Wales, and my dad's father was from London, the East End, back when it was nothing but immigrants and working class. After the war, he came over here and settled in Portland. And my grandmother, the one from Sweden, was born and raised in a town called Sundsvall. She came to the States when she was thirty and was married to my grandfather that same year. As far as I know, her people have been in Sundsvall for generations."

"If I were you, I wouldn't lie to us," Roach said. "Nobody really gives a shit if you're part nigger or kike or whatever, but if you tell me you're not, and I find out you are, well, we'll have a beef then. And I think you know you don't want a beef with me."

"Look, Roach, I figure you guys're trying to find out if I'm pure enough to join EK, and to be truthful, if I'm right, I'm glad you're thinking that way. But the truth is, I'm not so sure I want to join. No offense."

"None taken. Why wouldn't you want to join us? You know you're gonna get shanked in here, and I know you don't want to go back into segregation."

"I'm hoping I might just be able to keep to myself and lay low is all."

"You can try that if you want," said Semper. "But I heard Chitlin's got a hard-on for you now. That's the spook from the chow line yesterday. I heard there's a pool about how long you're gonna last. Guys are betting on when you'll get shanked, whether or not you'll go back to Ad Seg, when you'll get hit, how hard—just about anything. Trust us when we say it ain't gonna be long, Bad. We know what we're talking about. You want us as friends."

"Speaking of our buddy Chitlin," I said, "he told me that me and all the EK cracker bitches I'm sleeping with better grow eyes in the back of their heads cuz he's got friends in here, too. Just letting you know. It kind of sounded like he was throwing the gauntlet down."

Panhead sneered. "Them fuckin' porch monkeys. They're always looking for an excuse to start shit with us. You're their new excuse, Bad. Still think you don't want us at your back? I believe you used to refer to that as 'cover.'"

I hated that I had to actually get in bed with guys like Roach and Panhead, guys I would have shaken down and busted just a few short months ago. If you would have told me that I'd be invited to become a member of European Kindred a year ago, I'd have called you crazy.

Theirs was a one-time offer. It wouldn't be made twice.

"Ok, I may be having a hard time converting, but fuck yes, I want in," I said, meaning every word.

Roach said, "I figured as much. I got some boys on the outside looking into your background now, Bad. I'm taking you at your word. Tell me now if you're part Jewish or tainted dark even a little, then we'll just part ways, and I wish you good luck. But if you join us, and I find out you lied, I'll make you dead by my own hand. You understand that, don't you?"

"I'm not lying. No Jew and no black. No minorities."

"Ok. We had church before you came in, and its unanimous. If you want in, we're willing to see if you're a good fit. I kinda like the idea of having an ex-cop on the roster."

"Ok. What do I gotta do?"

"You gotta earn your bones. Panhead here, he thinks taking care of Chitlin might be a good way to start."

"Unless you're afraid of him, that is," said Panhead. "In that case, you can always tell the principal your bein' bullied. Maybe you could be excused from recess."

"Fuck," I said. "When and where?"

"Seems like the chow line would be an appropriate place, doesn't it?"

"Yeah, I guess it does," I said, trying to keep the misery out of my voice. This was a nightmare from which I wouldn't wake. I had to do something. If I didn't, EK was out, which meant no protection for me, but beyond that, I would have the reputation of being a coward, which would make me ten times the target I already was as an ex-cop. A rep like that would follow me for the remainder of my days in prison. EK would probably be a bigger threat to me than anyone else.

No, I had to do something. The problem was I didn't know *what* to do. Chitlin had disrespected both me and the European Kindred. EK had assigned me, as a prospect, to avenge the reputation of the gang. What was I supposed to do, shank the guy?

That night, after lights out, I whispered to Roach, "So, do you have any words of wisdom for me?"

The way he'd befriended me, I kind of thought he would be happy to mentor me along in my first prison assault, but instead he didn't utter a sound. His silence was unnerving.

"Roach?"

"Shut the fuck up, prospect. You got yourself into this; you figure it out. And don't fuckin' bother me again until the deed is done, either!"

Clearly, this was something I had to do on my own. The first test of my mettle. In the gang, it was called earning my bones. I was on my own until after my confrontation with Chitlin.

Needless to say, I didn't get much sleep that night.

The next morning, Roach and I didn't exchange a word. Panhead was nowhere to be seen, and no other EK member would even look at me. I went through the morning chow line without a clue what I was going to do, but Chitlin wasn't there. His absence, relief that it was, was also a bit of a disappointment. I just wanted this to be done.

I stayed out in the day room in the hopes of seeing Chitlin after morning chow, but he was nowhere to be found. In fact, I couldn't even see one black face anywhere. Their absence was ominous. It was as if the very air was charged with anticipation, as if everyone was waiting for the confrontation.

I tried to remember what my uncle Phil had told me in high school: things like attack first, don't stop, take the pain. He had said it didn't matter if I won or lost, as long as I fought. I wondered if that still held true here and now.

I still didn't know what to do. If Chitlin did show up at afternoon chow, my basic plan was to eyefuck him, and if that didn't provoke a fight, I'd verbally insult or challenge him. Once he attacked me, I would do my best to fight dirty and end it quickly by gouging an eye or punching him in the throat. I wanted to win, and I wanted it to be self-defense, but I had no illusions. I expected to get hurt. Bad.

Afternoon chow finally came around. The air was crackling, and I knew somehow Chitlin would be serving.

He was.

He looked at me when I was still three people away and smiled. He didn't seem to be too nervous. I tried to glare at him, but I had no nerve, and I'm sure it came off as a timid attempt to see if an attack was coming. My eyes were the ones to break away first.

I slid my tray forward, still two people away from getting served. I felt like I was going to wet myself. Chitlin glared malevolently at me and sneered his way into a contemptible grin. I only looked at him in quick glances, defeated already, and I was still ten feet from him. I knew I was about to get my ass kicked.

But then the rage began to build in me. I *hated* the fact that I was here in this situation. Yes, I put myself in prison, but all I wanted was to do my time and get the hell out. I didn't want to join a segregationist white power prison gang. I didn't believe in white supremacy. I didn't hate blacks. It wasn't me that created this conflict. It was *him*. It was Chitlin. It was all him.

That fucking *nigger*!

My mind went blank; my thoughts were replaced with blinding rage. I couldn't think about anything other than Chitlin and how this was all *his* fault. I lost track of everything but the distance between me and him. I looked up at him, and this time, I didn't disengage. He was standing there dropping a brown, gooey paste on the tray of the man ahead of me, his eyes boring right into me.

My eyes went from his eyes to his neck, now seven feet away from me. Seven feet.

In fact, it was only five, but I remembered something else my uncle had said.

With my hands still gripping the fiberglass lunch tray, I sprang forward like a lion up and over the counter upon which we were sliding our trays. In one fluid motion, I dove through the serving area past the guy next to me, using the counter as a springboard from which to launch myself like a rocket, tray first, at my chosen target.

The edge of the tray caught Chitlin midway between his lower jaw and his shoulders, square in the middle of his throat. His face plopped down on the tray as we went crashing backward onto the kitchen floor. By this time, I was in the zone, entirely out of control. Rage had replaced fear, and I had been utterly stripped of mercy.

Chitlin never had a chance. He was done from the moment I initiated the attack, but I wasn't. I stood over him and beat him with the tray until it broke over his head. I was aware of the crowd screaming and yelling, and of the fact that they were letting this play out without interfering. After the tray broke, I began to pummel his face with my fists. His head went from side to side with every blow.

I fell into a straddling position with one knee on either side of his face and beat his unconscious body until I was so exhausted I could barely breathe. Still, no one intervened. When I became so tired I could hardly raise a fist, I rolled off him, panting.

I stood up and turned around. Hacks were fighting their way through the crowd, which now relented a bit and let them pass. As they grabbed me, I looked down at Chitlin. He looked dead. Just before they tackled me to the floor, I spit into his face and managed to croak for the benefit of the crowd, "Courtesy of EK, *Sambo*!"

Then my own face was bloodied as five hacks beat me into a pair of flex cuffs.

Chapter 24

I was dragged to the Intensive Management Unit and thrown into an isolation cell. My rage and toughness drained away with the slamming of the door, and I found myself fighting tears. *Don't cry*, said the voice of my Uncle Phil, *never cry. If you cry, they'll know. Word will get around.*

The fear of losing status is the only thing that kept me from breaking down. Gone now was whatever had driven me to beat Chitlin to death (at the time, I thought I had killed him). A touch of compassion, of the old sense of right and wrong, now replaced it. I didn't hate him. He wasn't a fucking nigger; he was just some dude who was probably as scared as me deep down inside. Someone trying his best to survive, like me. Just doing what he had to.

I knew the fight would give me status. I knew I would no longer be looked upon as a victim, at least for a little while. I knew it had given me the street creds I would need to be accepted into EK. But I also knew it wasn't free. Membership in this club would cost me. A bit of humanity here; a piece of my soul there. I'd have to keep paying, piece by piece, until there was nothing left.

I didn't know if I could do it.

For the immediate future, though, I was safe. I was in IMU, and nobody could touch me in here. When I got out, I'd have the protection of the European Kindred. Safety in numbers. It was hard to comprehend that acceptance into such a group was important to me, was actually vital to my survival. I'd made a life out of judging and rejecting such people, and now I was forced to rely on them to be my brothers. Hell, in my mind, I still considered *cops* to be my brothers. What a difference a day makes.

I did six long weeks in the hole, and it sucked. At first, though, it wasn't so bad. I felt more relaxed those first few days than I had in a long time. Even before prison, in my other life as a cop, I never could completely relax. I always had the specter of some future problem hanging over my head—my risk-taking cravings. It was as if I always knew it would be my undoing.

Then, of course, there was no relaxing at all in prison. I had to learn to sleep with one eye open. At least in the hole, if nothing else, I was untouchable. Literally. My only physical contact came from being handcuffed once a week for my hour in the yard. Meals were delivered to me through the slot in the door, but only after I was seated against the wall on the opposite side of my six-by-eight cell. The hacks who delivered them didn't say a word and only grumbled when I made the attempt to start conversation.

After about five days, I began to crave contact again. I found myself missing my cell and at least seeing and hearing other living human beings, such as they were here. I survived the first week, but I dreaded the remaining five.

After the second week, I didn't think I could hack it any longer. Time seemed to come to a standstill. There was no good way to measure it; I had no clock, and the light was left on twenty-four hours a day. I lost track of day and night, and I slept when I got tired and tried not to wake up. Meals were the only way I could gauge time.

I was given books and took to reading anything they brought me. Nothing was interesting, but everything took time, and I had plenty of that.

Weeks passed, but when time passes moment by moment, it doesn't seem to pass at all. One day blended into the next, one week into another. Then, at some point, which I think must have been somewhat past the midpoint of my sentence, a new hack I had never met before brought me my evening meal. After he passed it through, he bent down and looked at me through the open slot and spoke the first sentences I'd heard since arriving here.

"Here you go, Bad. I think it's ham and mashed potatoes, but I'm not sure. Doesn't smell that godawful, though."

"Uh, thanks," I said. "I'm not used to hearing anyone speak. I gotta admit, after a couple of weeks, it feels pretty good to talk."

"Yeah, well, I never understood the mentality of the C.O.s down here. I mean, we talk to you guys in your cellblocks, so why not here? There's just some kind of unwritten rule—don't talk to the cons in the hole. I don't get it, so I don't do it."

"Well, I appreciate it."

"Hey, no problem. My name's Leonard Scott."

"DJ Appleby, AKA Bad. My pleasure."

"So, Bad. I guess I know why they call you that."

"It's a better name than some I can think of," I said for maybe the twenty-fifth time.

"I'll grant you that. But after your little dance with DeShawn Davis, I'm pretty sure you've earned it."

"DeShawn Davis, I take it that's Chitlin's real name?"

"Yep."

"So, how's he doing?"

"Not good. He's gonna live, but he'll be fucked up a long time. Maybe the rest of his life. You crushed his larynx, among other things. It's been almost four weeks, and he's still breathing and eating out of a tube in the infirmary. They say maybe for the rest of his life 'cause of the scarring from surgery. You really did a number on him."

"Well, I didn't want any of it. I just wanted to keep to myself and do my time when I came here. So, what does assaulting Davis mean for me?"

"For you? Status, man, that's what. You're gonna be hot shit among your EK friends when you go back to general pop. But I hope you're prepared to live up to the rep because sometime, someone's gonna come along and want their own rep, and then it'll be on. That's just the way things work in here. It'll be a while, especially now that you're joining EK. In the meantime, enjoy your new status as a badass, Bad. You know, if the shoe fits . . . "

"Yeah, well, I figure some of the blacks won't decide to go so easy on me."

"They will for a while because of your EK buddies, but the blacks and the white power groups have been like a powder keg for a long time around here, and I'm guessing you might be the spark that eventually sets it all off."

"Aside from all that," I said, dismissing what could be a deadly situation for me with the wave of a hand, "what's it mean for me here? What are *you* guys gonna do to me?"

He laughed. "Us? We just did it. Detention, man, this is it. I mean, what're we gonna do, Bad, send you to jail? Make you do a second life sentence after you die of old age? Do your time here, man, it'll be over before you know it. Two more weeks."

Over the course of the next two weeks, Leonard kept me sane simply by providing a little companionship Thursdays through Mondays at dinnertime. To me, he was a link to my old life. He was interested in my SERT experiences, and I entertained him at every visit with some slightly embellished stories.

It turns out that Leonard was a colorful guy. He and the Oregon State Penitentiary had a bit of their own familial history. Leonard's father was executed in this very facility thirty-five years earlier after killing a woman and her unborn baby during a mugging gone bad. The execution happened during a three-year window when executions were still going on in Oregon between two of the numerous court-ordered moratoriums prohibiting them. They only started up again after the governor resigned in shame last year.

Leonard was three when his dad was executed and has no independent recollection of him. But the execution haunted his childhood, driving him toward a career in law enforcement, and he'd tried, but failed, to get a job as a police officer virtually all of his adult life. Becoming a corrections officer was the closest he could get.

Leonard was a likable guy who was trying to advance himself. His goal in the Department of Corrections was to rise at least to the rank of captain to better provide for his wife and two daughters, who were fiercely proud of their dad. Leonard was the kind of guy I would have liked if I was the kind of guy who liked people and who was capable of having actual relationships with them. Unfortunately, I was neither.

Thanks to him, my remaining time passed relatively quickly, and I didn't leave the hole a wild-eyed zombie. One day, Leonard told me I'd be going back to general pop the next day and shook my hand. The following morning I was led without ceremony down a hall, across the yard, and back to my own cellblock. My ordeal was over.

I couldn't believe it. You maim a guy, damn near kill him, and you get six weeks in time out. Like Leonard said, what could they do, put me in jail?

From the moment I walked onto the yard, I immediately noticed that things were different. I didn't know what to expect. I knew enough to know that word of my return would have preceded me; therefore, I was worried the black gangs would attack me from the beginning.

But they didn't. The blacks didn't give me a second glance, and when we did make eye contact, they nodded and looked away first. It was respect. Part of it was because of the beating I had laid on Davis, AKA Chitlin, but I think most of it was that they couldn't touch me without starting a war they weren't prepared to fight. I had EK solid at my back.

When I entered my cell, Roach treated me more as a peer or a friend than a cellie. He was friendly and accepting, and we actually got along well. All the EK members accepted and even seemed to like me. I was still a prospect as far as I knew, but Panhead, Semper, and a dozen other guys I didn't yet know all treated me as brothers. Billy and the other prospects looked up to me. There was acceptance here, much as there had been at the department. It wasn't as difficult as I had thought it would be to switch allegiances and cling to this group.

In the weeks following my return, I was given several books to read, including works by ultra-conservative former white house press secretary Patrick Buchanan and the Chinese general / philosopher Sun Tzu. I was even quizzed as to whether I had read them. I spent time being a gopher and servant to Roach and Panhead, the top two EK guys here, and I was eventually told that as a final test, I had to "do something good" for the club.

I'd learned that EK was big on controlling the meth market around Oregon. I also knew that my uncle Phil, who had helped me out in my youth, had been here back in the day and wondered if he might be able to give me some advice on what to do. There were rumors in the family that he had been mixed up with pretty high level drug trading after he'd gotten out, but nobody had ever bothered to check. Uncle Phil had pretty much dropped off the family radar for the past three decades. Surprisingly, after just a few hours in the library, I had his number.

A week later, I had my first visitor in prison. Uncle Phil had grown old and frail looking since I'd last seen him as a kid, but his eyes were still hard and sharp. I remember when he was the black sheep of the family, back before I took that mantle from him.

"Well damn, boy," he said over the phone from the opposite side of the glass. "You look like your old man, you know that?"

"Bet you never saw my old man on this side of the glass, did you?"

"Ain't never saw him on this side, neither. He never did come visit me any of the times I was in. But that don't matter. He had a family, and that was best, I guess. You look like you're doin' ok in here. How's the joint treating you?"

"Could be worse. I did a stint in PC because I was a cop, but I couldn't take it and decided to take my chances in general pop. Fell in with some boys who are, uh, helping *shield* me from trouble, shall we say."

Phil smiled. "I know them boys well," he said. "I hung with some of their associates myself. He pulled up a sleeve and showed me an Aryan Brotherhood tattoo. "Never hurts to have friends in a place like this."

"Yeah, I kinda wanted to do something nice for them," I said. "Kind of an acceptance thing."

Uncle Phil nodded. He knew the code. "I know what them boys like. Don't you worry about it. You'll, uh, find something nice for them I'm sure. I can think of lots of things that might come your way."

"That'd be real nice. So what have you been doing the past couple of decades? I think the family pretty much wrote you off when I was just a kid."

"A little of this, a little of that. I made some money over the years. Had me a good woman who made a good move or two with it, but she passed a couple years back. Breast cancer. That shit sure does suck. She left me a little place out in Rockwood, and because of what she did with my money, I got pretty much everything I'll ever need, which ain't much. I just pretty much keep to myself nowadays. Actually, I'm glad to have you back in contact, even if you are in here. Gives an old con something to do."

"Yeah, well, up until very recently, I wouldn't have thought I'd feel the same, but I do. I guess I have a little different perspective on things nowadays."

"I reckon so, boy. Listen, you take it real easy in here. Watch your back, and let your buddies help you with that. You keep on the lookout for hidden surprises in this place. You never know what you might find."

"I will, Uncle Phil. You'll come see me from time to time?"

"Damn straight, boy. It ain't like I keep a full social calendar nowadays."

After a little more small talk, we said our goodbyes, and the visit was up.

Three days later, two hacks came in and kicked Roach and I out of our cell. We stood in the dayroom while they tossed the place looking for contraband.

"Don't worry about this shit," Roach said. "They do this whenever they want to hassle us. They rarely find anything, and sometimes I'll even leave a little half-baked shiv or something lying around just to make 'em happy. That way, they don't look too hard to find what I'm really hiding."

Fifteen minutes later, they left without a word. I returned to the cell and found my bed unmade and my few possessions scattered about. No real damage.

As I remade my bed, I found a rolled up washcloth under the pillow. Contained within it were four small plastic baggies, each containing what appeared to be a few grams of meth. No note, nothing to indicate how or why it was there, but I knew. Uncle Phil, it seems, had made some friends in high places.

The following day, I told Roach I had something good for the boys. That afternoon, Roach called for church to be held in our cell, and everyone, me included, sat back and had a snort. I dared not object and found that it was actually kind of fun. The meth gave me a kick I never expected. I was kind of glad it was a one-time deal; the last thing I needed was to become a tweaker.

Semper brought his jailhouse tattoo needle, which looked suspiciously like a guitar string wired to a small, blue electric motor. There was a brief ceremony, during which I swore a sacred oath of allegiance, and I was welcomed into the ranks as a full-fledged member of the European Kindred. Semper tattooed the EK shield on my right calf, and that was it.

I was glad to be a part of this gang, which spoke volumes as to how far I'd come in the six months since my fall from grace. But in my heart, I was not committed to this group. In my heart, I was more good guy than bad guy, and I knew this. Right now, I was doing what I had to do, and I recognized that I was going to have to do it for the rest of my life. I was trying as hard as I could, but I still didn't feel as if I fit in as a white supremacist.

I hadn't quite fit in there as a cop, either. I was a misfit, a broken toy. But there was no island for toys like me, not here or anywhere else. I was an island unto myself.

In the weeks following my induction into the European Kindred, I threw everything into reshaping myself as a badass prison gang member. I grew a biker's beard and started letting my hair grow long. I began working out with other EK members daily for hours in the yard. After a few months, I was noticeably buffed out. By the end of my first year in the joint, my left arm was covered in ink, and I was working on getting my right arm sleeved out.

My speech and mannerisms had become the same as other prisoners who had been in the joint the majority of their adult lives, and I'd pretty much acquired a lifer's attitude. Prison was my new home. It had become my entire world. I don't think I would have embraced it so much if I could get out in ten to twenty, but I was doing "all day and a night," which was prison vernacular for life with no possibility of parole. I knew damn well that I'd never leave this place alive. I recognized early on that if I wanted to avoid going insane, I'd have to actually *become* a lifer and forget about the outside and everything I used to be.

When I looked at my distorted reflection in the stainless steel plate bolted to the wall that served as a mirror, I was glad my older sister never lived to see what had become of her baby boo.

Chapter 25

The only time I ever remotely felt like my old self was when I was doing a stretch in the hole. During my first two years, I did four stretches, all for fighting. I didn't always win, but I never backed down and won more than my share. Ya gotta do what ya gotta do to survive. It had become my mantra.

With all the time to reflect in the hole, I couldn't help but think about my old life. I still missed being a good guy during these times. I recalled the way I respected myself. I had worn the badge with a certain degree of pride, and I had enjoyed being a cop on several levels, not the least of which was the thrill of it.

In the joint, there were no more risks to take to fill that particular need, so I'd had to take a giant step backward, instead seeking thrills. That's pretty much what drove me to not shy away from a fight—hence my four stints in the hole.

What really made me miss my old life were my conversations with Leonard, who was still the only hack willing to talk to me in solitary. Leonard constantly wanted to talk about my experiences on SERT and CNT, and conversations with him made me feel nostalgic and melancholic. But then I'd go back to general pop, and instantly I'd find myself reassimilated into my new life. Still, lying in my bunk during the still part of the night when the doubts come, I inventoried the ways I might kill myself if I ever wanted to, just so I'd be prepared for the time when I could no longer face another three or four decades of prison.

It was just a natural consequence of living here.

One day, an EK guy named Kevin Durst, also known as Kickstart, called the guys together for an impromptu church meeting in the dayroom. Once we were all gathered, he didn't beat around the bush: "I want to grease one of the hacks," he said.

We all looked at Roach, but nobody said anything.

After a moment, Durst said, "Did you hear me? I want to put a hit on one of the hacks."

Killing a guard was about the biggest thing that could happen in the joint short of a riot. For the most part, the hacks treated us fairly as long as we didn't sling them too much shit. When we did, they had a way of slinging it back, only a lot harder and a lot more of it, too.

There was a lot of head shaking and low whistles at Durst's proposal. Roach said, "We can't just waste a hack, Kick. We couldn't survive that. They'd break us up, separate us, and transfer us all around the country. Right now, we got it good here. We're at the top of the food chain, and we're getting stronger. Who the fuck do you want to hit, and why?"

Without batting an eye, Durst said, "It's Don Porter, that bald motherfucker who thinks he's God. I found out that motherfucker's layin' the track on my old lady."

"How do you know that?" Roach asked.

"I could tell from the way that prick's been treating me the past couple weeks that something's been up. The way he looks at me, with this little sneer on his fat face. It started right after JoAnne started coming around again to see me. Hell, I even knew something was up with her, too. Right about the same time, she started acting weird. Disconnected, you know, like I didn't own her no more? Well, we just had a big ass fight, and she told me straight up she's been fucking Porter for a month. She said he's the reason she started coming back around, so she could see *him*, not me. She said Porter's gettin' a divorce, so now she can fuck him in his own bed, so she don't need to come around here to meet him no more. Hell, she even said she's packing my shit up and taking it down to the club and not to bother coming home when I get out."

"Jesus, I'm sorry to hear that, Kicky," said Panhead. "She knows she can't just do that. She knows the rules. Roach, what say I have some of the boys on the outside tune her up a little?"

Roach turned to Durst. "That's the way it should be handled, Kevin. How hard you want her hit? You want her gone? Just say the word."

"It ain't that fuckin' whore I care about, Roach. It's that asshole Porter. I want *that* fucker dead!"

"Calm down, Kevin. We can't just go waste a badge over this. It's not worth the consequences. Panhead's got the right idea, only we'll do Porter instead of JoAnne. You want him gone? Fine, we'll have the boys on the outside pay a little visit to C.O. Porter when he's off-duty. They can make it look like a robbery or something, but make sure that *he* knows exactly why he's getting hit before he dies."

"No!" yelled Durst. "I want to be the one to gut that fucker myself!"

"Well, Kick, I'm sure as hell not gonna stop you from doing what you need to do, but I can't put the EK stamp on it. Not in here."

"You can't just let them think they can steal someone else's shit like that can you? How can you do that? That fucker *brags* about it with his eyes. I guaran-goddam-tee you that fucker's told all his buddies he's plowing JoAnne, and there ain't shit I can do about it. Come on, Roach, I thought an attack on one of us is an attack on all of us!"

"Goddamn it, Kevin, I know you're pissed, but did you not hear me? They'll break us up! Do you know how long it would take us to reestablish the juice we got in here now? We're at the top. Them fuckin' niggers'll be running this joint for the next five years if we're busted. No, you want EK to do it, it's going to happen on the outside. That's what I'd do, man. But if you want it your way, you gotta do it by yourself, apart from the group."

"Then I guess I know what I gotta do."

"Fine. Obviously, you've thought this thing out. So what's the plan?"

"I'm gonna blood that motherfucker out. I been making a nice shank from a broken screwdriver I bought from a guy in D Block. Blade's almost three inches long and filed real sharp, and I mounted it on a nice wooden handle. I been watching Porter real close for three weeks, and on Tuesdays, when he's partnered with Fryer, he's usually alone in the cage for fifteen minutes or so right after their lunch hour. I think Fryer takes a long shit then or something. Anyways, what I need is for someone to collapse in the yard, or fake an injury, or something during that time. Porter'll come out of the cage, and it'll be at least a minute or two before one of the other hacks gets here from the other side of the block. That's when I'll do it."

"How long's your bit?"

"I'm doing two dimes C.C. for armed robbery and kidnapping," he said, meaning two consecutive ten-year sentences. "I'm almost done. Got eighteen more months."

"A year-and-a-half? You're gonna walk in a year-and-a-half, and you want to give that up for a fuckin' *hack*? You'll never leave here, you do this. You know that, don't you?"

"Fuck it, man. Fuck *him*. I already thought about it. I'm doing it. Hell, I'd be back in here six months after my release anyway."

"Long as you know what you're getting into. I'll tell you what. We can't do it as an EK thing, but if you can get a volunteer to help you out in an unofficial capacity, I'm good with that."

"Fine. Who wants to help a brother out?"

Nobody spoke up. "Come on, you pussies. Bad, what about you? You're already a lifer. Come on, man."

"I'm a lifer for killing a cop, Kick. I kill another one, and they'll give me the big jab." The big jab is pretty self-explanatory. "But I gotta tell you, murder while incarcerated, especially the murder of a correctional officer, is aggravated murder under Oregon law. *You'll* get the big jab if you do it."

"I don't give a fuck."

Roach said, "We get that, but you can't ask one of us to take a fall like that. I'll tell you what. Billy Balls is trying to earn his bones. Ask him, and if he does it, I propose we patch him in. What say you?"

"Aye."

"Aye."

"Aye."

"Unanimous. Tell Billy if he helps you out, he's in."

And with that, the plan was set.

That was on a Thursday. By Saturday, I was getting pretty mentally screwed up over the upcoming murder. I'd been a con for over two years now. I was twenty-six months into a life sentence. During that time, I had changed dramatically. My hair was down to my shoulders, I had a five-inch beard I planned never to cut, and colorful sleeve tattoos covering thick, muscular arms. A child would instinctively shy away at the sight of me.

But as still occasionally happened, I really began feeling the dichotomy that I actually was. The outside may be all con, but there was still a good guy buried inside who was alive and well, lying dormant, just waiting for a time such as this.

Durst was going to kill a correctional officer, the closest thing there was to a cop in here. He had no proof that his old lady was sleeping with this guy, but even if he was, he shouldn't die over it. I knew the guard, Porter, and he was never an asshole to me. He seemed like a straight up guy. In fact, he'd told me he was in the Marines before he came here. He did a couple tours in Afghanistan. I remember him talking about a daughter.

Knowing that he was going to die was gnawing at me. I ignored it at first because it wasn't my deal, but the more I ignored it, the worse I felt. I could stop this, but that was totally at odds with everything I had strived to become in here. I had become a member of EK to survive. I didn't beat Chitlin near to death because he was black or because I wanted to join EK; I'd done it because I had to in order to survive.

So really, other than not wanting to get on their bad side, I had no lasting loyalty to the Kindred. If I was somehow miracled out of here on parole, I wouldn't take up with them on the outside like so many do. I'd just disappear, and my status as a member would be forgotten forever, unless I ever had to come back.

But I was going to live in this place until the day I died, and therefore, I had to have eternal loyalty to them. So, I thought, I should keep my fat mouth shut because the fastest way for me to die was to cross EK. Nothing was lower in the joint than a snitch, not even a diaper sniper.

But the idea of watching a CO get hit for something like this just didn't set well with me. I didn't know what to do. Snitching on EK would present one of the biggest risks I'd ever taken, and in the end, that's pretty much what swayed me. After all, there weren't many ways to fill that particular need in here.

Once I made the decision, I could feel it building in me just like the old days, and damn, I liked the anticipation! I let it build until it was so strong I had to do something or burst, just like when I walked into Killer Burger.

On Monday, the day before the hit, I went out into the yard after lunch in search of a victim. It didn't take long to find one. A big Hispanic was doing pull-ups by himself, not far from a pair of hacks who were taking shelter from the August sun under an eave. I walked past him, maddogging him all the way. Predictably, he muttered something under his breath as I passed.

I stopped and turned around. "What did you just call me, you fucking wetback?"

He looked at me with an almost puzzled expression. He was a lot bigger than me, and we'd never had a problem in the past, so this was probably a little bizarre to him.

"Get lost, bolillos, before I fuck you up," he said.

I flew at him and managed to land one good punch to the side of his head before he commenced to kicking my ass. Fortunately, before he could lay too good a whooping on me, hacks flooded the yard, and we were pulled apart.

That night, in the hole, the talkative Leonard Scott brought me my dinner.

Chapter 26

A week later when I returned to E Block, I went outside to hang with some Kindred in the yard. Two of the guys were spotting for Panhead, who could bench three-fifty. After finishing a set, he saw me. He stood up and said, "So what'd that spic say to get you all riled up for another trip to the hole?"

"I don't know man, nothing, really. He called me a bolillos. I don't even know what that shit is, but it was the way he said it. I was having a bad day anyway. It just pissed me off."

"It just means 'white bread,' man. Was it worth a week in the hole?"

"Hell no. I hate that fucking place."

"Well, you missed all the action around here."

"Oh, yeah, that's right. Kickstart hit that guard. How'd that all go down anyway? Does Kevin still walk among us?

"Nothing happened, man. Hacks came around after lights out the night you went away and shook down all the EK cells. They found Durst's shank along with some weed Scarlini was holding. Semper lost his tattoo gun, and you lost your brass knuckles. But worst of all, they found Roach's cell phone."

"Fuck! That phone's gonna be hard to replace."

"Yeah, but what really bothers me is, how'd they know?"

"What, you think someone ratted? Nobody knew but us."

"I know."

"You think it was one of *us*? I can't see that, man. Not even Billy Balls. No, I bet they either just smelled something was up, or they're going around shaking everyone down, and it was just our turn. Nobody here would rat. Not for something as stupid as Durst's old lady."

A shadow fell next to me. I looked up, and it was Kevin Durst. Before I could say anything, Roach stepped in on the other side. He was standing way too close, and at that moment, I knew my goose was cooked.

Roach said, "One of the COs occasionally snitches for me, Bad. He told me Porter heard it from a hack named Scanlon. Scanlon is the sergeant of the hacks working the hole. He told Porter that EK had put a hit out on him for fucking one of their bitches."

I didn't say anything. The circle closed a little tighter.

Roach said, "Scott, you know the hack who likes to chat with cons in the hole? Well, it turns out he was on duty that night, which just happens to be the night you picked a fight with that spic."

"Jesus, Roach. I been EK for a long time. Two fuckin' *years*, man. Come on, you know I wouldn't do something like that!"

"You were five-o for a lot longer than that."

Two guys grabbed Panhead's barbell off the rack, while at the same time Panhead grabbed me in a bear hug and wrestled me to the ground. A hand went over my mouth, and they dropped the barbell across my neck, pinning me to the ground and just about crushing my windpipe. They all dropped down and commenced to beating me to death with kicks, fists, and hammer blows, raining a nonstop deluge on me while two guys held my arms, so I couldn't protect myself. The last thing I remember was Durst's foot coming down on the bridge of my nose.

The next thing I recall was looking up and seeing two hacks and a paramedic. They were swaying in unison while they worked on me, which I didn't understand at all. It turned out to be the motion of the ambulance in transit. I wasn't sure if the noise was a siren or something going on inside my head. I was in an out a lot those first few days.

I spent nearly two weeks in the intensive care unit at the Oregon Health Sciences University hospital in Portland, under guard. My friends in the Kindred had done quite a number on me. I had a concussion, a shattered orbit, a broken cheek, two broken teeth, two broken ribs, a ruptured spleen, bruised kidneys, a dislocated shoulder, and swelling in my throat from the barbell. I pissed blood for three weeks after the attack.

I spent a total of four-and-a-half weeks in the hospital before being transferred to the prison infirmary. I was given a choice when I came out:

protective custody in Ad Seg again or transfer to the Intensive Management Unit at Oregon's Snake River Correctional Institution.

Even under a prison death sentence, I refused Ad Seg. I just couldn't handle that again, so I chose Snake River, not that it would do me much good. The European Kindred was not only Oregon's largest and most violent prison gang, but it was also well represented at SNCI. Additionally, EK was affiliated with the Aryan Brotherhood, the largest white supremacist gang in the country, so it really wouldn't matter where they sent me. Word travels quickly from prison to prison. Regardless of your affiliations, there's nothing more offensive to *anyone* in prison than a snitch.

When I was finally healthy enough to be reintegrated back into general pop, I was immediately placed on a bus and taken to Snake River, a five-hour drive from the Oregon State Pen. Upon my arrival, I was sent to Unit B in Intensive Management, which houses inmates who are at risk from fellow inmates. The thing I liked about IMU was that inmates are housed in single-occupancy cells, forty-eight per unit. But even there, I had a feeling that I wouldn't feel secure until I was safely tucked away in my cell at lights out.

I found out that there was at least one other EK guy in the IMU, but he was housed in Unit A. I don't know why he was there, but he was a problem child on the unit, and he never rose above a level I offender status. There are four levels in IMU, with level I being the most unmanageable prisoners with next to no privileges and level IV being the highest, with the most privileges.

I started off, like everyone else, as a level II, but after six months of good behavior and without any safety incidents, the threat to my safety got recategorized as low, and I was transferred up to unit D, which is where level III and IV offenders are housed together. This still afforded me the protection of IMU but gave me a higher level of privileges.

One of those privileges was the right to work as a trustee. I got a job in the prison kitchen scrubbing pots and pans and cleaning grease out of the fryers and oven hoods. Doesn't sound like much, but it was a distraction, got me off the unit every day, and gave me a little cash to hold.

It turned out that all my fretting seemed to be for naught. My reputation as a snitch never came back to haunt me in IMU. I had spent months worrying about it, but it had become a non-issue. In fact, my reputation as a badass had followed me.

After another couple of months without incident, I was recategorized as a Level IV prisoner, with the most privileges allowed. I was now at the highest level Oregon offered for protective custody.

The Intensive Management Unit at Snake River was different than general pop at OSP. Here, no longer did I blend in with every other prison badass. Most of the inmates in the protective segregation unit were guys who didn't fit the badass prison profile: child molesters, effeminate gays, a few easily managed, nonviolent mentally impaired prisoners we called tards, and a bunch of soft white collar criminals who wouldn't last an hour in general pop. With my rep, my attitude, my long hair and tats, I went to the top of the food chain by default. Within months, I was running the unit.

I used this position not for power or intimidation, but more in an advisory capacity for the other inmates. Despite my exterior shell, the good guy in me had a tendency to come out in unexpected ways. I didn't tolerate excessive bullying, for example—even of the lowest of the low, the child molesters. I made sure that those guys got the most shit, but I also made sure they weren't handed out more than they could take. I can't say why I did this other than, perhaps, as a way to hang onto a shred of civility. Maybe it was a way to atone for my wanton destruction of Chitlin for no real reason. It could have been my way of making up for compromising the tolerant, non-racist views I'd always held by joining EK. Perhaps it was just my way of making amends for killing Horace Anderson.

I think it was all of that and more. Just a general way of ensuring that I felt good about myself. We are all the sum of our life experiences, from our earliest moments to how the consequences of our decisions continually shape us.

I expect it was for that reason that I ended up doing what I did in Unit D.

Any block or housing unit experiences a slow but constant change of characters. Guys get released, transferred, or occasionally die, and new guys come along to take their places. The Oregon State Pen had been there for decades, and one day I came, and then one day I left. Same with Snake

River. One day, I'd leave here and go somewhere else. Hopefully, it wouldn't be Unit C at OSP. That was death row, and guys only leave there one way.

Every now and then an EK guy would come in, but by the time they made it up to Unit D, they wanted to keep their noses clean, so there was never any trouble beyond a few nasty words. There was one guy who wanted to challenge me. He attacked me, but I just defended myself without striking back. He got busted back to Level I, and I stayed where I was. He never made it back to IV, so I don't know what happened to him, and I don't care.

But for the most part, despite the slow change in role players, things didn't change too much. I still ran the unit, and everyone was happy. New guys would roll into Unit D and spend a day or two getting the lay of the land. Pretty soon, they'd talk to someone and find out who the boss was. They'd come pay me a visit. I'd lay down the rules, tell them what I expected from them, and gain their cooperation. Most just accepted it.

Those few who didn't want to play by the rules rarely lasted more than a week. It was the hacks themselves who'd provoke them, just to bust them down and off the unit. Because the way I ran it, guys weren't getting stepped on, which made the prisoners happy. The hacks were happy because the system worked; there were far fewer disciplinary problems than before, and it was a well-run unit. I was happy because I felt like I was doing what I could to make up for all I'd done wrong. If it ain't broke, don't fix it.

But then a new prisoner rolled onto the floor, and the well-oiled machine I'd built began to break down.

I will never forget the date he showed up. August 17, 2017.

Chapter 27

Randy Denton, a dayshift hack, told me we were getting a new guy later that afternoon. He was a softie, a predatory sex offender with a penchant for juveniles—a diaper sniper, the lowest of the low. When these types arrive, they are generally the most obedient. They've usually been in the system long enough to know how much they need a protective custody unit, so they are more than willing to do whatever they have to in order to not make trouble. My biggest job with guys like this is keeping the others off their backs.

Everything you've ever heard about child molesters in prison is true. They are eschewed and tormented by all. They're the most likely to be assaulted (including sexually assaulted) and the least likely to be able to resist. They have the highest suicide rate in prison. They also have very high recidivism rates, which means they're quite likely to return after they're released. They are hated and reviled by everyone in the joint and are constantly harassed, assaulted, and fucked with.

As a consequence, they seek out protection and are willing to do anything to get it. Therefore, they are utterly obedient and entirely manageable to the boss, which seems like a good thing for them, but it rarely is since most bosses quietly orchestrate their misery. I did that, too, but like I said, I took care to ensure that they were never dealt more shit than I thought they could handle.

New transferees usually come in between lunch and dinner. It generally takes most guys a day or two before they show up in my cell for our little come-to-Jesus chat, but child molesters usually show up within hours, sometimes minutes, of arriving. They know they need protection, even in protective custody, and it doesn't take them long to find out where to get it.

After noon chow, I went to my cell and lay on my bunk reading. I spent a fair amount of time there as opposed to the day room anyway. Can't fraternize too much with the underlings, I guess. It's good for me because I don't really fit in with anyone, and my position as boss is a good excuse to be a loner.

An hour or so after chow, there was a knock at the door.

"Come."

The new guy walked in, and when he did, the world as I knew it stopped turning. My heart took an adrenaline dump that felt fatal, and the blood drained out of my face. His red hair had gone mostly gray, and he'd lost some, but certainly not all, of his weight. I recognized him instantly, but he showed no sign whatsoever of recognizing me. How could he? I was a nine-year-old runt when we last saw each other the day he stripped me naked and molested me in his office.

Dr. Douglas McNab.

I stared at him with what to me was fear, but it must have looked like malevolent hatred to him. I felt that same weird mix of fear, shame, and guilt that I learned to live with in the years following the molestation. He was the authority figure who had dangled my entire future over my head and used it to gain my compliance in his perverted sexual desires.

For the moment, I forgot about everything that had ever happened in the intervening decades. I was too afraid to speak. But then McNab lowered his gaze, a hound yielding to the alpha of the pack, and I somehow clawed my way back to the present. I had no reason to fear Dr. McNab anymore. Dr. McNab had every reason to fear *me*.

To him, I wasn't a scared, easily victimized nine-year-old underdeveloped boy. He was looking at a hardcore con. If he wanted to survive in here, he had to submit to the authority. He had to submit to me.

"They . . . they said I needed to come see you," he said hesitantly. He was clearly frightened. Dr. McNab was just as soft as he was thirty-four years ago, but it was his voice that haunted me the most. It took me a moment to get myself together before I was confident enough to speak.

"What's your name, slick?"

"McNab. Uh, Douglas."

"No, it's not. It's Karma. What are you in for, Karma?"

"Ah, you know, all the usual child stuff."

I burned my eyes into his. "No, I don't know. What were you convicted of?"

"S-Sex Abuse I, Rape I of a child, Sodomy I, Sexual Corruption of a Minor, and one count each of Distribution and Manufacturing Child Pornography."

"Did you take a deal?"

"Yes."

"What were you originally charged with?"

"Well, it was all the same stuff, you know, only with eight victims. But there were two thousand counts of child porn."

"And your sentence?"

"Two-hundred-forty months."

"When *can* you get out?"

"The way my lawyer explained it, eighty-four months before parole, but that could be reduced to sixty under the right circumstances."

"How old are you?"

"Sixty-two."

"How long ago were you arrested?"

"Eight months."

"Well, you're going to find things a little different here at Snake River than they were in county, Karma. Even here, in protective custody, they'll tear you apart. I seen guys like you die in here. More'n once. Really, the only thing between you and the guys that'll do that to you is me. And quite frankly, Chester, I don't give a shit what happens to you. If I keep them off you, it's only because I don't want your death fucking up my record with the hacks. I run a tight ship, and the hacks like it that way, so I got it nice and good in here."

"Look, I know there's something very wrong with me to make me the way I am," McNab said. Dismissing it with a wave of his hand, he continued, "Well, I guess that doesn't matter anymore, but I'm old, and I'm going to be in my eighties if I ever leave here. I'm not a tough guy, Mr. Bad. Jail hasn't been easy for me. I was beaten, badly, in Multnomah County Jail before trial, and when they sent me here, I got . . . assaulted . . . in Unit B. And that's still administrative segregation! I don't want any more of that. I don't think I could take any more of that. All I want to do is keep to myself and do my time. I won't have any friends, and I can live with that, but please, I won't make any trouble. I just want to be left alone in here."

His tone was pitiful. He really wouldn't survive without protection. People like him were what this place was all about. How could I fear such a man? The feelings that had overcome me at the unexpected sight of him were just left over from when I was a small child. From when *he*, as the authority figure, victimized *me*. Way back when. When the shoe was on the other foot.

He hadn't sounded like a crybaby pussy when he stripped me naked and tried to penetrate me with his pathetic little hard-on as part of my "therapy." I felt my blood beginning to boil.

"You know why I call you Karma?"

He just shook his head.

"It's because guys like you? Sometimes shit has a way of coming back around again. You never know, maybe you'll run into one of your victims in here. Wouldn't that be something?"

"That's why I need help!" he whined.

"Get out of here."

"But are you—"

"I said get the fuck out of my sight!"

He fled to his cell.

I lay awake that night with my head pounding. Douglas McNab had been the author of virtually all my adult troubles. Yes, I had been somewhat fucked up before him (after all, I did light my room on fire), but I don't think there was anything too screwed up in me that couldn't have been unscrewed with *proper* counseling. I applaud my mother for getting me into treatment in the first place. She had done the right thing, just with the wrong person, but there was no way she could have known about McNab.

I kept to myself for the next day and a half, spending hours alone in my cell, mentally processing the damage McNab had done to me, and how I felt about his sudden appearance. I knew I was going to do something, but I didn't want to go off half-cocked. I wanted to do the right thing.

A few years after my thing with Julie Albatross ended, when I caught her doing another little freshman boy, I took care of that problem. Though

I didn't know the proper terminology, I realized that she too was a predatory sex offender, and that even though the boys considered themselves the luckiest kids in the world, they weren't. I know in my case, by using me, she had destroyed a part of me.

After giving the matter a lot of thought, I came up with a way to get back at her in what I considered equal proportion to the damage she had done me. I felt a little bad about it at the time, but I don't regret what I did. Julie destroyed me, so I destroyed Julie. I'll never forget the satisfaction I felt in the days and weeks after I watched them lead her away in handcuffs.

I had paid Julie Albatross back, but Douglas McNab had destroyed me far worse than she had and gotten away with it. How many hundreds of other children had he victimized and destroyed before he finally got caught? What had become of the others?

But now, he was here. With me. *Under* me. And he had no idea. I liked that.

I've never really been a big believer in karma. Perhaps it was time to rethink that notion.

I kept an eye on the goings-on of the unit during my seclusion. It became known within the first hours of McNab's arrival that he was a child molester. I think guys like him exude their filth from their very pores, and for that reason, they are easily spotted in an environment such as this. Regardless of the reason, I knew he would receive more than his share of harassment from the other prisoners, no matter where he went.

So far, it had mostly been limited to shoulder bumps and verbal threats, both veiled and outright, but there was at least one incident in which he had been punched in the face. After that, I made it known to the unit that he was not to be physically injured, but anything would go as far as verbal threats and physical intimidation.

Two days after McNab's arrival, I sent for him. When he showed up in my cell, he had a black eye and was as timid as a whipped dog.

I made him stand there while I lay on my bunk reading. After about a minute, I said, "So how do you like protective custody, Karma?"

"It's no better here than anywhere else. Nobody but the other chesters will talk to me, and frankly, I don't like any of them. Everyone threatens me all the time, and I know it won't be long before I get beaten again. Please, Bad, I was told you could protect me."

I sat up and turned a hardcore stare on him. He immediately wilted. "Exactly why the fuck should I protect you?"

He answered right up, as if he'd prepared himself for the question. "Because I'm not a bad man! Yes, I admit I've done bad things, terrible things, and I'm neither proud nor happy I've done them. I *hate* that I've done them! You see, I don't know if you're aware of this or not, but I'm a highly educated man. I'm a doctor, a psychiatrist. A child psychiatrist, which is really the worst thing a man like me can be. But what makes me the way I am is a . . . well, a genetic flaw, really. It's not a learned thing or a choice. It's something I was born with. It's a damaged gene if you will, something over which I have absolutely no control. Actually, it's a lot like homosexuality in that respect. It's not a choice one makes, but the way one is; only unlike homosexuality, my flaw, the sexual attraction to children, is not acceptable to society. To *any* society in the known world, although it has been proven to exist in even some of the most primitive cultures ever studied. And not only is it not accepted, it is considered criminal, something with which I wholeheartedly agree.

"I've been aware of my . . . condition from the time I was a teenager. The reason I gravitated toward medicine, and psychiatry to be specific, was to teach myself to defeat it. But like homosexuality, it simply cannot be "conditioned out." It is the way I am. I can no more change my sexual preference than I can will myself to grow taller. I—"

"What you're saying is that I should protect you because you don't *want* to fuck children, but you do it anyway."

"That's a rough way of putting it, but in a way, yes. I'm a good man at heart. I have tried to have sex with women, and even men, but there's no attraction there. Therefore, there's no fulfillment. I'm not physically able to perform, probably any more than you could if you tried to have sex with a partner not of your preferred gender, or, abhorrent as it may seem to you, with a child. I've tried to live without sex, but as you know, the sexual drive in men is second only to that of survival, and I've found this impossible."

"And why, exactly, am I supposed to give a shit about all this?"

"Because I'm harmless now, and I need help! Look, obviously I can't have sex with children in here, nor can I engage in sexual fulfillment from child pornography. All I can do is masturbate to fantasies within my own mind, where, thankfully, nobody else can see what it is that torments me. Therefore, all that is left of me here is the good part. I can *help* people in here. A lot of the inmates must have problems, and helping people with problems is exactly what I've been trained and certified to do! I don't know what comes after this life, Bad, but I believe in heaven and hell. I hope that if I can help people, if I can finally stop hurting the children, even if it's only because I'm locked up, that maybe I can make up for some of it and not burn in hell. And failing that, I can at least lead a miserable, lonely existence without getting beat up. That's all I'm asking."

Old Dr. McNab didn't want to burn, eh? That gave me an idea.

I took a long pause, as if I was only now considering his request. Finally, I said, "You ever see the movie *The Silence of the Lambs*?"

"Of course."

"Like Agent Starling was to Hannibal Lecter, you are an item of interest to me. Remember their deal, their quid-pro-quo thing? As long as you entertain me, I'll protect you. You tell me anything I ask you about yourself, and I'll keep these goons off your back. You don't, and . . . well, you can probably imagine what will happen."

He reached out to shake my hand, "Yes, yes, I can do that! Thank you, Bad, thank you very much!"

Ignoring his outstretched hand, I told him that I'd call him when I wanted him and in the meantime to get the fuck out of my cell.

Chapter 28

Along with my daughter Grace, my parents had written me off after my arrest. Since my case was adjudicated and I had no further need of a lawyer, I have had exactly one visitor since my arrest—my Uncle Phil, who had pulled strings to smuggle me some meth for the boys in EK.

Here in Snake River, since I had earned my way up to a Level IV status in Unit D, I was allowed to have actual face-to-face visits, albeit with family only. Fortunately, the definition of family extended to aunts and uncles. I made a call to Uncle Phil, and a week later, we had a very productive visit.

Uncle Phil was excited when I asked him for a favor and especially when I explained exactly why. He didn't have much to live for, so he was thrilled to have been given what he considered a noble task. Since I was allowed family visits twice per month, Phil promised to see me at least two more times, on the first and fifteenth of September. After that, we both knew I wouldn't be allowed visitors anymore.

A couple days later, I walked into the dayroom for evening chow. As usual, McNab was seated by himself, as far apart from everyone as he could get. I took up a seat next to him; the closeness clearly made him feel uncomfortable. "Tell me about how you got caught," I said.

McNab looked stricken. "Well," he said hesitantly, "like I told you, I'm sick. Flawed, I think, is a better way of putting it. Because of the nature of what I like, it's extremely difficult to come by. I wouldn't want you to think that I've used my profession solely to find victims, either, because that's not the way it was. I had a private practice, and I have done far more good for children without ever laying a finger on them than I have bad. Far more. But . . ."

"But still, you diddled some of your patients."

He hung his head. "Yes. The police had done an investigation a little less than a year before my arrest, in which the parents of a young boy complained that I spent the majority of the session holding him while he cried. Apparently the boy had felt uncomfortable with it, but I assure you nothing happened in that instance. It was purely—"

"I don't want to listen to you sugarcoating this, Karma. You were grooming the kid. He wasn't ready for the full monty yet. So don't say nothing happened. Say nothing happened *yet*."

"But that's not accurate. You . . . well, I don't mean to be rude, but you weren't there. You may think you have an idea of how it was, but I assure you, this type of therapy has its legitimate place in child psychiatry. Not every—"

"Hey Zero! Come here," I called to the inmate who had punched McNab when he first arrived. "This chester here needs a tune up."

Zero—a black gang member who for some reason had been marked for death by his own gang—came over and without a word mashed McNab's face down into his food and held it there. After about twenty seconds, McNab's arms started flailing about and slapping the table. His mouth and nose were submerged in a bowl of soup, and Zero held him there until he was clearly in distress, at which point I nodded to him. When he let McNab up, Zero smiled and said, "Seeya in the shower tomorrow, sugar," and he walked away.

McNab looked at me, a chicken noodle and a small drizzle of blood oozing out of his left nostril. "You see, Karma, you interest me only with a *truthful* account of your sins."

My face clouded up, and I snarled, "Look at where you are, man. You're in the fuckin' joint! Do you think I'm recording a confession for your trial?"

"No, I—"

"If you're not truthful with me, I will torment you until you find a way to kill yourself."

As I stood, McNab said desperately, "No, please wait. You're right; I was grooming him. I was hoping that the hugs would lead to fondling, but so far, it hadn't gone that far. But yes, that . . . that was my intent."

I sat back down. "So there had been a complaint, which means the police were on to you. Maybe looking for evidence or at least other complaints."

"Yes. The boy's mother complained to the medical board. It was actually the third complaint of this nature, so I was sanctioned, and my medical license was suspended for six months. I had to sign an agreement not to in any way get physical with the patients before they'd allow me to practice again. The police were notified, and a file was generated, but it went nowhere since no crime had been committed."

"So what got you busted?"

"About a year later, the nighttime cleaning woman discovered a camera I had set up in my office. This was on a Friday night, and because it was hidden in such a way as to appear suspicious, she called the police. They notified detectives, and due to the past complaints, a search warrant was obtained. They raided my office and, well, on my laptop, they discovered, uh, evidence."

"Karma . . ."

McNab's eyes welled up, and his face got blotchy: "Ok, ok. There were recordings of sessions with children. Some were of kids I thought might be . . . you know, future prospects. Those were just innocuous counseling sessions, in which I appear extraordinarily compassionate. But seven of them contained various degrees of . . . encounters, of a sexual nature."

"Molestations."

He looked around as if others might be listening, even though we were entirely alone and nodded. "Please don't share this with the other inmates, Bad. You can see I'm a good man at heart, can't you? I never liked doing this! In fact, I would go home and cry afterwards. I went to church, but when I tried to confess, I became afraid the priest would notify the authorities. Once I drove three hours to Seattle to go to church anonymously, but I still couldn't say the words. I . . . I just want you to understand how difficult this is for me."

I didn't want to hear his blathering about how bad he felt. I knew exactly what his "flaw" had done to me and my life. It was everything I could do not to choke him to death right there. "What about those kids,

Karma? You think it might have been 'difficult' for them? What about the fucking children?"

"I never forced myself on any of them. I was really quite gentle—"

I had vivid memories of how "gentle" he could be. Suddenly, I couldn't stand any more of this. I boiled over and elbowed him sharply in the face. He fell off the stool and lay there holding his nose, crying. Three other guys ran over to join the beat down, but I regained control before they could put the boots to him.

"No!" I said, standing protectively over him. "Leave him alone. Zero, that means tomorrow in the showers, too."

A crowd had begun to gather, and I could see the hacks working their way through. I stood like a lion over a wounded gazelle I was saving for a later meal and shouted to the entire dayroom: "You hear me? This chester is off limits to everyone until I say so!"

"What the fuck's going on here, Bad?" said the first hack to get to us.

"Nothing. He fell, and I'm helping him up."

"That . . . that's right, Officer," said McNab through tears, the dribble of blood now a full-blown mess covering the lower half of his face. "Bad here was nice enough to help me out."

My next session with McNab was even more productive. He told me he had molested a total of twelve children over the years, but investigators had only been able to locate eight victims. That left four who had not come forward, one of whom was me.

Nine of his victims had been boys, and three had been girls. Ages ranged from five to eleven. The eleven-year-old was a girl whose mother had brought her to McNab because of her early and increasing promiscuity, which had been triggered by sexual molestation by her older brother. In her case, she willingly complied with McNab, and he paid her a hundred dollars per session. His argument to me was that, though he readily admitted to victimizing her (he was unconvincing of this and probably said it because he feared another elbow to the face), it was far less traumatic to her because she was not only a willing participant, but an eager one, for the money. The majority of the videos shot in his office that they discovered on his laptop were of him having every sort of sex imaginable with this victim.

The youngest was a five-year-old boy who had quit speaking after having survived a fatal collision that took both his parents. The child's grandparents had brought him to McNab four weeks after the crash because he hadn't uttered a word since, desperate to help the boy. McNab had been unable to help him, but he had digitally sodomized him during his "therapy." McNab was proud of himself because he felt so badly about what he'd done that he turned down future opportunities to see the boy after the second molestation incident.

After hearing just these two stories, I was unable to continue. The timing, however, was good for me because the following day was the first of September, and Uncle Phil was scheduled to visit me.

The morning of the visit, I went to see an overweight sex offender who'd earned the nickname Dudley Do-Right by his constant acts of kindness in the joint, which he did as penance for his past sins. Dudley would do just about anything you wanted as long as it didn't involve hurting another inmate.

"Hey Dudley, I need a favor, man. It's gonna sound crazy, but I want to borrow a pair of your pants."

"Well, sure Bad, but how come?"

"My uncle's visiting me today, and he's always telling me how much weight I've lost, so I just thought it'd be funny if I went in there wearing your pants. You know, like a joke."

"Sure. These ones are almost clean," he said, tossing a pair my way.

Two hours later, hoping my pants wouldn't fall down, I was led to the visitor's area, where my old uncle was waiting for me. He was wearing a long sleeve flannel shirt this hot September day, which thankfully, nobody seemed to care about.

Uncle Phil and I talked of his deteriorating condition due to cancer (a condition we made up at our last visit) and how this might be our last chance to see each other while the hack stood by haplessly. We pissed away our half-hour talking about nothing. Finally, when the visit was over, Uncle Phil and I stood.

"Uh, Guard," said Phil. "Can you see it in your heart to let me give my nephew a hug? It's awful late in our lives to renew a relationship, but sometimes prison and cancer'll do that to folks. I'd sure appreciate it."

The hack half rolled his eyes and gave a listless nod. Uncle Phil stood and encircled me with his arms. He smelled like he could benefit from a bath.

I felt him shake his left arm behind my back, and then he reached his hand down my pants and into my underwear, letting the reason for the visit slip from his sleeve into my drawers. It was cold and squishy.

"Don't sit down, kid," he whispered.

"I love you, Uncle Phil," I said for the hack. "If you feel up to it, see if you can come see me again."

"I will, boy. In the meantime, don't do nothin' I wouldn't do."

Back in my cell, I bit into the bottom of my mattress under the corner by the wall, tearing a four-inch gash into the fabric. I then transferred the package into the mattress, pushing it deep into the fiberfill and covering it up with the sheet. If they shook down my cell, it would be discovered, but there hadn't been any shakedowns since I'd been here, and I wasn't expecting any soon. Besides, if everything went according to plan, it wouldn't be there long. All I had to do now was be patient and await another visit from Uncle Phil.

In the meantime, I made sure to keep the other inmates off McNab's back, but I maintained some sort of contact with him every couple of days. Every now and then, I'd have Zero or someone lean on him a little, and then I'd come to his rescue. In this way, I kept him conditioned to the idea that I was his only protection. The truth of it was that most of the guys in this unit were just like him, and those who weren't, like Zero, were smart enough to know that since it took so long to make it up to a Level IV status in this unit, a guy like McNab wasn't worth getting busted down to a Level II or I. In other words, nobody would have messed with him too much anyway, so my "protection" was actually a lot worse for him than it would have otherwise been without me.

Once a week, I'd enter McNab's cell and make him talk to me about his crimes. These sessions were very difficult for me to endure, but still, I had a mysterious fascination with them. Aside from the obvious personal aspect of it, I had a kind of professional one. Back when I was a cop, I'd had an interest in joining CAT, the multi-agency Child Abuse Team, which deals with cases such as his. Through McNab, I was being afforded a unique view into the mind of a very fucked-up individual who, I'm sure, had been the subject of a major CAT investigation.

I forced him to be extremely specific about his victims and what he'd done to them. I don't know if this made McNab feel any better to get it off his chest or not, but it sure made me feel better about what I was planning for him. McNab's stories were full of self-pity about the monster inside him and the terrible feelings he had before, during, and after his "sessions" with children.

He admitted to viewing every patient as a potential victim and fantasizing about those he never touched. It was always in the back of his mind, and he described his anticipation of new patients with a higher level of excitement than he was, no doubt, aware of. It both scared me (as he described the acts of abuse, I would involuntarily relive the dread I felt before going to see him) and enraged me.

One of the most telling things about all this was the fact that McNab never mentioned the effects of his molestation on the children. He was full of excuses about how he never used force to gain compliance from them, how he took care to stay gentle and loving, and how his abuse was often the first real feelings of love (misguided and perverted as it was, by his own admission) some of these kids had ever experienced, but he never speculated on the long-term effects it would have on their lives.

The more of his narrative I heard, the more I wanted to strangle the life out of him right then and there, especially when he touched on the case of a little boy who tried to burn his house down after his older sister had died of cancer, causing more family turmoil than he could handle. He lumped my case together with two others in which he talked the victims out of their clothes, but he maintained that nothing sexual happened. I remembered turning around while he furiously pumped his little dick after he fondled me and tried to penetrate me, but according to him, "nothing sexual happened." What other lies had he told me?

After that, I didn't want to hear any more, but I had set myself up as McNab's judge, jury, and executioner, and as such, I was duty bound to hear all the evidence first.

During this time, I got my second and last visit from Uncle Phil. We made a lot of small talk for the allotted half-hour and finally he said, "I ain't doing so well, boy. I wish I'd be able to come see you again, but I don't think I'm going to be able to. I think this may be the last time we ever get to see each other."

"I'm real sorry, Uncle Phil. We haven't known each other too much over the years, but every time you've ever come into my life, good things have happened. I remember you saving my ass with some advice when I was in high school. I still use that advice to this day, especially in here."

"I guess you've covered a lot of ground since then, boy. Lord knows, you been on both sides of the fence. If I could give you one last piece of advice, I'd tell you to be very careful in here." His blue eyes narrowed and bore into me with a laser-like focus. "Doing what you do in this place is a lot like playing with fire. You got to be real careful cuz it's easy as hell to get burnt."

"Thanks, Uncle Phil. I'll try to keep that in mind."

"You'd best. Now stand up, boy. Your old uncle wants to give you one last hug. I reckon one of us'll be dead afore we can see each other again."

The hack, a different one from the last, spoke up: "Sorry, old timer. No physical contact allowed."

"God damn it, this boy is my only kin, and I'm a dying old man. Fuck your rules, sonny. I'm giving my nephew a hug. You can stand here and watch if you like. Hell, you can whip it out and jerk off if you like, but I'm giving my only kin a hug."

The hack rolled his eyes. "You sound like you've been a guest here yourself, gramps. Aw, what the hell. Just make it quick."

We stood, and Uncle Phil grabbed my shoulders and spun me around so I ended up with my back facing away from the guard. "Lemme have a look at you, boy. You sure did grow up to look like your pa."

He put his skinny arms around me and shook his left arm. I felt his hand slide into Dudley Do-Right's pants and down into my underwear. When he slid it out, he left a cold, soft bulge.

"I'm proud of you, DJ," he said. "I'd be lying if I said I didn't like the way you turned out."

And with that, he walked out of the room.

Chapter 29

I waited several days contemplating what I was about to do and trying to process it all. From my screwed-up childhood, to my career in law enforcement, to my fall from grace, to prison, it was a long road I'd been traveling. Frankly, I had grown weary of it.

I've never been the kind of guy to seriously contemplate suicide. I had given the matter considerable thought when I was holed up with SERT surrounding me, but back then, I just wasn't ready. A lot has changed since then, and I'd already made my decision. Once I was done with McNab, I'd be ready.

I knew I wasn't a monster or some psychiatric anomaly. I was just a guy who had been subjected to more crap than he could deal with. No different than any of the thousands of screwed up combat vets from WW-I through Afghanistan. People can only take so much before they break. There's nothing new in that. If I had a second chance, I could get proper therapy, learn to deal with my shit, and lead a halfway normal life. But in prison, there are no second chances. I can't go back and do the right thing. I could only do the right thing from this point forward.

The laughable thing is, there is no right thing in here. Should I forgive McNab and let him live? To what end? So he can get out in five years and molest another kid?

I'm a broken toy. I've known this for a long time. It's too late for me. Since the moment McNab walked into my unit, I knew I was going to kill him. Killing him would make me feel better. Killing him would avenge his past crimes. Killing him would prevent him from victimizing and fucking up another child.

On the other hand, letting him live would . . .

How very interesting. I couldn't think of a single benefit of letting him live. With regards to McNab, I figured killing him is the only right thing.

Three days after my uncle's last visit, it was time. I reached into my mattress and withdrew the two sealed freezer bags full of gasoline, and the tiny Bic lighter he'd smuggled in to me. Stuffing them down the front of my pants, I set my jaw and headed over to McNab's cell.

As usual, he was lying alone on his bunk. In the month that he'd been here, McNab hadn't made any friends, even among the other chesters. He kept to himself and probably would for his entire stretch. He looked up and nodded when I darkened the doorway to his cell. I think he'd come to look forward to our little sessions, as if he was finding some kind of redemption through confession.

If McNab was looking to pay for his sins, then I was exactly who he wanted to see. Like Walter White, my favorite TV character, I was the one who knocks. Only I didn't knock, I just strode right on in. Upon my entry, McNab sat up on the edge of the bed, and I sat down next to him. There was something I wanted to hear before recogging him to Jesus.

"Where do you want to start today," he asked.

"You mentioned one kid whose sister had died. Tell me about that one."

"He was small and weak, but I could tell he was smart. He'd tried to burn his house down. I think he was around ten or eleven as I recall. This was a long time ago."

"How did you seduce him?"

"As I remember, that boy had issues with love. After his sister had died, he felt nobody loved him. It was easy to step in and offer him love."

"You gave him just what he was looking for, huh?"

"Look, Bad, we've talked enough for you to know it wasn't like that, and that's not what I'm saying. I perverted love in my own self-interest. But, as was normally the case, it wasn't just all one-sided. Though I hurt him, I also helped him with other issues—things like trust and getting over the death of his sister. I like to think I was instrumental in helping him over some real problems in his life in addition to the, you know, molestation."

"Did you penetrate him?"

"No! I told you I only got that far a couple of times. But before you get mad, yes, I, I probably would have, if he hadn't been so . . . bothered by it."

"What did you do with him?"

"I talked him into removing his clothes, and then I . . . we just cuddled. Naked. Both of us were naked. All we did was cuddle."

We—as in both of us did this willingly. I maintained a cool exterior, but in my mind, I was right back there in his office. I could see it all as clear as if it were happening right now through the nine-year-old eyes of my memory: his sagging man boobs with their blotchy, ovular nipples; that pale fishbelly gut; his thin, hairless legs like spindly little sticks; and that tiny penis almost buried in a pad of fat, looking like a button in a red fur coat. The expression on his face was desperate, almost pleading. I squeezed my eyes closed at the memory of him turning me around and trying to force himself between by buttocks.

"And what about the kid, Dr. McNab? What the fuck happened to the kid?"

He looked at me with a shocked expression. I had never once referred to him as anything other than Chester or Karma.

"Why, nothing, I suppose. This only happened that one time. I gave his mother a favorable report for the courts and told her I didn't need to see him anymore, and I never saw him again."

"You filthy little baby fucker, what do you *think* happened to him? Do you think he just walked away from that and forgot about it? You're a fucking psychiatrist. What happens to the kids?"

"Whoa, Bad, cool down. Generally, kids have a tendency to get past traumatic incidents such as this and move on. This boy was very resilient. Yes, there are extreme cases in which some children don't get past it. Depression could set in, or other forms of psychological trauma. Acting out, drugs, even sometimes a tendency to become molesters themselves. But these are relatively rare reactions. This boy was smart, savvy even. I remember him. He knew the score. He knew I could put him away. As I said, he had tried to burn his house down. He knew he was messed up and wouldn't have passed any psychological testing. He really would have gone to juvie and was smart enough to know I saved him from that. Putting up with me was something he was willing to do, but he made me aware that there was only so much he could take, and I respected those boundaries. He was willing to go to the lengths we did to get my favorable report. I'm not trying to lessen the impact, but we both benefitted from it. Believe me, Bad, he partook willingly, so he could get his report. It was a you-scratch-my-back-I'll-scratch-yours kind of thing. And when he let me know what was too much, I stopped. Yes, I admit I have hurt children, but not *this* child. I'd venture to say this particular patient went on to lead a rather productive life. I'd wager that, though his experience was traumatic, it did not have any long-lasting effects on his life."

"You lose the bet, *Doctor*. It had a big effect on his life."

"Why would you say that? How could you *possibly* know that? I treated this boy for months, and I don't think he was adversely affected."

"Shut up, Karma. Just shut the fuck up. You really are a dumbshit, you know that? I know exactly what happened to that little boy, and I'm pretty sure if you use that doctor brain of yours, you can figure out why."

His eyes grew wide. "You . . . you're not . . ."

This was the moment I'd been waiting for. All the events of my life—beginning with Connie's illness and ending with me in my position as boss in this particular unit in this particular prison—had led up to this moment. What went around for Douglas McNab has finally come back around. I would kill him for his sins, and when it was done, I would feel just fine about checking myself out. My heart went black, and my smile became evil.

"Oh, yes I am. Why do you think I call you Karma?"

"Oh, my God . . ." His head dropped to his chest like an old dog's when the vet gives the final injection. "You're him," he said, more to himself than to me. "You're Dean Appleby."

"You're goddamn right I am. And now it's time for you to pay for your sins."

"I'm a sick man, Bad. I've *told* you. I never meant to hurt any one of you. Can't you see that I've been hurt, too? I've lived a *lifetime* of hurt."

"Shut up, and get off that rack," I commanded.

He immediately complied.

"Strip the bed."

The beds here were different than in OSP. Here, they consisted of a metal frame with a wire mesh, upon which lay a flimsy mattress. Perfect for what I had in mind. McNab pulled the sheets off, and I threw them onto the floor for now.

"I remembered each and every one of your names," he whispered. "Because . . . because I've always known one of you would come for me. You, probably. Or Jason Fitzwarren. Maybe even Veronica Taylor. I've *waited* for you. Whatever you're doing now, it's all right. It's ok. I want you to know that, Bad—Dean. I won't fight you, and I won't scream." He began crying, and lowered his voice even more. "Just please, don't make it hurt."

"Shut up."

"If you hadn't come, I would have gotten released, you know, and I would have hurt more children. I, I can't help it."

I pulled the mattress off the wire mesh suspension frame and threw it on the floor. I kicked it beneath the bed. "Lie down on the wire mesh."

Keeping his eyes squeezed shut, McNab complied. A solitary tear tracked down his cheek. He said nothing, but his mouth was moving silently. He might have been praying.

I pulled out the two baggies of gasoline and the lighter, but then, unexpectedly, I paused. His simpering did nothing to soften me. My doubts came from inside me, not from him. I think they were my last shred of humanity. I think Bad wanted to burn him alive, but DJ was having second thoughts. I had thought that DJ was pretty much gone, and there wasn't anything left but Bad, but that wasn't really the case. After all, it was DJ who had ratted out EK to the hacks.

But it was also DJ who had been molested. It was DJ who still felt the rage over the loss of his sister. It was DJ who remembered McNab's pathetic attempts to sodomize him.

And it was Bad who could do something about it.

It was Bad who opened the first bag of gas and poured it over McNab, making sure to thoroughly soak his prison jumpsuit, hair, and face. McNab, his eyes still squeezed shut, jumped and whimpered, "Oh,

God . . . Please, forgive me." Due to the overpowering smell, he had to know what was coming, but still, he didn't resist.

It was Bad who poured the second bag on the mattress beneath him, so the flames would roast him alive like a pig on a spit. It was Bad who used the last of the gasoline to soak the sheets and drape them over McNab's prostrate body.

I wished McNab wasn't being so compliant in his demise. I wished he struggled, or screamed, or fought me. His compliance was unnerving. It magnified the struggle between Bad and DJ. It felt like an epic battle within me.

Finally, despite all of Bad's preparations, it was DJ who prevailed. At the last second, I hauled off and punched McNab in the left temple with every ounce of strength in my buffed out body. He never saw the blow coming, and it knocked him unconscious immediately.

I tried to listen for his breathing, but the sound of violent, rushing water in my head was so loud that it completely eclipsed all other noises.

The overwhelming odor of gasoline had yet to draw anyone to the cell. I stepped away from the bed and glanced into the dayroom. The inmates all knew something was up, and by the unwritten code of jail ethics, they were giving me my space. Nobody was anywhere near this cell.

I was suddenly exhausted. I wanted nothing more than to go to sleep and not wake up. At this moment, I would have traded everything for a month—six months—in the hole, but I wasn't finished yet. I knew I would be put to death for this, but I had already decided I wouldn't wait for the state of Oregon to do it for me. Even on death row, there were ways for a determined inmate to kill himself, and I would find one. But first, I had more work to do here. I turned my attention back to McNab.

He was breathing, but he was out cold.

Despite what he did to me, I couldn't burn him alive. All the planning I'd done, all the risk I'd gone through to have Uncle Phil smuggle in two quarts of gasoline and a lighter. All of it was for naught. DJ was back.

But Bad was here, too. McNab had caused me immeasurable damage, and he was right about me: I am intelligent, and I am strong, yet look how I had turned out. What of his other victims? What of the weak and of the stupid? What of the average? How badly had he ruined them? How badly had they gone on to ruin others? How far would it go? How about the future victims still to come after his release?

I had appointed myself as the doer of justice to Douglas McNab. I had made myself his judge and having heard all the testimony, I had found him guilty. I had already determined his sentence in advance, so now, as his executioner, all that remained was for me to carry it out.

I pulled his feet down, straightening out his legs, and lay down next to him, almost as if we were spooning. This is probably how he'd like to go.

McNab was stirring as my right arm snaked under his fat chin and around his neck. I made a fist and grabbed it with my left hand, laying my head against the back of his, and positioned the crook of my arm over his throat. My bicep was along the right side of his neck and my forearm along the left. Pulling on my fist, I compressed his jugular and carotid arteries as hard as I possibly could, choking off the flow of blood to his brain.

I'd been taught this method of restraint, commonly known as a sleeper hold, in the police academy. I'd used it many times in the field, and it was a favorite of mine. When properly applied, the subject, denied blood to the brain, loses consciousness within seconds. The thing they drummed into us over and over in the Academy was to release the hold the moment the subject went out because if held too long, it would be fatal. For that reason, it was considered deadly force.

McNab was now completely limp, entirely unconscious. Now would be the time to release him. Instead, I squeezed even harder. I counted off the seconds in my mind. After ninety, my arms were so tired it was hard to continue. I kept up the pressure until my arms finally gave out.

Sweating, I rolled off the bed, allowing McNab to roll onto his back. He was dead. His eyes were open, but he didn't look scared. He looked peaceful.

The hard work was already done. Now I would make a statement about McNab and what he had done to me. I grabbed the bic lighter, held it to the corner of the mattress and gave it a flick.

There was a *whump* and a flash, and the entire room exploded into flame. I was instantly engulfed in a conflagration of burning fumes, and turned to run. But instead of running toward the door, I ran into the wall in a panic.

My shirt was ablaze, as was my beard and my hair. I sucked in a lungful of flame and felt as if I was burning from the inside. Wildly, I flailed, but I was overcome with panic and had no idea where the door was. I fell to the ground, entirely aware that I had killed myself in a manner I had deemed too cruel even for McNab. Oh, the irony.

I became aware of yelling and of being dragged out. Hands beat me, and a blanket was tossed over me, extinguishing the fire, but I could still hear the cell next to me burning. It sounded like a flag snapping in the wind. Through it, I heard crackling and sizzling, like eggs frying on a pan.

I knew the latter was the good doctor, and I smiled.

Chapter 30

I'd never felt such pain in my life. My face felt like it was still on fire, and I could see the skin hanging off my right arm like a thin layer of rotted clothing. Much of the arm was charred and black. Oddly, it seemed to be the only part of me that didn't hurt.

I felt like I was out of breath from strenuous exercise, but no matter how much I gasped, I couldn't get enough air into my lungs. Every breath I managed to take caused stabbing pains in my chest and panic set in. I was not getting enough air to sustain myself, and I realized that no matter how bad the burns were, I was actually going to die of suffocation.

I could still see McNab's cell. Corrections officers were standing outside of it, and though I couldn't see the fire, it was still burning furiously. Black smoke was pouring out, and the smell was horrendous. A firefighting team of hacks pushed through the crowd bearing fire extinguishers and a hose. There was a lot of yelling, and it took them several minutes, but they finally got the fire out.

During this time, other hacks hovered over me. Within minutes, the dayroom was clear, and everyone was back in the cells. By the time a paramedic crew came in, I was losing consciousness.

I closed my eyes and heard a voice say, "I'm not sure exactly what happened, but the room he was in just . . . exploded in flames. His arm is the worst, but his face is also burned, and he's been doing that gasping thing since we brought him out."

"He's got a lower airway inhalation burn," a woman's voice said "from inhaling superheated air. Hard to believe, but it's actually much worse than the visible burns. His lungs are damaged. Swollen, maybe even collapsed. We need to intubate him immediately."

I forced my eyes open. A female paramedic hovered directly over my face. "Look," she said as she worked, "I know you're in pain. We're going to have to place an endotracheal tube down your throat. It's going to hurt, and you're going to feel as if you're being choked, but it's the only way to ensure that you'll keep breathing. Do you understand?"

I nodded, my eyes wide with fear. I've seen paramedics intubate people before but never someone conscious. It looked bad enough when they were out.

A male paramedic stabilized my head and held me down, and the female inserted a lighted scope in my mouth. I was fading fast, faster than she could work. I concentrated on the light, but it dimmed as I lost consciousness. Faintly, I was aware of a tube being shoved down my throat and then nothing.

I wasn't out for thirty seconds. Suddenly, there was sufficient air in my lungs, which was the most refreshing feeling I had ever experienced. There wasn't as much as I would have wanted, but it was enough to keep me panting, as if I had just finished a long-distance run.

The other paramedic was wrapping my face and arm with wet gauze, and I felt a needle jab into my right arm. I was then lifted and packed onto a gurney.

I remember how good the fresh air felt on my skin as I was rushed out the main gate to the waiting ambulance. Once inside, I was driven to an open area of the parking lot, slowly and without lights and sirens. Shortly after we stopped, the unmistakable sound of an approaching helicopter grew louder and louder.

As it landed, I was transferred to another gurney and roughly loaded aboard the LifeFlight helicopter. One of the hacks tried to get on, but the crew wouldn't allow it.

"We'll have police waiting at Emanuel," shouted the doctor.

Seconds later, the helicopter spiraled into the sky.

I felt like I was dying. I was still unable to get sufficient air, but I was no longer in danger of suffocating. The medical crew kept bathing my arm and monitoring me, but there was little else they could do.

We were going to the Oregon Burn Unit at Emanuel Hospital in northeast Portland. I knew the hospital well; it had been on my beat for over a year when I worked north precinct. I'd been to the ER with various suspects and victims more times than I could count. The flight seemed to take forever, but soon, we were landing.

Rolling from the helipad into the ER, I noted two Portland police officers and three security guards flanking me, staying well out of the way of the medical team. The cops were both young, and I didn't know either of them.

I was rushed directly into a surgical prep room where a flock of medical staff swarmed me like a NASCAR pit crew. Twenty minutes after the helicopter touched down, they finished whatever they were doing, and I was wheeled into the OR.

I slowly awoke in a private room. I wasn't cuffed to the bed, but I was no less shackled to it than if I had been. A plastic tube ran from a ventilator into my mouth and down my throat, I was catheterized, I had IVs going into both hands, and I was connected to various monitors by at least ten wire leads. My right arm was swathed in thick bandages, but my face seemed to be uncovered.

A female physician, maybe fifty years old, stood over me, as did two nurses and a state corrections officer in green with a paper mask over his face.

"Mr. Appleby," said the doctor. "You're out of surgery. Can you understand me?"

I nodded, and she continued: "Ok, here's a rundown on your condition. You've suffered a lower airway burn, which is the most concerning to us of your various injuries. You inhaled a lot of direct heat and smoke, which has caused considerable damage to your pulmonary system. The alveoli, the air sacs, in both of your lungs have been seriously impaired. Your left lung has suffered the worst damage and is about sixty percent collapsed—the right lung, maybe thirty percent. Currently, we have you breathing through a ventilator, which is keeping your lungs under constant positive pressure with humidified oxygen to prevent the further collapse of the air sacs and to try to reinflate the lungs.

"As to the rest of your injuries, you have significant third degree burns on your left arm, side, and chest, and you have moderate-to-serious second degree burns on your left hand, neck, and face. These were caused by your clothes burning, fueled by an accelerant, which, I'm told, you used to kill another inmate. I suspect there was some accidental transfer of this accelerant to your clothing, which you were unaware of."

I closed my eyes. I lose track of the bigger picture when under stress; I always have. It was no different than when I locked all the hostages in a room with cell phones at Killer Burger. I had soaked McNab with gas, but then, out of mercy, I had laid down next to him and killed him with the sleeper hold, and in so doing, I had soaked myself in all that gas without even thinking about it. Then I flicked the bic. I couldn't believe I had been so stupid.

The doctor continued, "I expect those burns to heal relatively well. You will have significant scarring, though, particularly on the arm and torso. We may end up needing grafts from your buttocks or legs to help cover the arm. We'll see how the burns heal before making that determination.

"The rest of the burns can be treated mostly by exposure therapy. They will eventually crust over with eschar, which is overlying dead skin. As they dry in the open air, we will apply saline to help the eschar slough off naturally, allowing the skin beneath it to redevelop. You won't have to worry about bulky facial dressings, but the pain will be somewhat worse as it heals than on your arm. The pain can be self-managed with a morphine drip which you will control, with certain limitations, of course.

"Of all your external injuries, the arm and torso are the most severe. Because these injuries are more susceptible to infection, we're going to have to use occlusive bandaging to treat them. We use an antibacterial cream under the dressing, which you'll probably find very soothing. However, because of the heat your body generates at the wound site, bacteria still grows rampant even with the cream, so the dressings will need to be changed frequently. You may not feel an excessive amount of pain associated with the arm and torso burns at the moment, which is due to the fact that the burn was intense enough to actually destroy the nerve endings, but as they heal, you will. Unfortunately, the changing of the dressings can be quite painful. I'm sorry about that, but just as with your other injuries, the pain can be self-managed with the morphine drip. Do you have any questions?"

I shook my head.

"I have one," said the corrections officer. "How long until he can be transferred to the prison infirmary? Because we're gonna have to keep a guy here around the clock as long as he's here."

"I'm sorry about that," said the doctor. "But my main concern is the patient's health. With these types of injuries, I'd say you're looking at several weeks. It could be longer, depending on the actual intensity of the pulmonary damage."

"Wonderful. How long until he's up and mobile?"

"On his own? Weeks. Months, maybe. But eventually, in maybe two weeks, we'll start taking him every day to an immersion tank. The solution will help keep the wounds clean and stave off bacterial infection and ultimately aid in the removal of dead tissue. You'll be able to accompany him on these trips, of course. It's not far."

"Well, I'm glad to hear you say that because we're not about to let him out of our sight."

"Yes. Well, at any rate, you can expect to be here for a while."

After the doctor left, the correctional officer stood over my bed and said, "Gee-zooey, you sure did a number on yourself, didn't you? I don't know exactly what you used, but it smelled just like gasoline. Whatever it was, you sure as hell made Douglas McNab a crispy critter. Looks like you didn't get the hell outta Dodge fast enough, though. You know, this reminds me of this video I saw a long time ago where these Arab kids were all riled up, throwing stones and bottles and such at soldiers, yelling shit about Allah and all that. Well, this one kid lights a molotov cocktail, then hauls back to throw it, and when he launches it forward, the burning gas sloshes out and spreads all over his arm. I gotta say, it was pretty damn funny watching him running around like a chicken with his head cut off, only on fire, too. Uh, you know, not that I'm making fun of you or anything.

"Anyway, you probably already know this, but killing an incarcerated person can be a capital crime. It's your *second* capital crime. This won't be of any surprise, but when you finally get out of here, you're going directly into Ad Seg, and I suspect from there, your next stop will be death row. Isn't that something? You escape the needle for killing a cop, but you get the big jab for killing a con. Actually, that really pisses me off. Should be the other way around, you know? Anyway, it's all kind of ironic, isn't it? I mean, you're gonna spend weeks in here at the taxpayers' expense just to get well enough to be executed. I sure hope that miserable blob of shit McNab was worth it."

I tried saying something around the tube in my throat: "Eee ulested eee."

"What? Can't understand you, man. You wanna write it down?"

I nodded, and he gave me his notebook and pen. With my good hand I wrote, "He molested me when I was a child."

The hack looked at it, and his eyes got wide. "No shit? Damn, Bad, now I wish you hadn't got burned. Jesus Christ."

I smiled. It felt good to let someone know.

"Where'd you get the gas from? I know your EK buddies didn't help you. Hell, they'da used it to light *you* on fire! Yeah, I know you dimed EK off to us 'bout a hit on one of our guys. I gotta say, that goes a long way with us. We don't forget about that kind of thing. I think instead of calling you Bad, we ought to start calling you Good."

This was the most talkative hack I had ever met. I had tubes running down my throat, and I was on a bunch of medications, and to say I was in a tad bit of pain would be a slight understatement. The last thing I wanted was to listen to an extended one-way conversation with this guy, but I was what you'd call a captive audience. My whole upper body flared like someone had a blowtorch on it, and I pressed the button for the morphine drip.

The hack wouldn't shut up. He went on talking, telling prison stories, and never seemed to mind that I couldn't answer back, but I toned him out and tried to go to sleep. He was droning on about how a con once stabbed a child molester one hundred and thirty-two times before anyone could stop him when I drifted off to sleep.

The doctor was right. At first, the only real pain I had was from my neck and face and also my hand. The arm, side, and chest weren't that bad. After several days though, that pain started lighting up like a shuttle launch. The pain during the changing of the dressings on my arm every eight to ten hours was probably the worst I'd ever endured.

Despite these levels of pain, I began to ration the amount of morphine I'd give myself, waiting until I literally couldn't take it any more before hitting the button. I'd seen too many guys get strung out on heroin and other opiates, and I didn't want to add withdrawals to my list of ailments when I finally got out of here. I'd power through the bandage changes until it was just too much, and then I'd take only enough to take the edge off. The nurses even commented on how little I was using.

The hacks worked in ten-hour shifts. They set up a table and chair next to an outlet outside my door. Most were guys I didn't know, though every couple days the talkative guy, whose name I learned was Hank Lindano, showed up, mostly on the night shift. Everyone else kept to themselves, but Hank would always come into the room to see if I was awake at the beginning of his shift. If so, he would start his one-way conversation, which would last until I either fell asleep or pretended to. After a while, I learned to pretend to be sleeping at shift change just to shut him the hell up.

Chapter 31

I'd been in the burn unit for two weeks, and the doctors said I was doing very well. I was off the ventilator, and the burns were starting to show signs of healing. They began to talk of transferring me out of the burn unit and into a regular hospital room, possibly in Salem, in a week or two if things kept going well. But as long as I needed saline baths, I had to stay here. The saline baths were actually very comfortable and soothing, though afterwards, the scrubbing of the dead skin was excruciating.

On my eighteenth day, I was told that tomorrow, I would be transferred out of the burn unit to a regular hospital room. I would spend perhaps three or four days there, and by then, I would be well enough to go to the infirmary at the Oregon State Penitentiary.

Sometime in the middle of that last night, I was awakened by the sound of voices just outside my room, which quickly grew heated. The talkative hack, Lindano, was on duty at the desk just to the right of my room door, which was the last room at the end of a dead-end hallway. I didn't know what time it was, but I knew it was late. Middle of the night late.

I heard a man snarl and curse, followed immediately by the sounds of a scuffle. There was a lot of yelling, and finally, a sharp crash. I was too befuddled to figure out what was going on, but it clearly wasn't good. I sat up in the bed, tense and alert. Then, just outside the door, there was the unmistakable crack of a gunshot.

I half rolled, half fell off the bed, the IV ripping painfully out of my hand and the leads flying off my body. I hit the floor with both hands, sending white flames of pain through my arm and chest. Before I could make it under the bed, there was a second gunshot, and then the sound of someone running away. Now there was screaming up and down the hall, in addition to a man's voice moaning.

Ten seconds after the first gunshot, I peeked around the corner. Lindano lay on the floor in a growing pool of his own blood, bleeding profusely from what looked like stab wounds to the neck and forearms. I recognized the cuts on his arms as defensive wounds.

A man lay facedown next to him, a large, sharp hunting knife still in his hand. The facedown man had long hair and was wearing shorts. On his calf was a tattoo of a shield with the letters EK inside, just like mine.

Lindano's Glock lay on the floor between them.

Lindano wasn't going to make it; I could see that right off. The neck wound was pumping out a thick, ever-weakening jet of bright red blood. Arterial spurting. He didn't have a minute left.

I took his face in my hands: "Lindano," I croaked. "Thanks, man. You killed him. He was EK, coming for me. Because of what I did for you guys. But you saved me."

His pleading eyes locked onto mine, but the light in them was already fading. I wished I could remember his first name, but I couldn't.

"Lindano, I . . . I want you to know that I listened to every word you said. Thanks for talking to me, man. You're gonna be ok, you know? The doctors are almost here."

The blood stopped spurting, and the light went out.

I looked up, and though I could hear screaming, I couldn't see anyone. "Nurse!" I yelled. "Help this guy!"

I looked back at my room. I needed what was in there. I needed the treatment the hospital afforded me and the sterility of this environment. I was still subject to infection, which is the leading cause of fatality among serious burn survivors.

I looked down the hallway. There was screaming, but as of yet, nobody had come out to investigate. With all the recent active shooter incidents over the past few years, people had been conditioned to shelter in place in such situations, but it wouldn't last long. The police were no doubt already en-route. Somewhere down there was an exit, and beyond it, freedom.

I've been a con for over three years, but I'd been a police officer for eighteen years before that and a law-abiding citizen for my entire life, up until my addiction changed all that. Prison conditions you to obey the rules. What time you eat, what time you sleep, what you do, where you go—everything goes by the rules. With all that behind me, I am a man whose first instinct is to follow the rules. My thought process was that I'm a prisoner; I'm not *allowed* to leave. I have to go back and wait for the police.

I wasted a good couple seconds just shaking my head at the notion. I was going to be put to death, and in the intervening years before that happened, I would go insane while housed on death row, the most isolated place in our society today: not for days, not for weeks, not even months, but years, a decade or more, until they killed me. I had already planned my death row suicide for God's sake (a twisted sheet around my neck, somehow secured to the bed or sink, and a backflip would probably do it), yet I was actually considering staying?

I picked up the Glock and turned to leave. Before I did, I grabbed the knife off Lindano's belt and took his spare mags, cuffs and radio. I stuffed them into the backpack he'd brought, but I kept his gun in my hand and started down the hallway. Ten feet away, a blood trail began. There had been two EK guys and two gunshots. Apparently, Lindano had hit both of them.

I came to a T-intersection. The blood trail went to the left, so I went to the right. After only a moment, I heard someone yell "Hey—" from somewhere far behind me. This was immediately followed by the sound of another gunshot. Two more in rapid succession followed. As the third shot faded, the hospital fell silent. Even the screaming from the rooms had been silenced.

I found what looked like a service elevator and pressed the button. As I waited for it to come up, I heard another muffled gunshot from somewhere far behind me. The elevator door opened, and I hit the button for the basement.

When I came out, a strobe was flashing, and a metallic voice was chanting "Code Silver, Burn Center. Code Silver, Main Entry. Code Silver, Burn Center. Code Silver, Main Entry."

I could go right or left. I chose right. I passed the laundry and several large wheeled baskets containing dirty gowns, sheets, and scrubs. I fished out a long sleeve green scrub top and bottom, and I found some slippers with rubberized soles. I completed my ensemble with a hair cap and green surgical mask.

I continued down the hall and eventually found my way to the loading dock, and then I was outside.

Sirens filled the warm night air. I walked out into a parking lot where I came upon a female employee getting out of her car after a smoke break. Entirely unaware of the trouble, she waved as I walked toward her.

"I wonder what's going on with all the sirens," she said, probably thinking we were going to share a smoke.

"I think they're about me," I answered, producing the pistol from under my scrub top. "I'm sorry, but I'm going to need your car and your purse."

Her eyes grew wide, but she was smart enough to hold her purse out to me.

"Get your keys out first," I said. "And there better not be anything but keys in your hand when it comes out of there."

She handed me her keys and purse. "Please, don't kill me," she said.

"What's your name?" I asked.

"Kim."

"Look, Kim. I'm not really a bad guy, ok? I don't want to hurt you. I just want to get the hell away from here. I need your car. I'm sorry, but I need a little time, too, so I'm going to handcuff you to that fence."

I led her to a chain-link fence twenty yards away. Kim was entirely cooperative as I handcuffed her wrist to the fence.

"You're the guy from the burn center, aren't you? The prisoner?"

"I was," I said. I smiled at her, and though she was crying, she smiled back. I got into her Hyundai Accent and drove away.

I was on the back side of the hospital, the west side, which was as far away from the police response as I could be. By this time, though, I was getting lightheaded. I slowed to a normal speed, trying desperately not to draw attention to myself. The place had to be crawling with cops, but so far, I hadn't seen any.

I knew a back way out, which would be the least likely place for me to encounter the police. I headed down Russell intending to go south on N. Interstate and eventually take I-84 out to Gresham, where I hoped to somehow find my uncle Phil's house. I figured if I took the more direct route down N. Vancouver toward I-5, I wouldn't make it a half-mile before running into the police.

As I approached the light at Russell and N. Interstate, vertigo overtook me, and I momentarily blacked out. When I was able to focus, I saw I was about to hit the back of a car stopped at the light. I swerved to the right, but I caught the right rear corner of the car with my left front end in a glancing blow, pushing the car into the intersection and sending me onto the sidewalk at the northeast corner.

Recovering quickly, I drove off the sidewalk and sped up, now heading north. A glance into the rearview mirror showed the other driver, a man, getting out of his car and flipping me off. I was now headed in the opposite direction from where I wanted to go, directly toward the most likely police response.

I immediately realized that the man I'd hit would be able to say I went north, and the woman I'd left chained to the fence would give them the plate and vehicle description. I had to lose the car, and fast.

The first thing I had to do was get off N. Interstate Avenue. As soon as I was out of sight of the guy I'd hit, I took the first right, which put me on N. Graham. Unfortunately, I was now heading directly back to the hospital, toward N. Kirby Avenue, which circles the hospital on the west side. I took Kirby heading north, passing the emergency department and ambulance entry and began heading to one of the several parking structures on the other side of the hospital. The problem was that's where the police were all headed.

As I drove around the north end of the campus, I passed a southbound police car, which was rolling code three. I almost floored it, but the officer wasn't even looking in my direction, and we passed without incident. Ahead, toward the front of the hospital, I saw at least ten police cars swarmed about, all with lights flashing. Sirens still pierced the air.

Finally, I pulled into the relative safety of the first of three parking structures and found a tight spot between two parked cars. I nosed in, hiding the crunched-up front end. I lay down across the front seat and started rummaging through the woman's purse until I found her cell phone.

Thankfully, I knew Uncle Phil's phone number by heart and dialed it with shaking fingers. But just before I hit send, I realized what I was doing. Not only would a check of her cell phone records show who I called, but she, or the police, could find her phone with just a few clicks of any computer in the world.

Reluctantly, I powered the phone down and did my best to destroy it by puncturing it with her house key.

Looking around, the parking structure surrounding me appeared to be entirely devoid of people. Cautiously, I got out and headed over to the side facing the hospital. Officers who had been inside were now stepping outside the main entrance.

More police cars, ambulances, and firetrucks began pulling up to the scene. A dozen police officers formed a protective cordon for firemen, who pulled a gurney out of the ambulance and went into the main entrance. A moment later, they brought out what had to be the second EK guy and loaded him into the ambulance. It was impossible to tell if he was alive or dead. I hoped he was dead.

By now, officers were leading employees and ambulatory patients outside. They were directed toward the parking lots and structures, where they began milling about. As I watched, the first SERT units arrived. They would be used to search the buildings—looking for me. It would take every team in the tri-county area to effectively clear the hospital. Ten minutes after the arrival of SERT, the CNT Sprinter showed up as well.

I just shook my head. It was all too surreal to comprehend.

The earliest dayshift employees were also beginning to arrive for work, unaware that anything was going on. Officers were keeping them in the parking lots and structures as well. Pretty soon, cars began filling up the parking structure and curious employees gathered in clusters, trying to figure out what was happening.

I approached one such group, counting on the fact that in a place the size of Emanuel Hospital, not everyone could be expected to know everyone else. I was counting on the scrubs to not only conceal my burns and bandages, but to fool them into thinking I was an employee.

"I heard there was a shooting," a young woman said to another.

"Raphael said there were like ten people killed in the Burn Center."

"I heard the guy was still in there and took a bunch of hostages," someone else said.

I approached the group and said, "Hey, can I borrow someone's phone? They made me leave, and I didn't have a chance to grab mine. I need to tell my wife I'm ok."

"Sure, but what happened?" a custodian said, handing me a cheap TracFone.

"I don't know. I didn't hear a thing, and then the alarms went off. Everyone started running around screaming. Security came through and told us all to leave. I thought there was a fire, but I've talked to other people that said there had been a shooting."

That got them all talking. I took the phone and dialed Uncle Phil's number, praying that he would answer. The clock on the phone read 5:52 AM.

"Who the hell is calling me so damned early!" answered Phil, clearly pissed that someone had woken him up.

"Uncle Phil, it's me, DJ! Listen carefully! I'm in Portland, at Emanuel Hospital. I've escaped, and I need you to come pick me up!"

"Well damn, boy! How the hell did you manage that? I read that you blew your damn self up killin' that chester, and got burnt pret' near to death."

"That's true. I've been here in the burn center for the past three weeks. I'll tell you all about it later, but right now I really need your help. Now shut up and listen carefully. I'm in parking garage one, on the second level, in a black Hyundai Accent, parked nose-in facing the hospital. Cops are everywhere, and they know what kind of car to look for. Just get here as soon as you can."

"What do you need for your burns?" he asked, all business now.

"I don't know. They have my left arm wrapped in bandages, which they change twice a day. And some kind of antibacterial burn cream. I think other than that, they just monitor my lung functions and stuff like that."

"Ok. Don't go anywhere. I'll be there as soon as I can," he said.

"I won't have a phone, so don't try calling back. I borrowed this from somebody who works here. They think I'm an employee. I'll be in the car. Hurry!"

"Black Hyundai, parking garage one, second floor, got it. Don't do anything else, kid, just stay out of sight in that car. I'm proud as hell of you."

Uncle Phil. He had an excitement in his voice I'd never heard before. I think he lived for this kind of thing. We hung up, and I erased the call before giving the phone back. The little group of people wanted to talk, but I said I was tired after the night shift, and since I couldn't go back in, I was going to catch a nap in the car.

By this time, the pain in my arm was worse than it had been for a while, and the bandages needed to be changed. By now, my face wasn't much worse than a severe sunburn, but the arm was still wet and hot, a definite infection risk. Given the pain level from all the exertion, I could use a morphine dump, but I didn't have access to so much as an aspirin.

I got back in the car and leaned the front seat back. I was sound asleep when a sharp rap at the window jolted me awake. The dashboard clock read 8:55 AM.

It was Uncle Phil.

"Get back here," he said, gesturing toward his pickup and camper, which was idling behind the stolen Hyundai. He opened the door to the camper, and I piled in. He ran around to the front, and then we were moving.

Looking around, I could see that Phil had been to the grocery store. I counted five large jars of TriDERMA burn cream, bandages of all sizes, and lots of boxed food. I crawled into the camper's small bed and let the motion of the truck lure me into semi-consciousness. My arm haunted my every attempt to sleep since the escape, and the pain was so bad I'd have taken a hit of heroin if I had some.

Uncle Phil could tell I was in distress. "Here, take these," he said, handing me two white pills and an open beer.

Grateful, I swallowed them without question. Whatever they were, they made the pain and the world fade to almost nothing, and put me out within minutes. When I awoke, we were parked, and Uncle Phil was seated at the tiny dinette. It was already the next morning. Whatever he had given me had worked like a charm. I'd slept the entire day and the following night.

"God damn, boy, you escaped from prison!" he exclaimed when he saw that I was awake. "That's a damn sight more'n I ever did. I recon you're the newest, baddest black sheep this family ever seen now."

I smiled. "Hardly the great escape, Uncle Phil. All I did was screw up, get myself burned, and then walk out of the hospital."

"It's the biggest thing on the news, all anyone can talk about. The news is reportin' you were sent to the hospital in critical condition after you burned another prisoner to death and accidentally torched yourself in the process. They said the cops think some of your prison gang buddies came to spring you, but the hack guarding you got two of them, and the rest ran away. How much of that did they get right?"

"Not much. First of all, I couldn't bring myself to burn the good doctor alive, so I choked him to death first. But like a dumbshit, I choked him out after I soaked him in the gas, getting it all over my own clothes and hair. When I lit him up, I just exploded in flames. And as for my European Kindred buddies, they weren't coming to rescue me, they were coming to kill me 'cause I dropped a dime on their plan to kill a hack. The guy guarding me saved my life. They damn near cut his head off, but he got off a shot that killed one outright. I think he may have wounded the other one. There was more shooting, and I really don't know what happened."

"Well, no matter what, you're the subject of the biggest manhunt since . . . well shit, since the last time they were looking for you! Hoo-wee, you are one badass ex-cop convict, boy!"

I couldn't contain a smile. Uncle Phil was really impressed. "Where are we, anyway?" I asked him.

"Long term parking lot at the airport. The farthest end of the farthest lot. This camper can stay here for months without being found."

"Are they looking for it?"

"I don't know. But they'll sure as hell be watching me. And that daughter of yours, and your folks, too. Stay the hell away from everybody."

"I figured that. I'm really sorry to put you through all this, Uncle Phil."

"Don't mention it. You got no idea how boring my shitty old life has been these past couple of years since Blaire died. You comin' back into my life made me realize I ain't all alone. Hell, I can't blame your old man for disowning me. Apart from him, I ain't had no real kinfolk left. 'Til you come along, that is. Kinfolk means a lot."

"Well, I'm kinda in the same boat now. My daughter hasn't talked to me since I got arrested, and I have no contact with my folks any more. Like you said, I can't really blame them."

"You and me, we're a lot alike, least we are now, anyway. I figure you're about the only family I got now and likewise for you, too. 'Cept your daughter's still young, and maybe the book ain't closed on that one yet. So, how's the arm doin?"

"Arm's killing me. I gotta change my bandage."

"I got that. I was a medic in 'Nam, you know. I changed a burn dressing or two in my day." And with that, Uncle Phil proceeded to do an excellent job changing my bandages. He didn't have any more of whatever it was he gave me that first day, but I dosed up on the extra-strength Tylenol he'd brought, and I took the pain just like he'd taught me to in high school.

Chapter 32

Uncle Phil bought two cheap cell phones, the type without a plan where you pay for minutes ahead of time. We spoke daily, and he came to visit me a couple times a week. He said the police had been watching his house off and on, so he always took great pains to ensure he wasn't being followed whenever he came to see me.

I was healing well. There had been no sign of infection, but I was taking the antibiotics Uncle Phil provided anyway, just in case. My face and chest had faded to a darker shade of red, and my arm was healing nicely.

Uncle Phil kept me in food, water, and medical supplies, showing up every few days with a care package and some much-needed company. Five days into my stay in the camper at the airport, he showed up one day grinning from ear to ear.

"Boy," he said, "I may be a old fart, but I still got a trick or two up my sleeve. I pulled a good one for you yesterday."

"Jesus, Uncle Phil, you've already done so much for me; I have no idea how to thank you."

"Ain't a damn thing, sonny. I gotta be truthful. I've been having the time of my life 'cause of you."

"So what'd you do?"

He winked at me. "I put the cops hot on your trail. 'Ceptin', mebbe they're heading in the wrong direction now."

"How?"

"Yesterday, I took a cab back up to the hospital where you parked that car you swiped, and guess what? Sure as shit, it was still parked right there where you left it, right along with the owner's purse stuffed down under the front seat. So, I took the purse down to Eugene and dumped it by the college down there."

"You're shitting me, so now they're looking for me in Eugene?"

"Yep. I figure that ought to keep 'em busy for a while."

I was incredulous. "You really think it'll work?"

"News this morning said the cops found evidence that tells 'em you're heading to California, maybe even makin' a run for the border."

I laughed. "Jesus, Uncle Phil, I don't know what to say. I'm sure glad you didn't get caught."

"Campus cop caught me walkin' around just after I dumped the purse," he said. "I told him I was walking my little dog Princess, and she got away from me. Pretended not to know where I parked my car. He actually drove me around looking for the dog, then found my car for me. Hell, they're still lookin' for a little Chihuahua with a pink rhinestone-studded collar down there. Stupid ass cops," he said. "I love fuckin' with 'em. No offense to anyone present who mighta used to be one, o'course."

Even though I'd spent time in protective custody and should be used to confinement, by the third week, I was fighting the urge to get out and take a walk every now and then. I didn't because I knew my freedom depended on strict discipline, but it was hard. The only time I ever got out was to drag the black water drain hose to the ditch behind the camper to dump the tanks every few days, only in the middle of the night.

My phone had the ability to get on the internet, which I used mostly to keep up with the story of my escape. I read that the correctional officer had died at the scene, but before succumbing to his injuries, he had managed to kill one of his assailants outright. I already knew that after witnessing the aftermath firsthand. The officer had also shot and superficially wounded the other assailant. That guy had made his way toward the front entrance of the hospital, where he was confronted by an unarmed security guard, whom he shot and killed. He never made it outside though because the police had already arrived, and an active shooter team confronted him just inside the doors. Some shots were exchanged, and he was gravely wounded. They said he would never walk again.

Both were EK, and the fact that they were there to kill me rather than spring me had never made it into the news. I was said to be armed with the correctional officer's gun and extremely dangerous. There was evidence I was headed south and might be seeking refuge with white power groups anywhere from southern Oregon to Mexico.

Uncle Phil and I talked extensively about when would be the best time for me to go. Finally, when the burn on my arm had healed over to the point where it no longer needed regular dressing changes and the danger of infection was greatly reduced, we agreed the time had come. It was just over three weeks since my escape from the hospital. The cops were looking down south, and the heat around here had died down tremendously.

On the day we agreed I would leave, Uncle Phil showed up bearing a heavy hiking pack and bedroll.

We went over the plan one final time. He produced a binder containing several maps printed from the Internet, along with bus and train schedules in major cities in Canada, from Vancouver to Toronto.

"This here's got your maps and public transit schedules and such. Now let's go over this one more time. I'll take you up here," he said, pointing to a map of northern Washington State. "Northport Washington. I figure I can prob'ly get you to maybe within a mile or so of the border. I'll drop you off, and you're gonna have to make your way across and on up to the town of Rossland. Ain't but fifteen miles or so."

"I'll bet I can make it in one night without even seeing a car. I'll stay along the side of the road so that I can just disappear into the woods if one comes by."

"Right. From Rossland, you got two more towns within an easy walk. Warfield and Trail. I'm hopin' you'll be able to buy a car somewhere's along the line. Pay cash. Make sure the tags're good, no questions asked. If you get one or two raised eyebrows, just forget the deal, and move on. You got a long ass haul to Calgary, near about four hundred miles, so you're gonna need to pick up wheels somewhere's along the way."

"Right. I'll find a car."

"You know how to get one in a pinch if you need to," he reminded me.

"I know." Uncle Phil had given me a crash course on auto theft, using his own truck as an example.

"Them big cities up there, they know how to take care of their homeless folk. They feed em, clothe 'em, and shelter 'em. They give 'em all the medical attention they need, too. You'll do ok up there 'til you land on your feet."

"Yeah."

"In any case, the weather's gonna turn real soon. It's already gettin' cold at night. So's I brung you some stuff you might find useful."

"Uncle Phil, you've already gone to way too much trouble and risk for me," I said, meaning every word. "Everything you're doing puts you at risk of going back to the joint. That's the last thing you need, especially given your age and health. Being a criminal is a young man's game."

"I think you're gonna find out, boy, it's a lifelong career."

"Still, Uncle Phil, you don't need to do anything else for me. Seriously, I can't tell you how much I appreciate everything you've done so far. You've literally given me my life back. If you could just get me out of town and spare a few bucks, I think I could make it from there."

"Let me tell you something, sonny," he said. "I wasn't kiddin' you when I said I ain't got nobody else. You remember when you called me when you was a young'n, askin' for advice on how to fight?"

"Sure I do. I've used that advice ever since, especially when I was on the inside."

"Well, that was the first time in years that anybody ever made me feel useful. Your daddy and the whole family writ me off a long time before that. When you called, it weren't nobody but Blaire and me. And after she passed, I been alone and depressed and good for nothing. But then I get a call out of the blue from you in the can askin' for my help. And these past months has made me feel like I got kin folk that ain't ashamed of me and even need me. You ain't got a idea what that done for me, boy."

"I'm glad to hear it, Uncle Phil. To tell you the truth, I've felt a lot like you, ever since the day I got busted. Even before that, I never really had anyone. My marriage sucked, and then my daughter disowned me. As a cop, I never had any close friends, even among other cops."

"You always been a bit of a loner."

"Yeah, I guess I have been, ever since my sister died. I can make friends, but it's not like, I don't know, like they're *real*, if you know what I mean."

"I know exactly what you mean. Me, I always been the same way. The black sheep. As good as your pa was, I was just the opposite. He was outgoing and friendly and the straightest dude I know. Still is. Way I see it, when you were born, you took after him, but then you just kinda got messed up somewhere along the way. It weren't your fault. Seems like the older you get, the more you started taking after me than him. And look at you now. Hell, boy, in just the past couple months, you made me feel like you was more my son than my nephew."

"I don't know what to say."

"I'm gonna tell you somethin', and I don't want to hear no bitchin' about it. Don't say nothing; just hear me out." I nodded, and he continued, "I done some wheelin' and dealin' in my days, and I made a penny or two. Back when meth was first startin' to hit the big time. Blaire, she was good at handlin' money, and she made some halfway decent moves with it. I ain't got nothing else to do with it, so I figured I'd help you along a bit."

"Uncle Phil, I—"

"Didn't I say shut up and listen? Well, I was gonna leave it to your daddy, but he don't need it, and you do. Problem is, I can't just will it to you. What are you gonna do when I croak? Turn yourself in to get it? So, what I'm sayin' is, I got a little something for you now."

He hefted the hiking pack up onto the tiny table where it landed with a thunk. "Open it up."

I did, expecting clothes and freeze-dried foods, which were among its contents, but mostly, it was filled with cash. Lots of it. I looked through it, my eyes growing ever wider. Most was Canadian, but some was U.S. It was all in twenties.

"There're some bundles of fifties in there, toward the bottom. You ain't gonna need those for a while. I figure you can pretty much live off the grid—"

"Uncle Phil, I can't take this!" I protested. "There must be . . ."

"Thirty thousand in there, and you will take it. The rest I'll send UPS when you land somewhere."

I looked at him with my mouth hanging open.

"Wipe that stupid look off your face, boy. I ain't got no need for it. I got my little house, my truck, and pret' near everything I need, which ain't what you'd call a damn sight. Just shut up, and take it. You want to say something, a simple thank you ought to do it."

"Uh, thank you."

Three nights later, we pulled off a dark road into a firebreak between Northport Washington and the Canadian border. It was 2:30 in the morning.

"Well, we're no more'n a half-mile from the border," my uncle said. "I figure this is as good a place as any. There ain't been another car for the past two hours, so you should be able to stay pretty much on the road. Any cars come your way, you'll see them long before they see you. Just melt into them woods, and you won't have nothin' to worry about."

We said our goodbyes, with promises to keep in occasional touch via our cell phones, if for no other reason than he could send me the rest of my "inheritance." Uncle Phil was truly a remarkable man.

Ten minutes later the border came into view. The area was brightly lit and there was a small brick-and-stone customs station on the west side of the road. The whole thing was very rustic looking. I couldn't tell if the crossing was manned or not, and didn't want to take any chances, so I chose a good place to enter the woods well before I got to the building. It didn't take me long to bypass it, and I made sure to keep to the woods for close to a mile before getting back onto the empty pavement.

Just like that, the crossing was done. I was in Canada. There was no fanfare to mark the end of one chapter of my life and beginning of the next, and that's exactly how I wanted it.

Epilogue

Thirteen Months Later, July, 2018

I've been in Saskatoon, Saskatchewan for just over a year. Thanks to Uncle Phil's money, I am able to live well. I'm even semi-legitimate now. I have a new, albeit fake, Canadian ID and two bank accounts, each containing ten thousand dollars. In a storage unit—which I have under a different name two kilometers from my apartment—there are two suitcases: one contains another fifty thousand dollars Canadian, and the other, fifty thousand U.S., all courtesy of my eccentric, but generous, Uncle Phil.

My new name is Julius McNab. The way I figure it, many killers like to take some kind of a trophy from their victims. I didn't, so I took their names. Julie wasn't really a victim in the classic sense, so perhaps my first name is more of a homage to her than a trophy. The truth is, I actually hope she turned out well.

I like this place. Saskatoon is a city of just about three hundred thousand, a little smaller than Portland, so it's pretty comfortable for me. It's clean and bright, and I live a very nondescript life in a nice apartment on the north side of town. I've taken to the outdoors: camping, hiking, and bicycling in the summer months. This area gets frequent summer thunderstorms, which I've learned to love, but the summers are short-lived here. Due to the harsh, freezing winters, I vegetate indoors: watching movies, doing puzzles, and trying to find various other ways to occupy myself when the cold weather sets in.

The truth is, it can get pretty lonely up here. Sometimes, especially during the winter, being "free" (being on the run is never free, but compared to prison, the word fits) isn't much better than being locked up. I can do what I want, but there's nothing to do and nobody to do it with.

It would help if I had a woman in my life, but any such relationship is out of the question. It would raise too many unanswerable questions, and frankly, as much as I like taking risks, I don't want to risk going back to prison for a woman. What I really miss, and what actually *is* worth the risk though, is my daughter. I've missed my relationship with her more than anything, and ever since my escape, I've flirted more than once with the idea of contacting her.

I doubt they've been wasting the time, effort, or expense to keep her phones bugged and her place under surveillance this entire past year. There's always the risk, of course, that she might turn me in. But I am a man who has been known to take risks, and as a professional risk-taker, I deem the odds to be entirely in my favor and totally worth it.

I keep asking myself, what if she does turn me in? It would mean going back to prison, facing the death penalty, and reliving all of those nightmares all over again. But the other thing I keep asking myself is, what if she doesn't? I am her father, and we both loved each other very much before Killer Burger. Had that really changed? What if she, too, longs for contact from her daddy?

So, I took a gamble. Two days ago, I drove all day to Canmore, a small village an hour east of Calgary and paid in advance for a week at a nice, secluded hunting lodge a couple miles out of town. It's spartan, but it is the perfect place for a reunion.

I spoke to Grace about four hours ago. I drove into Calgary to make the call, just in case. I was somewhat shocked, and greatly relieved, that she even spoke to me. She was angry and bitter, but in no time, the little girl in her who still loves her daddy came out, and we both had a good cry together. After almost an hour of conversation, Grace agreed to come see me.

Prior to the call, I had taken the liberty of researching travel options for her to get up here from Portland. I couldn't pay for it in advance since that required leaving a paper trail, but I did offer to reimburse her for all her expenses. I gave her the flight numbers and times, and by the time we hung up, I couldn't tell which of us was more excited for the reunion.

I will meet her at the airport in Calgary shortly after noon the day after tomorrow.

Seeing Uncle Phil the way he is now, and observing firsthand what our renewed relationship has done for him, is really what kindled my desire to renew my own relationship with my family. I don't want to end up the way he has. My plan is to enlist Grace's help in reconnecting me with my own folks, and I think she will understand and do it. I'm not asking for their support, but I owe them an explanation. I have a right to ask for their forgiveness, and maybe even, I dare to hope, their understanding.

Grace is almost twenty-two years old now, and she's very smart. She is old enough to hear about the abuse I suffered at the hands of my namesakes and all that it has led to. It is my hope that she will see how badly I feel about the death of Deputy Anderson and perhaps find a path to some understanding of it, if nothing else. Regardless if that happens or not, a hug from my little girl and an occasional call ought to be sufficient to buoy me for life.

If I am wrong, and she turns me in, the authorities will concentrate their search in Canada, though not where I actually live. I'm enough of a realist to know that sooner or later, it is inevitable that they will find me. Hopefully, I will have enough of a lead to get my money and clear out before they close in on me, at least giving me a good head start. But I know my daughter pretty well, and I can tell you she won't do that.

When I see her, I will feel complete, and for the very first time since I walked into that restaurant, truly free. I'm risking it all, as I did at Killer Burger, but this time, the reason is completely different. This time, it is noble, and I have a good feeling about it.

After talking to Grace, I went shopping for a nice gift for her. I bought an expensive dress and matching shoes at a fancy boutique in the city, confident that I still know her size. I bet she hasn't gained a pound since high school.

I'm planning to be at the airport the night before she gets there to keep an eye out for a trap, but I think that's being overly cautious. I just can't wait to see her.

On the way back to the hunting cabin, my mind keeps replaying happy moments from Grace's childhood. By the time I arrive, I'm in a better mood than I have been since the day I robbed Killer Burger.

I park and take the things I bought for Grace inside, then head back to the car to get a bag of groceries I picked up while I was out. As I step out of the car, I see a dust cloud rising in the distance, where the driveway disappears over the little ridge.

I stare at it, transfixed. Mine is not the only cabin out here. There are at least two others, though the proprietor told me they were vacant. That dirt road is the only way in and out of here.

I'm sure someone else has rented one of the other cabins. Still, you just can't be too cautious when on the lam.

I leave the groceries in the car and run into the bushes, fighting a sudden urge to pee. The vehicle is just about to come into view when I remember I left my gun in the car. Feeling stupid, I make a mad dash back to it and grab the stolen Glock from under the seat. I barely make it back to the woodline before the car comes into view.

Peeking out from behind a double birch tree, I see that is not one car, but a four-car train of Royal Canadian Mounted Police SUVs, each containing several officers. The last unit displays a warning for people to stay clear of it because of the dog.

Fighting tears, I turn and fade into the forest.

For sales, editorial information, subsidiary rights information
or a catalog, please write or phone or e-mail

iBooks
Manhanset House
Dering Harbor, New York 11965

www.ibooksinc.com
bricktower@aol.com

www.IngramContent.com

For sales in the UK and Europe please contact our distributor,
Gazelle Book Services
White Cross Mills
Lancaster, LA1 4XS, UK
Tel: (01524) 68765 Fax: (01524) 63232
email: jacky@gazellebooks.co.uk

www.ingramcontent.com/pod-product-compliance
Lightning Source LLC
Chambersburg PA
CBHW060557310726
48982CB00008B/1148/J

* 9 7 8 1 5 9 6 8 7 4 3 8 1 *